RENDEZ-VOUS IN CANNES

JENNIFER BOHNET

B

Boldwood

Books Ltd.

Paperback ISBN 978-1-83889-760-4

Ebook ISBN 978-1-83889-147-3

Kindle ISBN 978-1-83889-148-0

Audio CD ISBN 978-1-83889-238-8

MP3 CD ISBN 978-1-83889-757-4

Digital audio download ISBN 978-1-83889-145-9

Boldwood Books Ltd
23 Bowerdean Street
London SW6 3TN
www.boldwoodbooks.com

To my husband Richard with love

1

WELCOME TO CANNES IN THE MONTH OF MAY IN THE
YEAR 2010

The day before she was due to fly to the South of France for the Cannes Film Festival, Anna Carson was in Somerset looking at a possible location for the latest film she was involved with as Production Designer.

Marshland House lay at the end of a long drive flanked by flowering white rhododendron bushes. From the outside, the brick built Victorian mansion looked perfect for her purpose. The location agent had told her that the major part of the house was untouched since the nineteenth century and, importantly for the film, the basement kitchen still boasted its original fixtures.

Anna parked her car and glanced at her watch. Fifteen minutes before the agent was due. Time enough for her to have a quick look around the grounds on her own and take some photographs. Apart from the set designer needing some, she knew Leo would want to see photographs of the house and its location. A smile touched her lips as she thought about Leo.

Just over four months ago, she'd thought she was as happy as she was ever going to be. Falling in love at fifty-seven years old hadn't been on her radar. Not that it ever had been. Her default setting since her particularly disastrous teenage years had been the old saying 'Better to have loved and lost than never to have loved at all.' So instead of a husband and family, she had a successful career she enjoyed, her own home and money in the bank. If she'd ever felt that something was missing from her life, she'd firmly pushed the thought down and away. Everybody had regrets, didn't they? You learned to live with them.

Then, at a swanky London party on New Year's Eve, mutual friends had introduced her to widower Leo Hunter. It was one of those rare occasions when two people connected, forming an instant friendship. Leo worked for one of the big five publishers and was intrigued by Anna's job in the film industry. The noise of the party had faded into the background as they'd talked and discovered things they had in common. Two hours later when Big Ben struck and welcomed in the New Year, and fireworks lit up the night sky, Leo had taken her by the hand and pulled her towards him. Lifting her hand to his lips and placing a gentle kiss on it, all the time his gaze never leaving her face, he'd said, 'Happy New Year, Anna. I think we're going to have a wonderful year together.'

Unprepared for the feelings he'd stirred in her, Anna was wary when he telephoned the next day, inviting her to the theatre, but within days she knew she'd fallen unequivocally in love with him. The realisation in the following week that Leo felt the same way about her had been, and still was, overwhelming.

Anna smiled at the memory of their first meeting; the way they'd just clicked. Within days they were acting like lovesick teenagers.

Unexpectedly, too, she'd found herself being accepted as part of a family when Leo introduced her to his two grown-up children, Luke and Alison, who unselfishly welcomed her presence in their father's life, pleased to see him happy again. With her own parents dead for years, it was a long time since Anna had had anything resembling a family unit in her life. Leo and his children were everything a proper family should be. Loving and close to each other and, importantly, there for each other. A real loving family, the like of which she'd long ago stopped wishing for in her own life, knowing it was an impossible dream.

Wandering around the grounds of Marshland House, stopping to smell and admire the beautiful display of rhododendrons of different colours that were everywhere, Anna tried to banish all thoughts of Leo and concentrate instead on this latest film she was working on, *In the Shadow of Mrs Beaton*. A costume drama based on the life of a little-known Victorian culinary expert, Mrs Agnes Marshall. Even in pre-production days, it was already stirring up a lot of interest. With a script written by a famous writer and a couple of big name stars being approached to play the principal roles, it was being tipped for box office success.

Anna's mobile rang while she was standing looking out over the lake that was part of the landscaped gardens to the rear of the house. Leo.

Taking a deep breath, Anna answered the phone trying to speak naturally, but, try as she might, she'd never yet managed to stop her heart thumping or her hands shaking whenever she heard or saw Leo. This time was no different. She hadn't felt this way about anyone since those long ago giddy days of her first love.

'Hi, how are you, my darling? Have I told you how much I miss you when we're not together?'

'Missing you too.'

'Is the house all the agent promised it would be?' Leo asked, knowing how important it was for Anna to find the right location.

'If the inside of the house is as good as the outside and the grounds, it will be perfect,' Anna told him. 'I'm glad I made the effort to come today. At least it's one less thing to worry about while I'm in Cannes.'

'Ah, Cannes,' Leo said. There was a slight pause before he continued, 'I sincerely hope you know what you are doing, Anna my darling. Going back and raking up the past is not always a good idea.'

Even from two hundred miles away, Anna could hear the concern in his voice.

'Leo, I have no intention of "raking up the past", as you put it. I'm simply going to the film festival. I know I've managed to avoid it for forty years, but it's time to lay the past to rest now. Besides, how could I refuse to go this year? I know I've been in the business for what seems like forever, but it's the first time since I started my own company five years ago that one of the films I've been production designer on, is "In Competition" at Cannes. This year I have to be there for the premiere of *Future Promises*. No excuse will be acceptable.' Anna hesitated. 'And, there are certain ghosts I have to lay for both our sakes, Leo.'

She heard Leo sigh softly down the phone. 'I just worry about you pulling the past into your present. I don't want you to be hurt.'

Anna smiled. Picturing Leo and longing to feel

his arms around her, she said softly, 'I know. You are still joining me, aren't you?' she added anxiously. 'I'm so looking forward to our first holiday together and I can't wait to show off my own handsome leading man on the red carpet.'

'Of course I'm coming and I'll be there as soon as I can get away,' Leo promised. 'But right now I must go. I'll ring you tomorrow to make sure you've arrived safely. Love you.'

'Love you too,' Anna smiled happily to herself, her hands trembling as she switched off her phone.

Looking out over the countryside, Anna sighed, her fingers toying with the chain of the gold locket that she rarely took off. Was Leo right inferring she was tempting fate returning to Cannes after all these years? Her nemesis was certainly powerful enough to rear up in protest and throw the errors of her past into her present – maybe even destroy the future with Leo. It was a risk, though, she had to take to ensure a second chance at happiness. Surely, after forty years, closure was a mere formality?

Leo hadn't mentioned marriage in so many

words yet, but Anna suspected – hoped – he would soon.

Standing in the grounds of Marshland House, Anna resolved to talk to Leo again about her past. In detail. He deserved to know the whole truth. And where better to tell him than in the place where it had all begun? What she had told him so far had been the merest skeleton of events. Until she knew him better, she'd been afraid to tell him the whole sad story, but now she was confident of her strong love for him, and his for her, she wanted him to know the complete story. She was determined to be totally honest with Leo. It was the only way.

Hearing car tyres scrunch along the gravel on the drive, Anna made her way round to the front of the house, where the agent was parking his car alongside hers.

An hour later, as the agent left for another appointment, Anna switched on the car radio and sat for a few moments writing up her notes, half listening to a news bulletin.

Inside, the house had been everything she'd hoped it would be and she'd instructed the agent to draw up a contract to allow filming to begin there in the autumn and send it to her office. Now she was free to go to Cannes and do what she had to do before enjoying the festival and Leo's company when he arrived.

The next moment, the voice of the news presenter made her catch her breath in shock.

'Some news just in. The respected French film-maker Philippe Cambone has died in America. Responsible for some of the biggest blockbuster movies of the twentieth century, he was recently awarded an industry lifetime achievement Bafta which was to have been presented at this week's Cannes film Festival.'

Automatically, Anna reached out and turned off the radio, before closing her eyes and leaning back against her seat as a wave of numbness and unexpected desolation flooded her body.

How could Philippe be dead when she'd vowed this would be the year she'd confront her demons and lay the past to rest?

2

Daisy Harris dragged her suitcase through the crowded Arrivals Hall of Terminal 2 at Nice airport and out on to the concourse, where she stopped to take a deep breath, look up at the azure blue sky and feel the heat of the sun. After the stress of the last couple of days, it was just wonderful to be breathing in the air of the Riviera, a favourite place of hers.

The plane from Bristol had been packed with both media people heading to the Cannes film Festival and holidaymakers with young children. A peaceful flight it was not. Crying babies, toddlers who wouldn't sit still and men with loud voices talking importantly to each other as they overindulged with G & Ts from the drinks trolley. Thankfully, Daisy hadn't known any of the journalists on board so hadn't had to confide in anyone that she too was a bona fide reporter covering the festival, albeit for the first time.

Seeing the length of the taxi queue, Daisy briefly toyed with the idea of taking the airport bus into Nice and picking up a taxi from there but decided, as Nice was in the opposite direction to Cannes, it would only lengthen her travelling time and delay her getting to her sister's.

Taxis were coming and going non-stop and in the end Daisy only had to wait for fifteen minutes before she was opening the door of a smart Mercedes and telling the driver her sister's address. 'Villa Flora, Cannes, please.'

The taxi fairly whizzed along the busy A7 autoroute, changing lanes with such alacrity that at times Daisy felt quite dizzy, as if she was on a switchback ride. It was twenty minutes before the driver swung across to the nearside lane and took the Cannes exit and Daisy told him the name of the boulevard the villa was situated on.

Five minutes later, a happy-to-be-alive Daisy grabbed her suitcase, stepped out of the taxi, paid the driver and watched the Mercedes speed away, spinning gravel out from under its wheels.

'Well, that was an interesting ride,' Daisy muttered as her sister Poppy engulfed her in a hug. 'I think he was practising for the Monaco Grand Prix. Either that or he has a death wish.'

'That bad? Never mind, you're here now. Good flight?' Poppy asked.

'Had better,' Daisy said, hugging her sister back. 'Oh, it's so good to be back down here with you. I miss having my bossy big sister around so much.'

'Bossy? Me? Never,' Poppy answered, laughing. 'Come on, let's get you indoors.'

'I'm sorry to land on you last minute like this,' Daisy said. 'I really couldn't face sharing a small apartment with Marcus and his cronies and there's no hope of finding an empty hotel room in Cannes this week. Besides, I'd far rather stay here with you.'

'You know you're more than welcome any-time,' Poppy replied. 'Just so long as you don't mind camping out with Tom and me in the old cottage.'

At that moment, Tom himself came running out of the villa at full tilt before throwing himself at Daisy.

'Hi Tom. How you doing?' Daisy picked up her young nephew and swung him around before gently placing him back down on the ground. 'You, young man, are getting too big and heavy for swings. Reckon you're strong enough to pull my suitcase down to the cottage?' Catching hold of his hand she bent down and whispered in his ear. 'There might just be some Lego in it waiting to be unpacked.'

She and Poppy watched, smiling, as six year old Tom started to pull the suitcase down the path.

'So, who have you rented the villa to for the festival? Pleeease tell me Aidan Turner and his family are going to be in residence,' Daisy asked, turning to Poppy as they followed Tom down the path.

'Sorry to disappoint you but the villa has been booked in the name of Anna Carson. I've never heard of her, but that doesn't mean anything,' Poppy answered. 'You know what I'm like, haven't got a clue about celebrities.'

'Anna Carson,' Daisy said thoughtfully. 'Nope, it's not a name that rings any bells with me either. Obviously not gossip column material. Where's Dan by the way?'

'Convenient business trip to America. You know how he hates the whole festival scene. When I was asked to rent the villa for a sum that will put some money back in the coffers after all the renovations, he told me to go for it but that he wouldn't be here!'

'Fair enough, I suppose,' Daisy said, knowing her brother-in-law's views on film stars and so-called 'A list' personalities. 'Makes life easier for you that way as well. When does this Anna Carson get here and take up residence?'

'First day of the festival in the afternoon,' Poppy answered. 'She's asked me to arrange for a car to collect her.'

'So we've still got the place to ourselves this evening and tomorrow morning,' Daisy said. 'We can at least have a swim then when I get back later. I need to go and collect my press pack and accreditation pass today. Tomorrow will be frantic. I told Marcus, the photographer, I'd see him there down there at about four o'clock this afternoon.'

'Let's get you settled in the cottage then,' Poppy said. 'Tom and I are sharing the bedroom – I've put a clic-clac bed on the mezzanine for you. Hope that's OK.' Poppy glanced anxiously at her sister.

'It'll be fine,' Daisy assured her and followed Poppy down the hidden narrow path behind the swimming pool hedge towards the corner of the garden where the cottage was hidden away from view by a bank of roses, their perfume filling the late afternoon air as Daisy and Poppy walked past.

Once a home for the full-time housekeeper and gardener who looked after the villa, the cottage had fallen into disrepair and when Poppy and Dan had bought Villa Flora two years ago both the properties were in dire need of some tender loving care. The last time Daisy had visited, seven months before, the villa had been finished, but the small cottage was still in a state of disarray.

'Wow, what a transformation,' she said now, looking around the sitting room as they walked in. 'First the villa and now this place. You should have been an interior designer – you've got such a good eye. I love the Provençal colour scheme in here,' she added, looking around the sitting room with its terracotta floor tiles and yellow and blue furnishings. With French doors and windows down two sides, the room had a spacious feel about it and Poppy's colour scheme and shabby-chic furniture gave it a welcoming, homely feel. 'Are you still planning to rent it out as a gîte?'

Poppy nodded. 'That's the idea. Renting out the villa is a one-off for this year.' Daisy turned to Tom.

'I'll carry the suitcase upstairs, Tom.'

Poppy led the way up a flight of wooden stairs in the far corner to the mezzanine whose railing ran like a minstrel's galley along the width of the room. Daisy put her laptop bag on the chest of drawers standing between two varnished doors and her suitcase on the floor. Tom, hopping from foot to foot, watched her anxiously as she un-zipped it and pulled out a box.

'Here you go, Tom – add this to your collection.'

Tom gave a delighted whoop. 'Thank you, thank you,' and he ran downstairs to begin playing with his present.

'I'm hoping this will give you enough privacy,' Poppy said, pulling open a decorative wicker screen that would hide from view the bed she'd placed at the end of the mezzanine. 'There's the bathroom and this is where Tom and I are sleep-ing,' Poppy continued, opening one of the doors. 'I've left some hangers for you to use in the wardrobe so you can at least unpack. These drawers are empty,' she said indicating the chest. 'I've put towels and things out for you in the bath-room and—'

'Poppy, stop fussing. You're sounding more and more like Mum,' Daisy said. 'It's all fine. Inci-dentally, have you spoken to Mum recently?'

Poppy nodded. 'She and Dad are hoping to come over at the end of the month. Apparently, Dad's won some tickets to see the Monaco Grand

Prix. Goodness only knows where I'm expected to put them the first night,' Poppy shook her head and looked at Daisy. 'Anna Carson doesn't leave until the next day. Are you hungry? Fancy a sandwich?'

'Please, and then I must think about walking down to Cannes.'

Downstairs, in the kitchen Poppy had created in what had originally been a lean-to conservatory, Daisy picked up Oscar, Poppy's fat ginger and white cat, and absently stroked him as she looked out over the garden.

'Is Anna Carson staying on her own?'

Poppy shrugged as she concentrated on making sandwiches. 'Some of the time. She's asked me to make up the bed in the master bedroom and one of the guest rooms but just to leave bedding in the other two rooms in case she has guests. She's hoping her partner will arrive in the next couple of days. He's hiring a car at the airport, so at least I don't have to worry about organising transport for him.'

'Did she sound okay when you spoke to her?

Or does she have "showbiz attitude"?' Daisy rolled her eyes in mock horror.

Poppy laughed. 'No, she sounded really nice – friendly and down-to-earth. Let's take these out into the garden,' and she led the way out to the swing seat under the shade of the linden tree. 'So what's this photographer, Marcus, like? Replacement material for Ben?' Poppy asked hopefully.

Daisy laughed. 'I doubt it. I've only met him a couple of times when he's called into the paper to see Bill, our editor, they're old friends apparently and he gets a lot of freelance work from Bill. He does have a bit of a reputation as far as women are concerned and I definitely don't want to be another notch on his belt. It's going to be strictly business for the next ten days.'

'It's been months since Ben upped and left you for the delights of Australia. Life goes on. It's about time you found someone else,' Poppy said. 'I just want to see my little sister settle down happily.'

'To be honest I'm quite enjoying being single. Anyway, I don't think Marcus is my type. Far too flamboyant.' Daisy hesitated, wondering whether to tell Poppy about the letter she'd stuffed in her bag and decided she'd leave it until later, when they'd have more time to talk about it together. 'Talking of Marcus, I'd better get going.'

'You can bring him back for supper if you like,' Poppy offered. 'I'd like to meet him. Give him the third degree and see if he does have the potential to be a boyfriend for my little sister,' she added.

'No way,' Daisy said. 'Besides, you and I are having a girlie evening before the film festival takes over my life for the next ten days. Right, I'd better dash. See you later. Bye, Tom. Be good.'

3

Cannes was in countdown to festival time as Daisy walked along the bord de mer and made her way towards the old port and the Palais des Festivals. The events of the past few days had happened so fast, she could scarcely believe she was officially here as a journalist at one of the biggest annual show business events in the world.

Summoned by the editor, Bill, into his inner sanctum late in the afternoon just two days ago, Daisy had been nervous, wondering if she was about to be given the sack over some faux pas or other that she'd unintentionally made. But a distracted Bill had simply looked at her as he ran his hands over his thinning hair.

'Two things. First: you got anything on for the next fortnight?' Without waiting for her answer, he'd continued, 'If you have, cancel it.'

'Why?' Daisy had looked at him, shocked, wondering what was coming.

'Damien, the bloody fool, has broken his leg. I need you in Cannes for the film festival with Marcus. He's an old hand down there, so he'll fill you in on the details.'

'You want me to cover the Cannes Film Festival for the paper?' Daisy couldn't keep the surprise out of her voice.

'You got a problem with that?'

Daisy had shaken her head. 'No. I'm just surprised you're giving me the job.'

'I don't have a choice. Alex has family commitments and can't go. You're single and commitment free – I hope?'

Ah, so she was second best, but she didn't care. Covering the Cannes Film Festival would be a real step up from the dreary round of low key reporting and the 'women's features' she was usually handed. She'd been thrilled, joining the team on the small South Coast daily paper a couple of years ago, but covering local events and writing up the sentences handed out at the weekly magistrates' court was as exciting as it had got so far.

'Definitely commitment free,' Daisy had replied.

'Marcus says the apartment he's renting is tiny, but you can squeeze in there with him and the others. Probably be an airbed on the floor, but—' Bill had shrugged.

'Not a problem,' Daisy had said, knowing there was no way she'd even think about sleeping on the floor. She knew Poppy would find her a more comfortable bed than that. 'My sister lives down there. I can stay with her. You said there were two things?'

Bill had picked up an envelope from his desk. 'You'll have heard the rumours about lots of changes here – this is your official notification of possible redundancies. Enjoy Cannes.' Having delivered the bad news in his usual brusque manner, Bill turned his attention to his computer screen and waved Daisy away.

Daisy had left his office with mixed feelings – elated she had been given the opportunity to cover the Cannes Film Festival and worried about her future afterwards. Later that day, though, once she'd opened the envelope and seen the offer of voluntary redundancy, thoughts of freelancing once again began stirring in her brain as she began packing for the festival.

And now here she was in Cannes. She must remember to send Damien a postcard teasing him about breaking his leg and giving her the opportunity to report on Cannes.

The palm tree lined streets were more chaotic than usual, with nose-to-tail traffic stuttering its way around double-parked vans and lorries busy unloading last minute supplies to various exhibition venues and traders. Luxury cars – Porsche, Bugatti, Aston Martins – all caught up in the gridlocked roads, attracted envious glances from pedestrians. Impatient gun-toting gendarmes, standing in front of 'route barre' signs, directed frustrated motorists down narrow streets they knew would take them in the opposite direction to where they wanted to go.

As she approached the Palais des Festivals, Daisy could see men busy sweeping and checking the condition of the red carpet that now covered the most famous flight of twenty-four steps in the world. Dodging the crowds that were milling aimlessly around, hoping to rub shoulders with the few stars already in town, Daisy made her way to the back of the Palais. She recognised Marcus at once, leaning against the railings watching the crowds on the beach, his official photographer pass already strung around his neck, his camera at the ready.

'You settled in all right at your sister's place?' Marcus asked after they'd greeted each other.

Daisy nodded. 'Yes, thanks. Where do I go to register?'

Marcus pointed to a door in the Palais. 'Through there. You'll be ages – French paperwork and chaotic bureaucracy is at its best in there. I'll wait for you in the UK Film Centre Pavilion over in the Village International,' he said, gesturing in the direction of the large marquee and other tents that had been set up along the embankment. 'We'll go for a coffee afterwards and try to map out a plan of campaign.'

'Plan of campaign?'

'As well as a daily report and photos, Bill wants us to try to unearth some unusual stories – a scandal would be good, he says,' Marcus shrugged. 'You know what editors are like – always wanting a scoop.'

Daisy was thoughtful as she made her way to register in the Palais office. Fingers crossed that she could do a good job and get her byline in the paper noticed. If she was made redundant her future freelancing career could depend on her CV showing how good a journalist she was.

* * *

Marcus was right. It was nearly two hours before Daisy escaped from the Accreditation Centre, her press pass finally around her neck and clutching a mountain of booklets and other assorted festival papers. When she eventually tracked Marcus down in the Film Centre marquee, he was with a group of men – all photographers, Daisy guessed

from the amount of camera paraphernalia sur-
rounding them.

'Hi guys, this is Daisy, my new partner in
crime for the festival. I'll see you lot later. Daisy
and I have to talk.'

Marcus picked up his large canvas bag and
Daisy followed him across the road to a pavement
café in front of Square Brougham, where they
managed to grab a vacant corner table.

'Deux café au lait, s'il vous plaît,' Marcus ordered, raising his voice to be heard above the
noise of a group of vocal Italians at the next table,
some Russians who'd clearly been there for some
time sampling the house rosé and a nearby crowd
of Americans who seemed intent on taking over
the place. A Japanese tourist was busy videoing
the scene.

'Hope he's got his sound switched on,' Daisy
said. 'I've never heard so many languages all at
once.'

'Heard the news about Philippe Cambone?'
Marcus asked, as the waiter put their coffees on
the table.

Daisy shook her head. 'The big-shot film director? What's happened?'

'Died of a heart attack in Los Angeles. There's going to be some sort of tribute later in the week – the powers that be haven't decided what yet. Do you know anything about Cambone?'

'Only that he was French, was one of the top directors, wasn't married...' she glanced at Marcus. 'Wasn't gay, was he?'

Marcus shrugged. 'If he was, it was a well kept secret. Had a reputation of loving women but wouldn't commit to one. Anyway, I expect they've got all the info they need back at the office but maybe you could do a couple of paragraphs about how the news has been received down here? Cannes was his home town. Maybe interview a few people who knew him? You know the score – find a human-interest angle: the school he went to; name of his first love, et cetera.' Marcus drained his coffee and pushed the cup and saucer away before asking, 'You got a press conference tomorrow?'

'Not tomorrow. I'm hoping to get to a screening in the morning and then I'm having lunch with a friend of Poppy's who works for Chanel. She's promised to give me the lowdown on some of the accessories and clothes they'll be lending the stars. So I should have a spare hour in the morning to try to see if I can find someone to talk about Philippe Cambone. Then, in the afternoon, I'll file my first daily report.'

'Don't forget to keep your ears open for any juicy gossip,' Marcus said. 'It's what this place is good for – and, like I said, Bill is keen to hear some of it.'

'As you're an old hand at this lark, where's the best place to hang out to catch the gossip? See people?' Daisy asked. Marcus might have a reputation as being a bit of a wild boy and overly fond of leather trousers but he was a brilliant photographer and had 'done' the festival for several years now.

'Any of the cafés and bars in town. This place is good,' Marcus said, glancing around. 'Occasionally some of the up-and-coming stars like to come down here and hang out with the boules players over there. Too much security these days for the famous ones to do that, unfortunately. Mind you, if Jack Nicholson is in town, he's known to like an early morning stroll along the Croisette by himself.'

Marcus stood up. 'Right, I'm off. Want to come to a party tomorrow night? Bernard Audibert, who's a big name down here and knows anybody worth knowing, is having his usual opening party bash and I've got two tickets. It should be a good starting place for gossip. Meet me after the evening screening and we'll go together. Ten thirty outside the Palais. Party's being held in rue Victor Cousin.'

'Sounds fun.'

'He was a mate of Cambone's too, so that could be useful for your feature,' Marcus added.

'I'll definitely try to be there then.' Daisy hesitated. She really did want to spend the evening with Poppy having a good catch-up but felt she ought to at least make the offer for Marcus to join them. 'Are you doing anything tonight? Poppy and I are planning a girlie evening, but if you'd like to come to supper? I warn you, you're likely to get the third degree from my big sister.'

Marcus shook his head. 'Thanks, but I've

arranged to meet the guys for a quick drink and then a reasonably early night. Doubt that I'll see bed much before 3 or 4 a.m. most days while the festival is on. Expect you'll find the same once you get into the swing of things.' Unexpectedly, he leaned forward and kissed her cheek. 'When in France and all that,' he said. He picked up his camera gear. 'If you need me urgently, you've got my mobile number and you'll invariably find me in the paparazzi scrum at the side of the red car- pet. We've got a definite dinner date one evening before the festival ends – either the Carlton Ter- race or the Palm Beach. You choose. Bill can pick up the tab! See you tomorrow night. Ciao,' and he sauntered off in the direction of Palm Beach.

Thoughtfully, Daisy watched him go. Well, that was definitely the most unromantic dinner date invite she'd ever had, but dinner at the Carlton would be an experience.

Daisy gathered up her things and headed off in the opposite direction to Marcus. Passing the busy pizza restaurant on the corner brought back memories of the last time she'd eaten in there seven months ago. The four of them – Poppy,

Dan, Ben and herself – had been out for the evening at the end of their holiday. She'd been so happy that night. She and Ben had even talked about the possibility of moving to France or finding themselves a small cottage to do up and use as a holiday home. A first step on the property ladder together. It seemed like a logical next step to Daisy. They'd been a couple then for over a year – nearly eighteen months in fact, although they still both rented their own places, despite Ben spending more and more time with her. When Daisy suggested he moved in with her as her flat was bigger than his and they could save money for buying their own place, he said he'd think about it.

They'd been back in the UK a week after that holiday when her world had fallen apart. Apparently, all the talk that night of getting a mortgage, moving in together and settling down as a couple had freaked Ben out and he'd told her it was all over between them – 'I'm not ready for that sort of commitment, Daisy. I need some space.' A few weeks later it turned out that the space he craved was in Australia – Sydney to be precise – which seemed to emphasise his desperation to get away from her.

How ironic then that his first letter since then should arrive as she left to catch her flight down here where they'd spent that happy holiday. Unsure of how to reply Daisy had stuffed the letter into her bag. She'd get Poppy to read it later and see if she had any thoughts about Ben's latest suggestion.

Standing with several people on the pavement in front of a busy road junction waiting for a red pedestrian crossing light to change to green, Daisy smiled at a little girl waiting with a tall man.

'Nat, d'you think Daddy will be at the house when we get back?' Daisy overheard the girl ask hopefully, looking up at the man.

'Maybe, Cindy. His plane should have landed an hour ago and a car was picking him up to bring him straight to Cannes.'

'Good,' Cindy said. 'He can take me to the park tomorrow.'

'Sorry, Cindy, I think you'll have to make do with me for a few days. Daddy and Mummy are going to be really busy with the festival for the next week. That's why they've asked me to look after you.'

Daisy smiled sympathetically as the man looked up and saw her watching. He returned the smile but didn't speak. Just then the lights changed and the small crowd surged forward. Once across the road, Daisy stopped, on the pretence of rummaging for something in her bag, and let the man and girl walk past her, curious to see where they were going.

It was a few hundred yards or so before they stopped in front of a pair of large wrought-iron gates, where the man pressed a security button high in the wall and spoke into the intercom. One of the dark green gates with its golden spikes on top swung slowly open, giving pedestrian access, and the two disappeared into a private garden. Daisy caught a glimpse of immaculate grounds and, in the distance, a belle-époque villa covered with bougainvillea before the gate snapped shut behind them.

Daisy strolled on past and, ten minutes later, she and Poppy were sat at the table under the cottage loggia, with a glass of wine to hand, thumbing through the various film magazines and trade papers Daisy had collected in Cannes.

'So, you still enjoying being a journalist?' Poppy asked.

Daisy hesitated long enough for her sister to throw her a curious glance, before saying slowly. 'Chasing after news stories is losing its appeal. Anyway, I mightn't have a job much longer. Bill gave me my official redundancy warning letter this week, which contained an offer of voluntary redundancy if I wanted to take it. There are rumours flying around at work about the paper actually folding, so I'm seriously thinking of going freelance and finding some sort of specialism.' She shrugged. 'I could even move over here. I do love it down here. Live with you while I find something. I still like the idea of renovating a place, even if Ben couldn't hack it.'

'You could stay in the cottage if you wanted to be a bit more independent,' Poppy said. 'I know Dan would be pleased for me to have you near when he's away – his business trips seem to be on the increase. I, of course, would love a live-in childminder.' She poured some more wine. 'Any idea what you'd specialise in?'

'Lifestyle? Property? Quite fancy the idea of getting to look around posh houses. Incidentally, there's this gorgeous belle-époque villa below you. Dark green gates with gold spikes. D'you know it? Saw a little girl and her minder disappearing in there earlier.'

'If it's the one I think you mean,' Poppy said, 'it's someone with either a lot of money, good connections, or both, staying there. It's one of the original grand nineteenth century villas along that road. It was bought last year by some Russian who's spent a fortune renovating it. Apparently, it's now the latest word in twenty-first century opulence. Available only to those with the necessary funds.'

'Well, "Daddy" is clearly some festival VIP to warrant an official car. Shall have to do a bit of sleuthing tomorrow, I think,' Daisy said. 'The little girl's name was Cindy – not that usual a name. Somebody is bound to know who her VIP father is. Maybe she's got a famous mother too.'

'Don't any of your official booklets and papers

have potted biographies of important people attending the festival?' Poppy asked. 'Have a look while I go and check Tom is asleep and fetch another bottle of rosé.'

When she returned, Daisy waved a booklet at her. 'No luck with my mystery VIP, but I've found your Anna Carson. She's a well-respected production designer, worked on lots of films over the years. Set up her own company a few years ago. Apparently this is her first visit to Cannes.'

Later, sitting on the edge of her clic-clac bed, balancing her laptop on her knees, Daisy updated her 'To-do list'. Tomorrow she'd a) go to a screening, b) find someone to interview about Philippe Cambone, c) talk to the girl from Chanel, d) write up her first report, e) go to Bernard's party, f) try to uncover a scoop for Bill.

She smiled ruefully to herself as she wrote 'uncover a scoop'. She didn't doubt there would be several secret scandals floating around in a place like Cannes over the next week or so, but whether she was capable of unearthing one was something else.

4

It's Wednesday morning and I'm sitting at a seafront café, croissant and coffee to hand, watching Cannes come to life on the first full day of the festival. The morning sky is the brilliant blue that gives this stretch of the Riviera its other name, the Cote d'Azur, and the forecast is for a sunny day.

All around me, there are giant billboards advertising the films that will be screening here over the next few days. Although only 7.35 a.m., there is a general sense of bustle everywhere. Queues are already forming outside boulangeries, espresso machines are hissing into life, squirting the dark, strong liquid the French call coffee into small cups.

People are arriving, bleary-eyed, back at their hotels and apartments, hoping to catch a few hours' sleep after partying the night away. Others, still bright eyed and with a spring in their step, are on their way out to the first breakfast meetings of the festival.

Daisy took a swig of her coffee and a bite of croissant before continuing to type the first of her daily reports on her laptop.

I've collected all the daily trade magazines, signed up for a press conference tomorrow morning with a famous star – more of that later in the week – and now I'm off to view my first early morning screening. With over one hundred and twenty films to be shown during the festival, things start early around here.

Daisy pressed the save button and switched off. She'd add some more to it after lunch with the fashion assistant who had promised to explain how the stars managed to acquire the necessary glitz for film premieres.

After drinking the rest of her coffee, she set off for the Theatre Bazin on the third floor of the Palais des Festivals, where many of the press screenings would be held during the festival – far away from the glamour of the red carpet.

Emerging three hours later, her head buzzing from both the film and the Q & A session with the filmmakers that had followed, Daisy joined the lunchtime crowds that were thronging the Croisette: tourists and locals enjoying the spectacle of entertainers and starlets strutting their stuff – eager to catch the eye of any moviemaker that might be around.

As she walked, intriguing snippets of conversation floated in the air around her.

'Sharon was really upset when Michael gave the part to...'

'Gosh yes, a ticket to the Vanity Fair party would be to die for. Any chance of...'

'No. We can't meet there. It's too risky. What if we were seen?'

Marcus was right; there was gossip everywhere.

Surely that was Tom Hanks over there talking to Bruce Willis? And that glamorous actress getting into a limousine looked incredibly like Meryl Streep.

Wandering through the crowds, Daisy wondered again about the possibility of chasing down a scoop for the paper. She just wasn't that keen on investigative journalism. As she'd told Poppy, she much preferred to write feel-good stories about people rather than write ones that besmirched them.

Lingering near the carousel she spotted the young girl from the previous day, Cindy, riding around happily on one of the gaily decorated carousel horses, the tall man standing to one side attentively watching. He smiled in acknowledgement at Daisy when he saw her, before turning as the carousel slowed to a stop and helping Cindy off.

'Come on, let's go for those pizzas. Mummy said she'd meet us there and maybe Daddy as well.'

So Daddy had arrived then, Daisy thought, wishing she could follow them and at least put faces to Mummy and Daddy. But it was time for her to learn the trade secrets of how the stars managed their haute-couture appearances, so she crossed the Croisette and walked in the opposite direction, towards the luxury designer shops.

* * *

It was past three o'clock when she arrived back at the villa, intending to write up her notes, finish her report and do some internet research on Philippe Cambone. Having failed to unearth anyone locally who'd known the director and was willing to talk to her, the internet seemed to be her only option.

With luck too, she'd be able to grab some sleep before heading back down into Cannes for the first evening red-carpet screening and then on to the party with Marcus.

Poppy was on her mobile as Daisy walked into the cottage.

'Well, I'm glad you're *très desolé*, but it doesn't

help me this afternoon, does it?'

Poppy slammed the case cover down on her mobile before turning to face Daisy.

'Can you believe it? The car people have double booked and they're "very sorry", but they are unable to meet Anna Carson this afternoon.' Poppy ran her hands through her hair distractedly. 'What on earth am I going to do? It'll be impossible to find anyone else at this short notice.'

'I shouldn't worry. I expect she'll just grab a taxi,' Daisy said. 'Just hope it's not my Speedy Gonzales!'

'She's expecting to be met. I've got no way of telling her to take a taxi. My first booking for the villa and this happens.'

'What time is her flight landing?' Daisy asked.

'If it's on time, in an hour,' Poppy said, looking at her watch.

'I can look after Tom – is he at school? I know where that is and can walk there. You can go and collect Anna in your car.'

'Would you? Oh, no that won't work,' Poppy sighed. 'They don't know you so they won't let him come with you before I've officially introduced you. New stricter policy about strangers at the school gates these days.' She looked at Daisy. 'I don't suppose you—'

'Poppy, you know how much I hate driving down here,' Daisy said, but she took one look at her sister and sighed. 'Okay. Give me the flight details and the car keys and I'll go and meet your Anna Carson.'

* * *

Anna was relieved when the plane finally landed at Nice airport fifty minutes late. It had been an uncomfortable flight and she couldn't wait to collect her luggage and meet up with the car she'd ordered for the journey to the Villa Flora.

The Arrivals Hall when she walked through was crowded. Official-looking chauffeurs were everywhere, holding up boards with various names on them, none of them hers. Did the flight delay mean the chauffeur hadn't waited?

As people were shepherded off to their transport and the waiting crowds thinned slightly, Anna stood there at a loss to know what to do.

'Excuse me. You wouldn't be Anna Carson by any chance?' a voice at her side asked hesitantly.

'Yes,' she said, turning to face a young woman holding a small piece of paper with 'Anna Carson' scrawled across it.

'Hi, I'm Daisy – Poppy's sister. I'm afraid there was a difficulty with your hire car and Poppy asked me to meet you.'

'Oh, thank goodness. Being so late arriving, I was worried I might be stranded,' Anna said, smiling.

Following Daisy as she led the way through the car park, Anna listened as Daisy explained what had happened.

'So, instead of a proper chauffeur and a limo, you've got me and my sister's runaround,' Daisy apologised as she opened the boot and put Anna's two cases inside.

'I'm just grateful to be met,' Anna said. 'I'm not that fond of limos anyway. I like sitting in the front passenger seat and official chauffeurs aren't too keen on that.'

As Daisy concentrated on finding her way out

of the car park and back to the autoroute, Anna sat quietly looking out of the window.

When Daisy let out a muttered curse, she said, 'Something wrong?'

'I've missed the autoroute entry slip road. Do you mind if we go back along the bord de mer instead? It's not as quick, but at least I know my way.'

'I'd enjoy the scenic route,' Anna said. 'Do you live down here with your sister?'

'No. I'm staying with her for the festival. I'm a journalist,' Daisy replied. 'It's my first time covering the festival.' Waiting in a queue for the traffic lights to change, Daisy looked across at Anna. 'I gather this is your first festival too?'

'What makes you say that?' Anna said, surprised.

'Your bio in one of the trade papers says although you've been in the industry for some time, you've never been to Cannes before.'

'I've never had a film make its premiere here before,' Anna answered.

'Your film *Future Promises* is showing at the

weekend, isn't it? I expect you're looking forward to walking up the infamous steps?'

'Think so. I'm not used to being in the glare of the spotlight,' Anna said. 'I'd rather leave all that to the actors. To be truthful, I find the whole thing rather daunting. Much rather be in the background of things.' She smiled. 'So long as my partner, Leo, manages to get here in time, I'll be fine.'

'Personally I'm amazed at how large the whole festival is,' Daisy said. 'The number of trade stands is huge and everyone seems to be networking like mad.'

'My favourite festival is Deauville,' Anna replied. 'Less trade, far more about the films. Same with Venice, but Cannes is the big one, as I'm sure you're aware. The important one in the industry.'

'The public come to see the stars, but people in the film industry simply want to do deals. At least that's what Marcus, the photographer I'm working with, tells me. Is your company exhibiting here?' Daisy asked.

'Yes. I have to show my face at a couple of meetings with some American clients. And probably go to a couple of parties.' Anna paused as she took in the view of the Mediterranean glinting in the sunshine.

'Where are we now?'

'Skirting Antibes. A few more minutes and we'll be passing the celebrated Eden Roc Hotel, where, I'm told, the best people stay and fabulous parties are held. Another ten minutes and we should be on the outskirts of Cannes.'

'Spectacular views,' Anna said, looking out across the bay as they drove down the hill.

While Daisy concentrated on the narrow winding coast road as it made its way around the Cap d'Antibes and on through Juan-les-Pins, Anna enjoyed the changing scenery.

The sudden whoosh of a TGV train rushing past on the railway line that followed the road as it approached Golf-Juan made her jump. Approaching Cannes, the traffic began to build up and soon they were reduced to a crawl.

Anna saw Daisy glance at the dashboard clock before sighing and saying, 'At this rate, it's going to take us ages to get to the villa.'

'Have you got things lined up to do this

evening?' Anna asked, guiltily aware her plane being so late had probably created a few problems for Daisy.

Daisy nodded. 'I've got to finish and file my first report for the newspaper, do a spot of internet research on this big director who's just died, take a look at tonight's stars on the red carpet and then I get to go to a party later.' She glanced at Anna. 'Don't suppose you knew this Philippe Cambone, did you? Work with him even? Any info – personal anecdotes or anything – would be gratefully received.'

'No, I never worked with Philippe Cambone, so unfortunately I can't help you with anything other than what you'll find on the internet.' Anna turned to look out of her passenger window, effectively finishing the conversation.

'That's a shame,' Daisy said, disappointed. 'There's not much info out there. Seems Mr Cambone was a very private person. Oh good, the traffic is clearing, we're on the move again.'

'Are we going via the Croisette?' Anna asked.

'Only so far. The police will probably have barricaded the road before we reach The Bunker, ready for the evening screening.'

'The Bunker?'

'Local name for the Festival des Palais,' Daisy explained. 'We'll have to take a right and go round the back streets. Hopefully it won't add too much time to the journey.'

With a silent Anna beside her, Daisy concentrated on her driving and ten minutes later turned into the villa entrance. Poppy, hearing the electric gates opening, was waiting by the front door to greet them.

Daisy turned to Anna. 'Poppy will look after you now. Hope you don't think me terribly rude, but I must dash and try to catch up with a few things before I walk back down to Cannes. I expect we'll bump into each other over the next few days, either here or in town. Enjoy the festival.'

'Thanks for meeting me, Daisy. Do come over with Poppy and have glass of wine with me when you're not so frantic.'

'I'd like that,' Daisy said. 'Thank you. Ciao,' and she ran down the path to the cottage, leaving Anna with Poppy.

'This way,' Poppy said, taking Anna's suitcases

and leading the way into the Villa Flora. 'I've never rented the villa out before,' Poppy continued. 'I hope everything is okay for you,' she added anxiously as she showed Anna around and explained everything she needed to know, including the code for the entry gates. 'If there is anything I've forgotten to provide, you will tell me, won't you?'

'Please don't worry,' Anna said. 'I'm sure you've thought of everything. It looks fantastic.'

Long buttercup yellow curtains hung either side of the French doors and windows. A bookcase lined the wall alongside the fireplace and a small glass table holding some glossy magazines and candles was placed between a couple of inviting cream sofas with deep feather cushions. A large terracotta pot filled with lavender stood in the fireplace, infusing the whole villa with its perfume.

'There's a welcome box in the kitchen with a few basics – cheese, eggs, baguette, tomatoes, milk, butter – and there's a bottle of rosé in the fridge. Enough, I hope, to keep you going until you get to a supermarket,' Poppy said, going into the kitchen with its views out over the patio towards the swimming pool.

Just then Tom ran into the kitchen. 'Mummy, can I have one last swim before Miss Carson gets here? Oh, you're here already,' he added, seeing Anna.

'Tom, please say how do you do to Miss Carson,' Poppy said. 'Then go back to the cottage. I'll be there in a moment to get your supper.'

Anna held her hand out for Tom to shake. 'How do you do, Tom? My name is Anna.'

'How do you do, Anna,' Tom said seriously. 'Do you like swimming?'

'I do indeed and I guess you do too.'

Tom nodded. 'Only now I can't. Mummy says the pool is yours while you're here and nobody else can use it 'cause you're paying for it.'

'Tom!' Poppy exclaimed.

Anna bent down to talk to Tom. 'Ah. Well, I expect my friends will be coming for a swim, so if you're my friend I can invite you and Mummy won't mind then.'

'Now?' Tom asked hopefully.

'No,' Poppy answered before Anna could say

anything. 'Anna has to settle in this evening. Besides, it's almost your bedtime. Cottage,' and she held the kitchen door open for a reluctant Tom to leave. 'I'm sorry,' Poppy said, embarrassed. 'I'll keep him out of your way while you're here. I'll take him to the beach so he can swim.'

'Poppy, it's not a problem. Please let him come for a swim. I like having children around. Besides, I expect when Leo gets here, we'll be out and about most days.'

'If you're sure. Now, I think I'd better leave you in peace to settle in. If you want anything, just come over to the cottage. Bye for now.'

5

Closing the door behind Poppy, Anna went upstairs and pulled her swimming costume out of her case. The pool was too tempting to resist. The unpacking could wait.

The water was warm and inviting and Anna swam ten lengths before turning over and floating lazily on her back, allowing her mind to wander over the upcoming days.

So far her diary contained just four definite appointments: the gala screening of *Future Promises* at the weekend; a meeting with her company's French representative; dinner with the American producer who was keen to come on board for the Agnes Marshall film. The fourth un-confirmed date was for the company party she was planning to hold, sometime during the festi-val, here at the villa. The actual date would have to be confirmed soon to avoid clashing with one of the big VIP parties. She also needed to talk to Poppy about the catering for it. The fifth entry in the diary 'Ring Philippe' would now never hap-pen. Anna smothered a sigh. Telling Daisy she'd never worked with Philippe was true but perhaps she should have admitted to knowing him a long time ago? If his name ever came up in conversa-tion between them again, she'd definitely apolo-gise to Daisy for being economical with the truth.

The sun had disappeared behind a cloud layer as she made her way indoors to shower and start unpacking. Hanging the evening gown she in-tended wearing for the weekend premiere in the spacious wardrobe, her attention was caught by a series of postcard-size photographs grouped to-gether on the bedroom wall.

Moving closer, she saw that some were sepia in colour and showed the beach and harbour be-fore the Croisette was built. Another showed the old casino on the edge of the harbour with figures in Edwardian costume stiffly posing outside.

The one that caught Anna's attention was more recent: a black and white photo of a large building with square flat columns and a short flight of wide steps leading up to the entrance. Even as she bent closer to read the faded lettering at the base of the card, Anna had already recognised it as the old 'Palais des Festivals Cannes'. It had been a lovely building, she thought affectionately. Such a shame it had been deemed too small to host the ever growing festival and conferences that had been encouraged to come to Cannes. It looked so different to the concrete 'Bunker' she'd had a glimpse of before Daisy had turned off the Croisette.

Anna's mobile phone rang as she finished arranging the rest of her clothes in the closet.

Pressing the answer button with shaking fingers, she said, 'Hello, Leo,' as she ran downstairs to the kitchen.

'Anna, my darling. How was the flight?'

'Late and bumpy,' Anna answered. 'But I'm here now. Villa Flora is delightful – worth every euro the company is paying. A real find. You're going to love it.'

'Are you going out for dinner tonight?'

'No. I've just had a swim and I'm about to indulge in a baguette and some cheese with a glass of rosé that Poppy very kindly left for me, before having an early night. Tomorrow I'll wander down to Cannes and show my face. The office is doing all the major stuff – I just have to show up a couple of times and do as I'm told.'

'Haven't done any sightseeing yet then?'

Anna laughed. 'Leo, I've barely got here. I'll probably have a bit of a mooch around tomorrow, if the crowds aren't too large. I've got to do some food shopping anyway. How are things at your end?' she asked, knowing that Leo was spending a few days with his daughter and her husband. 'How's Alison?'

'She's blooming,' Leo laughed down the line. 'Literally. Told me tonight she's making me a grandfather before Christmas!'

'How wonderful. You must be so thrilled. Do give her my love and congratulations,' Anna said. 'And Luke? Have you managed to speak to him?'

Leo's son, Luke, was some sort of trou-bleshooter for one of the large international banks and was always flying off somewhere. Anna had only met him the once and was in awe of his business acumen.

'He's fine too. Got some sort of crisis going on at the moment in Dubai. Alison has just called out dinner is ready, so I'd better go. We'll speak to-morrow. Goodnight, my darling.'

'Goodnight. Enjoy the evening,' and Anna closed down her phone.

Thoughtfully she prepared herself a supper tray with the goodies from the welcome basket, poured herself a glass of wine and carried it all out to a small poolside table. The moon was rising in the darkening sky and solar garden lights placed randomly around were starting to illumi-nate the terrace and garden.

Sitting there, absently fingering the gold locket she always wore, memories about the past started to float into Anna's mind. Carefully, she slipped the chain and its locket over her head and pressed the catch. Two photographs, a few strands of hair wedged under the inside rim, were nestling together in the interior.

Anna brushed her tears away as she looked at the photos. For years she'd kept them as beloved mementoes. Not only were they a link to the past and a life never lived, they'd offered a degree of comfort, tricking her into believing that one day in the future, things would turn around. That past wrongs could be righted. But to make that dream come true, she'd needed to summon up the courage to tell the truth and shame the devil, as the old saying went. Her parents, though, had drummed that other old cliché, 'we don't wash our dirty linen in public', deep into her psyche, making it impossible for Anna to ever contemplate shaming the devil.

In recent years, every time she opened the locket, she'd always hoped that maybe one day her secret dream would come true of its own free will, without her doing anything. Then, she would replace the photo with a new, modern, colour version.

Tonight, though, Anna knew she had to accept the facts. The locket photos would never be replaced with modern versions. She'd left it too late and too much time had passed. Nostalgia and regrets were all very well, but it was the future that mattered now. Her future with Leo.

Leo. Just thinking about Leo brought a smile to Anna's face and she allowed herself a little daydream about the two of them. She'd never dreamt about being married before, but since meeting Leo she'd started fantasising about life as Mrs Leo Hunter. What would her life be like as a married woman – having a ready-made family to spend time with? Alison and Luke were far too grown-up to need a stepmum, instead she hoped the friendships they'd all recently started to forge would become even stronger, particularly the one between herself and Alison. If Leo did propose to her, she could be taking on the role of step-grandmother to Alison's new baby. A role she'd never expected to play in her life.

Carefully, Anna replaced the chain and locket around her neck before picking up her wine glass and taking a thoughtful sip. She was sure that Leo felt the same way about her as she did about him, but maybe he was happy with the way things were? Perhaps he wouldn't want to get married again. She was definitely getting ahead of herself here. Tempting fate. That would never do. Life had knocked her down before when she was at her happiest. Best not to take her current good fortune for granted.

After collecting Anna, Daisy had no time to do more than send her first report to Bill before doing a quick internet search for information on Philippe Cambone – which yielded very little of interest. Mainly the titles of the major films he'd been involved with. Not a hint of any scandal, which was what Daisy had secretly been hoping for.

As Marcus said, he'd obviously liked the ladies as there were lots of publicity shots taken down the years at various festivals and film premieres, though rarely with the same companion hanging from his arm.

No real gossip anywhere about his private life, other than he was a keen sailor and kept a boat in his home port of Cannes. Maybe she could locate that and get Marcus to take a photo. She sighed as she shut down her laptop. She'd have another go tomorrow; there had to be something out there about him.

A quick shower and Daisy dithered over what to wear that was practical for the first part of the evening but would look dressy enough for the party later, which she knew would almost certainly be full of skinny women dressed to impress. Her normal jeans and T-shirt definitely wouldn't do. In the end, she decided on her black velvet trouser suit with a glittery silver spaghetti strap top under the jacket. Evenings could turn cold down here after the sun had set, so she would at least be warm.

'You look great,' Poppy assured her. 'Have fun.'

'Don't know what time I'll be back. I promise to creep in as quietly as I can.'

Daisy took a shortcut down through Le Suquet, hoping to miss the crowds. A ploy that worked until she reached the top of rue Saint Antoine. From there on, the place was buzzing with people intent on enjoying themselves. Although still early, the restaurants were beginning to fill with the first diners of the evening, and Daisy caught tantalising whiffs of food being cooked as she passed the various eateries.

Men, Daisy privately nicknamed 'the suits' with their official festival passes hanging around their necks, and their loud important voices, were out in force, busy networking on their mobiles and laptops, setting up deals to be finalised later in the week.

Gendarmes and security men were everywhere too, nonchalantly watching the proceedings but alert to any possible trouble erupting. The paparazzi, ten deep around the Palais des Festivals steps, were busy photographing the stars arriving for the evening screening.

Daisy squeezed into a space next to a stepladder that had been positioned on the middle of the road island separating the wide Croisette from the bord de mer. The woman sitting on top of it looked down and said, 'You're welcome to stand on the bottom for a better view.'

'Great. Thanks,' Daisy replied. 'Amazing crowds.'

'Is it your first festival? I've been every year for the past ten,' the woman continued, not waiting for an answer. 'Can't stay away. Know now to bring this and get here early for the best view. Oooh look, there's my favourite, George Clooney. Fancy a coffee, George?' and she laughingly held out a flask in his direction.

By the time all the stars had arrived and walked up the red carpet, it was twilight and the lights were coming on. Declining her new friend's offer of going for a drink, Daisy opted instead to have a wander around the tents of Village International while she waited to meet up with Marcus.

It proved to be a long wait. The evening screening had run on late and then Marcus had wanted to get some shots of the celebrities being whisked off to a private yacht for a champagne party. It was gone eleven before they began to make their way through the crowds still milling around on the Croisette to the party that Marcus had invites for.

There was no mistaking their party venue as they turned into a narrow street off rue d'Antibes:

blazing lights and pounding music and a crush of people queuing to enter the building.

'I'm not sure I'm up for this,' Daisy said, stifling a yawn as they joined the tail end of the queue. 'It's been a long day. Might just call a taxi and go home.'

'Come on, Daisy, don't be a wimp, it's only the first day of the festival,' Marcus said. 'I did warn you about the late nights. Bernard's a good contact for you, he knows everyone worth knowing – you never know who might be inside.'

'Okay. If I fall down asleep, it's your fault.'

'Not a chance with this racket going on,' Marcus said, taking her by the hand and leading her into the building as the security men took their tickets. 'Now let's mingle and see if we can find our host.'

Bernard, when they eventually located him holding court on a first-floor balcony, welcomed Marcus enthusiastically and kissed Daisy on the cheek when Marcus introduced her.

'Bernard, you knew Philippe Cambone well, didn't you?' Marcus asked. 'Daisy's writing a piece for the paper.'

Bernard gave brief nod. 'We go way back. He was best man at my wedding. He's my son's godfather. A terrible shock.' Bernard bit his lip, clearly upset. 'He was supposed to be here tonight, helping me host this bash. Instead I have to help arrange a tribute for later, but his family are being difficult.'

'How?' Daisy asked.

'They say it's a private matter and Philippe wouldn't have wanted a fuss.' Bernard sighed. 'What they don't seem to realise is how big a name he is – was – in the industry. We can't just ignore his passing. C'est pas possible.' Bernard took a sip of champagne from the glass he was holding. 'His brother, Jacques, says it's complicated. That there are other people to be considered – presumably he means Agnes, their mother. At nearly a hundred, the news about Philippe dying has made her ill. So everything has to be low key to avoid upsetting her further. All Jacques will tell me so far is that the body will be back in France by the end of this week and an announcement will be made then about a memorial service.'

'Do you think anyone in the family would talk to me about Philippe for a feature for the paper?' Daisy asked hopefully but received the answer she'd expected.

Bernard shook his head. 'Doubt it. The whole Cambone family appear to have closed ranks. They're not even talking to the French press.'

'Talk down at the Palais this afternoon was that there's some sort of scandal about to blow up,' Marcus said. 'That Mr Nice Guy Cambone wasn't all he seemed.'

Bernard glanced at him sharply. 'Philippe was the original Mr Nice Guy, I can assure you.' He sighed. 'Of course he's got this playboy reputation because he loved women – he was French after all.' Bernard gave a gallic shrug. 'Women adored him. He stayed friends with all his ex-lovers.' Bernard stared into his champagne glass thoughtfully. 'Still can't believe he's gone.'

A loud burst of music drowned out his next remark and he smiled apologetically at Daisy. As the noise abated, he handed her a business card.

'Great to meet you. Ring me sometime if you want to talk more about Philippe. I'll do what I can to help,' and he turned to greet another guest.

Daisy looked around the crowded room, trying to see if she recognised anyone famous. Unlike Poppy, she did read the gossip magazines, purely in the name of research, of course, and knew the faces of most of the 'A list' celebrities. Right now though, she didn't recognise anyone.

'Just spotted an old mate over by the bar,' Marcus shouted in her ear. 'Didn't expect to see him down here this year, he's had a few problems. Come and meet him,' and catching hold of her hand he led her across the room.

Marcus tapped a tall man on his shoulder, saying, 'Nat, how you doing? Meet Daisy, she's covering the festival for the first time.'

Daisy recognised Cindy's minder instantly. She could see, too, that he recognised her.

They smiled at each other. 'You!' they said in unison.

'You two already know each other?' Marcus asked.

'We've just seen each other around,' Nat said. 'Good to meet properly.'

'Sorted your problem yet?' Marcus asked.

Nat shook his head. 'Still working on it. Hope to get it sorted during the festival.'

Marcus turned to Daisy. 'This guy is a brilliant writer but insists on working as a nanny.'

'A fellow's got to eat,' Nat protested, smiling at Daisy. 'Especially when the rogues in this business insist on pinching my ideas,' he shrugged. 'At least I've got a roof over my head. Besides, I like children. Now, if you'll excuse me, I'm hoping there's a taxi waiting for me downstairs. I'll see you around.'

Impulsively Daisy said, 'I think I'm staying in the same direction as you – could I share your taxi?'

'Sure,' Nat replied easily.

Daisy looked at Marcus apologetically. 'I'm sorry but I am about to drop from exhaustion.'

Marcus placed a kiss on her cheek. 'Go home. I'll ring you tomorrow.'

Daisy looked at him. Now, why had he done that? Still trying to act like a Frenchman rather than the cocky leather-clad Northerner he was?

Or trying to stake a claim in front of Nat for some reason?

'I'll see her home safely for you, Marcus,' Nat said.

Daisy bit her lip. Nat had obviously got the idea from the kiss that she and Marcus were an item. Was that deliberate on Marcus's part?

The taxi was waiting when they got downstairs and Nat held the door open for Daisy before climbing in himself.

'Where are you staying?' he asked.

'I'm lucky that my sister lives down here.' Daisy gave him the address and took a ten euro note out of her bag and offered it to Nat, who shook his head.

'Don't worry about it. It's almost on my doorstep.'

'Thanks,' Daisy said. 'The little girl you're looking after, Cindy?' she said. 'Are her parents famous?'

'Verity Raymond and Teddy Wickham the director.'

'Her mum is the actress Verity Raymond?'

Nat nodded. 'Cindy's a sweet kid. Bit lonely at

the moment. Misses her friends. At least her father is here now. She adores him. Not that she's going to see a lot of him during the festival. He's head of the jury this year.'

'Would she like to meet up with Tom, my nephew, d'you think? Tom is six. Be a new friend for her.'

'That's a great idea. Cindy is almost six – big day next week! You and I could have a coffee together then? Look here's my number, give me a ring. I guess it will be easier for me to fit in a time around you as you're here to report on the festival.'

Daisy put the card Nat handed her in her bag. 'I'll find out what Tom is up to over the next few days and give you a ring,' she promised. 'Many thanks for the lift home.'

Cleaning her teeth before collapsing into bed, Daisy thought about Bernard's remarks regarding Philippe Cambone. If he was such a nice guy, why were there rumours starting to fly about him? And what exactly were those rumours?

Before snuggling down under the duvet, Daisy opened her laptop and updated her 'To-do list': go to another screening tomorrow; write up her 'clothing the stars for the festival' piece; find more info about Philippe Cambone.

And, of course, there was still the little matter of trying to uncover a scoop for Bill.

6

Thursday morning and Anna was up early, wanting to fit in a swim before breakfast and getting ready to go down to her company's temporary office in one of the hotels on the Croisette. It was a beautiful morning and, sitting out in the garden eating her breakfast, she decided to walk down into Cannes rather than call a taxi. It wasn't as if she had to clock in at a certain time.

Unknown to Anna, she was following in Daisy's footsteps of the previous evening when she turned onto rue Saint Antoine and began the steep descent. Because of the relatively early hour, many of the shops still had their shutters closed, but the cafés were already busy serving breakfasts to bleary-eyed festival goers. By the time Anna reached the bottom of the rue, the souvenir shops, their pavements and windows full of Cannes Film Festival memorabilia were open for business and the enticing smell of coffee being roasted hung in the air.

As she turned left at the bottom, Anna caught a glimpse of the amazing large trompe l'oeil on one of the buildings opposite. A tribute to Hollywood and the important part cinema had played in the growth of Cannes, Anna smiled as she recognised the famous faces depicted so brilliantly in movie scenes across the wall.

Rick, her business partner and office manager back home, and Fran, their PR and Personal Assistant, were both already in the office when Anna reached the hotel room they regularly booked during the festival. She was immediately absorbed into the meticulous, detailed organisation events at the festival demanded.

'As you know, *Future Promises* is screening Sunday evening, so I've managed to get a hair appointment for you with the salon here in the hotel for the morning,' Fran said, handing Anna an embossed card with the details on it. 'You've got your dress and everything organised?' She glanced at Anna who nodded. 'The limo will collect you and Leo at seven o'clock to take you to the Palais des Festivals and again afterwards to take you down to the Palm Beach for the party. There's also a couple of invitations here for various other parties.' Fran glanced at Anna. 'I know you said you didn't really want to get involved with the party scene on your own, but this one in particular sounds fun. It's up in Super Californie in one of the big villas there tomorrow night.'

Anna hesitated and glanced across at Rick. As always he was in total charge of things for Cannes week. She knew he'd been surprised when she'd told him she was coming to Cannes this year. The deal had always been, Anna didn't do Cannes. A couple of the other festivals, yes, but Rick was on his own for Cannes. He'd never asked why; just accepted it as a perk that he got to spend nearly a fortnight in the South of France every year. The networking he did was invaluable to the business and Anna had no intention of cramping his style in that regard.

'It's usually a good evening,' he said now. 'The Americans attend this one in full force. There will be several people there who would love to meet you, including the eccentric Rosa Cruft.'

'Isn't she on our party guest list? I'll meet her then,' Anna said.

Rick nodded. 'Yes, she is. No guarantee that she'll come though. We can go together if you like,' he offered. 'Pick you up at nine o'clock.'

'Okay and thanks,' Anna said, glancing at him. 'Rick, did you ever have any contact with Philippe Cambone down here?'

Rick shook his head. 'Shared a couple of cocktails with him at various parties down the years, but that's about it. Different ends of the business, so we were never going to be in regular contact. Seemed an okay sort of bloke. Did hear on the grapevine that he was looking to cut back on work. Wanted to spend more time down here with his family and on his boat. Shame he didn't manage it. Why?'

'No reason, just that somebody at the villa I've

rented asked if I'd ever worked with him and could I pass on any anecdotes for a feature she was writing. I thought I might ask around and see if anyone could help her.'

Rick shrugged. 'Sorry can't help. Right, I'm off to the JW Marriott for a meeting.'

'I'll walk down with you,' Anna said. 'I thought I'd have a mooch around Cannes this morning before going back to the villa. I need to find a supermarché too. Stock up on some supplies.'

At the hotel exit, they went their separate ways.

'See you tomorrow evening,' Rick said, before disappearing into the crowd, leaving Anna to cross the road and wander along the Croisette in the direction of the Palais des Festivals, soaking up the atmosphere.

Flags fluttering in the light breeze, huge bill-boards, pictures of famous stars everywhere, po-lice dogs and their handlers creating wide paths before them as the slow-moving crowd parted to let them through, before surging back to close ranks again behind them. Buskers, clowns, starlets hoping to be discovered, locals out for some people watching and nannies bribing their young charges with ice cream as they gazed at the over-the-top glamour in the designer boutiques that lined the Croisette. Anna watched it all and marvelled.

Le Petit Train, still with a few vacant seats, was about to set off on its routine sightseeing trip around town and Anna fleetingly wondered about hopping on board with the tourists. As she stood there, undecided, the decision was made for her when the driver rang the bell and the train began to slowly manoeuvre its way through the crowds and traffic.

A small crowd had gathered around a middle-aged woman with startling henna-red hair preparing to play an accordion. Anna, about to move on, found herself rooted to the spot as the woman began to sing 'Jezebel' à la Edith Piaf.

With a voice eerily similar to that of the tragic star's, the modern-day singer sent a frisson of déjà vu running through Anna's body. Once a favourite song of hers, she'd bought and played the record over and over again until, in a fit of blind rage the summer her world fell apart, she'd jumped and stamped on it until it was broken into hundreds of pieces. To hear that special song unexpectedly like this, in the place where the words had once been whispered so intimately to her, was heart-stoppingly hard.

Anna turned and blindly followed a group of teenage would-be starlets crossing the road. As the girls made their way up a busy street towards the centre of town, Anna turned in the opposite direction and took a narrower, quieter street, away from the hurly-burly of the crowds.

A small park, a labyrinth of traffic-free roads, and Anna slowly regained her composure. Another left turn and this street was busier, housing a florist, a fashion boutique, a couple of cafés and restaurants, the inevitable pharmacy and a tabac.

Anna sat at a pavement table at the smaller of the cafés and ordered a coffee. Waiting for her drink to arrive, she looked along the street with its tall, narrow buildings, their window boxes over-flowing with scarlet geraniums, blue shutters fastened against walls, exuding an air of tranquility absorbed down the centuries.

A typical French street, it reminded Anna of countless others she'd seen before in towns up and down the country, but there was something familiar about this particular street that she couldn't place and it was niggling at her.

'Merci,' she said as the waiter placed the demitasse coffee on the table before her.

Sipping her drink, she watched a couple of women, locals she guessed from their capacious straw shopping baskets, talking animatedly together as they came out of the pharmacy.

A few doors down, a well-dressed woman was in earnest discussion with the florist, before buying a large bunch of white lilies. As the woman, carefully holding her flowers, walked purposefully past her, Anna wondered who the flowers were destined for. The woman crossed the road a few yards on and stopped outside a shuttered restaurant with a large 'Fermé' sign plastered across its door.

Its pavement tables and chairs were piled up haphazardly, and there were numerous bunches of flowers already placed in the doorway. With a jolt, Anna realised where she was, why the street seemed familiar. As the unknown woman placed the lilies in the shade of the doorway, she didn't need to read the gold embossed name, 'Chez Cambone', above the door to know it was Philippe's family restaurant, the flowers placed as a tribute to him.

Her hand was shaking as she picked up her cup to take a steadying drink. Two reminders of her past on only her first full day in Cannes. Was every day going to be like this? Her past forcing her to remember and wonder 'what if'?

7

'Are you home this evening?' Poppy asked as Daisy helped herself to a tumbler of water in the cottage kitchen late that afternoon. 'Or are you off partying again?'

Daisy shook her head. 'Not tonight. I've got to finish writing up my daily report and send it, do a bit more to the Philippe Cambone feature – which reminds me. I must phone Marcus and see if he's got a photograph of the floral tributes that are apparently being laid at the door of the family restaurant, to send with my piece.' She took a drink before asking, 'Where's Tom? I thought I'd play with him for a bit.'

'Anna invited him over for a swim,' Poppy answered. 'He'll be back soon.'

'She's really nice, isn't she?' Daisy said. 'Friendly and approachable.'

'She seemed to be a bit low when I saw her this afternoon. Sad almost. I've asked her to join us tonight.'

'She doesn't seem to be interested in getting involved in the festivities very much,' Daisy said thoughtfully. 'She must know people in the business that are down here, but she did tell me she doesn't like the limelight.'

'There's a big party tomorrow evening that she's apparently thinking of attending. Anyway, I've asked her to join us for supper in the garden later,' Poppy said. 'I've warned her it's nothing fancy. No probing journalistic questions from you, mind,' she added, glancing at her sister sharply.

Daisy smiled. 'I promise. Now, what about this playdate I said I'd try and arrange for Cindy? I told Nat I'd fix a time and ring him.'

'How about ice creams in the park tomorrow afternoon, see how they get on. Being the daughter of an actress, Cindy might be a bit precocious for Tom,' Poppy replied. 'If they get on, you can bring them back here for tea. Nat too.'

'Great. I'll ring Nat,' Daisy said. 'Want me to help with supper?'

'No thanks,' Poppy said. 'It's just the usual quiche and salad, cheese and baguettes. I'll get Tom to help me carry it out to the loggia table.' She looked at the kitchen clock. 'Think I'll go and fetch him – I'm sure Anna will have had enough of his chatter by now.'

'Okay. I'll go and do my report and email it. Might even find time to do some more research on Philippe Cambone,' Daisy said. 'See you in a bit.'

* * *

Anna swam another half dozen laps after Poppy had collected Tom before getting out and going indoors for a shower. She was towelling her hair dry when Leo rang.

As always, her heart lifted at the sound of his voice.

'Leo, darling. How's your day been? Mine's been...' she hesitated, 'interesting.'

'Do I detect a note of distress?' Leo asked, the concern in his voice clear. 'Has something happened? Are you all right? I know Philippe's death was a shock to you.'

Anna sighed. 'No, nothing has happened to me other than a couple of memory-lane incidents that I'll tell you about when you get here.'

'Which will be Saturday now,' Leo said. 'One of my business meetings has been cancelled, so I've rearranged my flight.'

'Oh Leo, that's wonderful.'

'Would you like to book a table for dinner somewhere? I hear Le Moulin De Mougins is excellent.'

'I'll see what I can do,' Anna promised. 'I'm having supper with Poppy this evening, I'll ask her if there is anywhere special she can recommend.'

'Anna my darling, I've got to go. Alison wants my opinion on a cradle she's keen to buy – not that I really have any idea on such things. I'll ring you tomorrow. Love you.'

Anna smiled fondly at the thought of Alison and the expected baby. She could tell that Leo was already relishing his role of grandfather-to-be.

Half an hour later, taking a bottle of rosé out of the fridge, Anna made her way across the garden to the loggia attached to the cottage where Poppy had said they'd be eating supper.

Tom was busy putting cutlery and glasses on the gaily patterned Provençal tablecloth, before folding the matching napkins and placing them carefully on plates. Oscar the cat was curled up on one of the cushioned terrace chairs and Daisy was typing away at her laptop on a corner of the table. She raised a hand in greeting as she mouthed 'Hi' in Anna's direction.

Poppy came out of the kitchen carrying bowls of salad and a quiche, which she placed on the table. 'Hi – oh, thank you, but really there was no need,' she said as Anna handed her the bottle. 'Daisy will be finished soon and we'll eat. I must just light some candles before the midges decide to descend en masse. Grab a chair. I'll pour you a drink in a moment,' and Poppy took a match to several citronella candles that were dotted around the terrace.

Daisy closed the lid of her laptop with a flourish. 'Finished. Today's report sent and my short piece about Philippe Cambone just needs the photo Marcus promised to take of the floral tributes being laid on Chez Cambone's restaurant doorstep.'

'Did you manage to uncover much information?' Anna asked curiously.

'Not a lot. I did find a film biography site that mentioned his love of sailing, so I put that in, and the fact that his twin brother still runs the family restaurant here in Cannes – not that he'll talk to me. I decided not to mention the rumours that are floating around. I can keep that snippet for another feature if my editor wants more.'

'What rumours are those?' Anna asked, but before Daisy could answer, Poppy returned and the question was forgotten.

'Let's eat,' Poppy said, placing a bowl of buttered asparagus and new potatoes on the table. 'Bon appétit.'

'How are you enjoying the festival?' Daisy asked, looking at Anna. 'Have to say I'm already feeling exhausted at the sheer pace of things.

Goodness knows how you people actually in the industry cope with the frantic networking and partying that is going on.'

'Haven't really seen a great deal of it yet,' Anna replied. 'It's certainly different to the first time I was here.'

Daisy looked at her in surprise. 'I thought—'

Anna looked at her. 'I think I owe you an apology, Daisy. The trade-paper bio you read got it wrong. Mind you, it was a very different festival in those days, so it does feel a lot like coming for the first time.' Anna swirled the wine in her glass reflectively before looking up and saying, 'I was here in '68, the year the festival was closed early. I was seventeen, in my first year at Art College and had managed to get a low paid job as a messenger for the duration of the festival for a small UK film company.' She smiled at Daisy. 'Unfortunately it didn't work out as planned. I've discovered since that that is true of life in general.'

'That's true,' Poppy said. 'I never expected to be living in France, but here I am. May I give you some quiche, Anna?'

Anna held her plate out. 'Please. And you, Daisy? Is life working out for you so far?'

Daisy considered the question. 'Well, my love life hasn't lived up to expectations, that's for sure. I guess I'm lucky with my career going very much the way I wanted since I left university. Lots of changes at my newspaper are beginning to happen, though, and I'm toying with the idea of finally going freelance, whether that will mess things up remains to be seen.'

'What sort of freelance writing?' Anna asked.

'Lifestyle features. Property. Anything but hard-nosed reporting,' Daisy answered. 'I'm finding it difficult to justify the kind of intrusive journalism that seems to be the norm these days. I guess I'm just not hard enough. I think people are entitled to their privacy – unless they've done something criminally wrong, of course, and it needs exposing "in the public interest", as they say.' She looked at Anna, 'How long did it take you to establish your business? Did you have many contacts before you went independent?'

'Oh, it was years before I felt brave enough to go solo. Meeting Rick – my business partner – was the catalyst,' Anna said. 'With hindsight there are lots of things I would do differently, but, in general, I suppose my working life has turned out fine.' She turned to Poppy. 'Talking of work, I need to host a small party for my company during the festival. Can you help me organise one here at the villa next week? Or tell me where I can get help? Now I know Leo will definitely be here, I think Tuesday evening will be best.'

'No problem,' Poppy answered. 'Glad to help. We'll get together in the next couple of days and work things out. Tom, no dessert until you've eaten your salad.'

'The other thing is, Leo suggested I booked a table for dinner the evening he arrives, any ideas? He mentioned a restaurant called Le Moulin De Mougins.' Anna said.

Poppy pulled a face. 'Difficult. I suspect that particular restaurant will already be fully booked. It's expensive and a favourite with the celebrities. Everywhere gets so busy this fortnight. You might have to go to Antibes or even Cagnes-sur-mer.'

'I can always do something here. I saw a couple of delicatessens with some mouth-watering food this morning when I was shopping,' Anna said. 'In fact, I think I'll do that. The villa's garden is so lovely, I'm sure Leo will enjoy supper al fresco here for his first evening on Saturday. I'm certainly enjoying eating out here this evening, thank you.'

The four of them ate in companionable silence for several moments before Poppy stood up. 'Come on, Tom. Time for that video call Dad promised you tonight and then it's bed for you. Say goodnight to Daisy and Anna. Daisy, help Anna to some more dessert and wine.'

'How many people are you inviting for your party next week?' Daisy asked as she offered Anna the bowl of fruit salad and some meringues.

'Thirty-five – maybe forty. I doubt everyone will come. Depends on what else is on the same evening. These meringues are delicious.'

A loud croak from a frog somewhere in the garden made them both smile.

'Now that's something I remember from my first visit down here,' Anna said. 'There were a lot of croaking frogs. I was staying in a run-down guest house with a stagnant pond in the over-grown garden; the noise was unbelievable.'

'It gets quite noisy in this garden too some-times,' Daisy said absently. 'Anna, please may I ask you something? You can say no obviously, if you hate the idea. Would you talk to me about the differences you find in the festival this time around? The way it's developed from those early days? Maybe we could walk around Cannes to-gether – a nostalgic walk for you, a history lesson for me.'

'Oh, Daisy, I don't know. I'm not sure that...' Anna shook her head, thinking about her memory lane incidents earlier in the day.

'So much must have changed in the last forty years – not just buildings being pulled down and rebuilt, but people's everyday lives have altered too. You could always remain anonymous if you want, but I think the comparison between then and now would be of interest to lots of people.' Daisy looked at Anna hopefully.

'I'm not sure I remember enough to highlight the differences,' Anna said slowly. 'I was barely seventeen. Of course I remember the atmosphere, the students and the old Palais des Festivals but —' Anna shook her head. 'No. I'd rather not.'

'That's okay,' Daisy said quickly. 'It was just a thought. I was probably way out of line asking you. I'm sorry.'

Anna waved her apology away with a smile as Poppy returned at that moment with a pot of coffee. Gratefully, Anna accepted a cup, glad to be able to change the subject. 'I meant to say earlier, you will both come to the party, won't you?'

'Love to,' Daisy said, picking up her mobile from the table. 'Excuse me, I've got a text from Marcus – oh, it's okay. It's just to tell me he's sent the photo to accompany my feature and forwarded me a copy too.'

As the sonar garden lights flickered into action, Anna stood up to leave.

'Thank you both for a lovely evening. I was feeling a bit low this afternoon and you've really cheered me up. Can I help clear the table? No, you're sure?' as Poppy shook her head. 'I'll see you tomorrow then. Goodnight,' and Anna began to make her way across the garden to the villa.

'Poppy, look at this,' Daisy said, holding her

mobile out so Poppy could see the picture. 'Is that who I think it is about to place a single rose with the other tributes to Philippe Cambone at the family restaurant?'

'Think so,' Poppy said, looking at the screen intently. 'The soft focus has given it a certain ethereal look, but, yes, that's Anna.'

They both looked across the garden and returned Anna's last goodnight wave as she disappeared into the villa.

'I wonder why she was leaving flowers for someone she says she didn't know?' Daisy said curiously, looking at Poppy. 'I wish I'd looked at this before she said goodnight.'

Poppy sighed. 'She was probably simply laying a tribute to a fellow film-maker. Somebody in the same business. You know, like people do when someone famous dies – a mark of respect even if they didn't know them.'

8

Friday morning and Poppy was in the kitchen urging Tom to hurry up and eat his breakfast when Daisy joined them.

'You're going to be late for school at this rate,' Poppy said, before turning to her sister. 'Croissant? Coffee'

Daisy shook her head. 'No thanks. I'm running late for a screening. I'll grab something in Cannes after it finishes. See you both later,' and Daisy ruffled Tom's hair as she passed him.

It was a couple of hours later before she made her way across to one of the many cafés on the square opposite the Palais des Festivals and ordered a couple of croissants to go with the coffee she now felt desperate for.

She was sitting there eavesdropping on the conversations going on around her and trying to get some coherent thoughts about the film she'd just seen onto her laptop when Marcus briefly kissed her cheek and sat down beside her. She really was going to have to have a word about all this kissing. He was English not French.

'Hi. How's it going?'

'Fine. You? Caught any celebrities in flagrante?' Daisy asked.

Marcus shook his head. 'Not yet, but I live in hope. Uncovered any interesting titbits for Bill?'

'No. Thanks for the photo by the way. Was...' she went to say Anna but realised in time that Marcus didn't know her name, 'the woman alone? Did you speak to her?' Daisy asked.

'Didn't see anyone else. And no, I didn't speak to her,' Marcus said slowly. 'Why? D'you know who she is?'

Daisy nodded. 'Yes. It's... the woman who's rented my sister's villa for the festival.'

'I'm surprised you recognised her. I deliberately went for a slightly out-of-focus shot because I wanted the poignancy of a mourner laying a tribute without identification. Who is she, anyway?'

'Anna runs a production company and she's really nice but...' Daisy hesitated. 'Very private,' she said finally, wondering how Anna would react if she ever saw the photograph.

'You talked to her about Cambone?'

'I tried. She's not very forthcoming about him. Says she never worked with him,' Daisy said.

Marcus yawned. 'Sorry. Didn't get to bed until three this morning. See if you can get her to open up a bit more. Whatever Bernard says, there is something bubbling behind the Cambone family's silence. The fact they won't talk to anyone is suspicious.'

'They might just want their privacy at a sad time?' Daisy suggested tentatively.

Marcus shrugged. 'Privacy is rarely an option in the film business. Did you get to the press conference this morning?'

Daisy shook her head. 'No, the screening ran over and I missed it.'

'There was a rumour flying about that the American actor, Sean Hamill, is somehow connected to Cambone. Nobody is saying yet what the connection is though. Right, I'm off to take some pics of the celebs on the beach. You want to come too?'

'No thanks. I'm going to have a wander around, see if I can pick up some gossip in the shopping mall before I have lunch with a PR from one of the film agencies. Thought I might go and take a look at the floral tributes too,' Daisy said.

* * *

The windows of the shopping mall that linked the Croisette with the rue d'Antibes were filled with expensive clothes, jewellery and the latest must-have handbags. As Daisy wandered around, advertising flyer after flyer was pressed into her hand by young girls and boys keen to publicise their talents and catch the eye of anybody who could turn them into the stars they dreamed of being. Or at the very least give them fifteen minutes of fame. Daisy stuffed the flyers into her bag. She'd look at them later – there might be an interesting story in there somewhere.

A couple were entertaining the crowd with a juggling act. Near the mall exit doorway, a violinist was setting up his music as the gendarmes moved a couple of beggars and their dogs on. Outside, the streets in the centre of town were teeming with hawkers, buskers and human statues. It was all very colourful and noisy.

It took Daisy nearly ten minutes to reach Chez Cambone after leaving the mall. Although still firmly closed to customers, she saw the flowers had been moved to one side, allowing access through the restaurant door.

Slowly Daisy began to read the tributes as she looked for the single rose she knew Anna had placed in the doorway.

A sad loss
One of the greats
You'll be missed

There were two single roses – both red and both with attached cards.

Au revoir. God bless you. A lifelong admirer

read one. The other card was unsigned and read:

One Life. One Love. Farewell

followed by three kisses. Thoughtfully, Daisy studied that card. One kiss for each sentiment?

As Daisy stood there holding them, wondering which rose Anna had placed there, which inscription was from her, the restaurant door opened. Bernard Audibert came out, accompanied by another man who Daisy guessed was Jacques Cambone, Philippe's twin brother. From the photos she'd seen searching the internet, she could see the likeness.

The two men shook hands and Jacques disappeared back indoors, closing the door firmly behind him, without as much as a glance in Daisy's direction.

Daisy smiled at Bernard. 'Hello. D'you remember me? Marcus introduced us at your party.'

'Bien sûr, I remember you – it's Daisy, isn't it?' Bernard leant in and kissed her cheek. 'You were asking me about Philippe and the Cambone family.' He gestured towards the closed restaurant door. 'Désolé, I don't think Jacques was in the mood to be introduced.'

'No worries,' Daisy said. 'I've heard something about an American actor called Sean Hamill being somehow involved in a scandal involving Philippe Cambone. Any truth in that, d'you think?' Daisy said, watching for Bernard's reaction.

He shrugged. 'I doubt it. I think it's a publicity stunt in very questionable taste. The Cambones have already got the police looking into him. But – and this is strictly off the record, understand?' Bernard paused before continuing. 'Two letters have been found amongst Philippe's effects from someone trying to trace their family tree.'

'Is this why the Cambones have closed ranks?' Bernard nodded his head in agreement.

'D'you know who the letters are from?' Daisy asked.

'No.' Bernard shrugged. 'I didn't get to see or read the letters and Jacques was being pretty coy about their contents. He certainly didn't name names, but it was clear that Philippe had replied to the first letter. The second one arrived in response to it the day Philippe died.' He took a deep breath. 'Anyway, I've finally got some dates out of Jacques for the funeral and the memorial service. The funeral will be on Monday – strictly private, family and close friends. No details will be issued to the public.'

'Are you going?' Daisy asked.

Bernard nodded. 'Of course. I'm doing a reading. Hoping my son will be able to get here in time too.'

'And the memorial service is when?' Daisy asked.

'The following Monday morning after the festival has closed, open to everyone.'

Bernard looked at the flowers Daisy was still holding. 'From you?'

'Oh. No,' Daisy said. 'I was just reading the

messages. They both have a certain regretful solicitous tone,' and she read the first one out to Bernard. 'The other one feels more personal somehow: One life. One love. Farewell.'

'Show me,' Bernard demanded, holding his hand out.

Daisy handed him the two roses and the cards and watched him, his face intent as he studied both the messages, muttering under his breath as he did so and shaking his head.

Daisy had just caught the words 'C'est pas possible,' when Bernard turned to face her.

'I'm sorry, I have to go. I'm running late for a meeting.' He leant in and kissed her on the cheek. 'Keep in touch and I'll let you know if there's any news. Au revoir.' Carefully he placed the flowers down on the step and was gone.

A bemused Daisy gazed after him, wondering what was not possible. And which of the cards had caused him to make that comment?

* * *

From her table at the Beach Restaurant, Anna had

a clear view of the numerous luxury yachts moored out in the bay. The noise from heli-copters, busily ferrying VIPs to the Palm Beach complex at the far eastern end of the Croisette, added to the hubbub of sounds all around. In the distance, the Isles of Sainte-Marguerite and Saint-Honorat lay serene in the midday sun. Anna turned her head to alter her line of vision, deter-mined not to let certain memories of Sainte-Mar-guerite flood into her mind right now.

Anna reached for her tumbler of water. Lunch had been delicious – tuna salade niçoise followed by a mouth-watering glacé with summer fruits and mascarpone. Reneé Porteous, the Parisian who represented the company in France, had been full of enthusiasm for the coming year. Now she'd left for another meeting, leaving Anna and Rick sitting there mulling over the things that had been discussed and taking in the atmosphere.

All around them, life, as one big social net-working event, was busy: People talking animat-edly on their mobiles; men in Armani suits and actresses dressed to seduce, air-kissed; ladies who lunched with coiffured hair and their inevitable toy dogs were busy seeing and being seen. Two gendarmes, arms folded across their chests, were standing regarding the diners seriously.

'Wonder who or what they're after,' Rick said, as one of the policemen, his gun visibly protruding from his waist holster, began to weave his way between the tables towards a large group of diners. Judging by the noise they were making and the number of empty bottles on the table, the party had clearly indulged themselves over lunch.

Turning her head to look, Anna felt her heart lurch in her chest. Sitting three tables away was Jacques Cambone. For a fraction of a second, Anna had believed it was Philippe – the likeness was so startling. Both Jacques and the man he was lunching with, were watching the police intently. There was something vaguely familiar about the other man too, but Anna couldn't quite place what it was.

The rowdy table had fallen silent as the policeman approached. A fair haired man, clearly the subject of the policeman's interest, had pushed his chair back and was standing up.

'Yeah. Sure. I'm Sean Hamill,' Anna heard him say in a drunken drawl. 'What's the problem?'

The officer's reply was lost in the general buzz as he reached in a pocket for a pair of handcuffs, which he proceeded to snap around Sean Hamill's wrists, before indicating with a jerk of his head and a pull of his arm that he was to accompany him.

'Hey, lighten up, man. It was just a publicity stunt. A joke.'

'Une blague in poor taste, monsieur,' one of the gendarmes answered.

As Sean and the policemen passed their table, Anna and Rick got a good look at him. Late thirties, tall, sunglasses pushed up into his fashionably long hair, expensive loafers on his feet, wearing white jeans and polo shirt, he appeared unfazed by his arrest.

'Interesting,' Rick said. 'That's the actor who's been claiming to be related to Philippe Cambone.'

Shocked, Anna looked at him before slowly turning and looking at Jacques in time to see him glance at his companion and mutter, 'Bien. It is to be hoped that that should put a stop to it.'

'Right,' Rick said, pushing his chair back and standing. 'I'm off. See you this evening. The party,' he added as Anna looked at him, puzzled. 'Super Californie?'

'Sorry, I'd completely forgotten,' Anna answered. 'See you later then.'

Anna sat for a few moments after Rick had left, lost in her thoughts. She turned to look at Jacques and his companion. Idly she found herself wondering how Jacques would react if she approached him to offer her condolences about Philippe. Would he recognise her – unlikely, it was so long ago they'd met – or simply accept her platitudes about his brother as coming from an ex-colleague? Would he introduce her to his companion?

One of the licensed African beach sellers approached, offering a selection of watches and sunglasses, kaftans and various other items. Anna shook her head, the interruption breaking into her thoughts. 'Non merci,' and the man continued his hopeful trawl around the beach restaurant tables.

Pensively, she looked out across the bay towards the islands – and this time she allowed a long-ago memory a little space in her thoughts. Was life over there still as simple and idyllic as it had appeared to be, forty years ago? If there was time, she'd suggest she and Leo take one of the local ferryboats and spend a couple of hours wandering around Saint-Honorat with its ancient Abbaye. She knew Leo would be intrigued by the story of the Man in the Iron Mask who'd been held captive for decades in the ancient fort on Sainte-Marguerite, but she wasn't ready to face down her own particular memories of that island just yet.

Jacques Cambone and his friend had stood up and were walking towards her table on their way to the beach exit. Anna felt a jolt of recognition as she saw the face of Jacques' companion. She couldn't remember his name, but she was certain he was a friend of Philippe's whom she'd met years ago.

She half stood up to speak to him, to claim acquaintance, to offer Jacques her condolences, but sank back down again onto her chair without speaking. What was the point? It couldn't possibly serve any purpose, so was best left. Once the festival was over, she'd be leaving with Leo and together they would make new memories. New happy memories that would push away the old, unhappy recollections that seemed to have taken over her mind recently.

9

Daisy and Nat stood on the Croisette waving at Tom and Cindy every time they whirled by sitting side by side on gaily painted carousel horses.

'They're getting on well, aren't they? Poppy was worried Cindy might be a bit precocious,' Daisy said.

'Cindy's a sweet kid,' Nat answered. 'Not your average spoilt monster with showbiz parents. Verity and Teddy are very down-to-earth, nice people.'

Daisy hesitated before asking. 'It's none of my business, but I was wondering what you meant by rogues in the business the other day?'

'Somebody, pretending to be interested in representing me, took my last script and got it commissioned as his own work,' Nat said, sighing ruefully.

'That's awful,' Daisy exclaimed. 'Couldn't you expose him?'

Nat shook his head. 'Unfortunately there's no copyright in ideas and he'd altered the script just enough to make it difficult for me to prove anything. So from now on I intend to be more careful who I trust and make sure I register everything with the scriptwriters' union and other places. I do admit to harbouring murderous thoughts about him, but in the end I had to accept it as a harsh life lesson and move on.'

'Did it become a big film?'

Nat nodded. 'Oh yes. It did very well at the box office – I wouldn't have had any money problems for years. C'est la vie,' and shrugging his shoulders, he smiled at Daisy.

'Can't Teddy Wickham help you get started? He must know all sorts of people in the business,' Daisy said.

'He's promised to introduce me to a couple of

producers this week,' Nat answered. 'Being head of the jury, he's very busy. It's Cindy's birthday next week too. He's hoping to be able to at least spend a couple of hours with her on the day.'

'Is Verity planning anything special for her?'

'Lots of presents and treats here, and then a big party when they get back home to Los Angeles.'

As the carousel glided to a stop, Daisy and Nat helped the two children off.

'Time for ice creams now,' Daisy said. 'Then back to the cottage for tea.'

* * *

When Daisy, Nat and the two children got back to the Villa Flora Poppy was sitting at the kitchen table writing a long list.

'Hi sis, meet Nat and Cindy,' Daisy said.

Poppy smiled at the two of them. 'Hi Nat, nice to meet you. Tea will be in ten minutes. Tom, why don't you show Cindy your tree house – but stay away from the villa. Anna's just gone for a siesta by the pool. Try not to disturb her.'

Daisy glanced at the list. 'You and Anna sorted things for her party?'

'Yes. She's decided she'd like a "1920s on the Cote d'Azur" theme. I've agreed to do the catering as she mainly only wants nibbles – I can source some of them from the market and make the rest here on the day. She's also asked me to try to find a pianist for the night – thank goodness I had the piano tuned last month!'

'Sounds fun,' Daisy said. 'As guests, do we get to wear flapper dresses? I've forgotten – which evening is it? Must make sure I'm not busy.'

'Tuesday. Don't know about flapper dresses – but I'm definitely going to be in a bit of a flap, I think. Can you help me with things? It's a bigger event than I thought it was going to be.' Poppy appealed to her sister. 'I'm already starting to panic at the thought of forty people in the garden. Good job Dan's well out of the way.'

'Tom can come and play with Cindy after school for a couple of hours on Monday and Tuesday, if that's any help,' Nat said. 'They seem to be getting on well,' he added, as a burst of childish laughter drifted across the garden from the tree house.

'That would be brilliant, thanks,' Poppy answered. 'Now all I need to do is work my way through this list before next week.'

'Don't worry, sis, it'll all work out,' Daisy said reassuringly. 'Right now, though, we'd better eat before Nat has to take Cindy home and I have to get back down to Cannes for a quick look at the stars on tonight's red carpet. Eating in the garden as usual? I'll lay the table and then go and get the children.'

Walking out into the garden, Daisy saw Anna asleep on a sunbed under one of the poolside parasols. Tom waved from the tree house and Daisy beckoned to them to come down, before turning to go back to the cottage.

As they tiptoed past the end of the swimming pool, Tom told Cindy in a loud stage whisper, 'That's my friend, Anna. She's really nice. She lets me swim in the pool with her. She's come for the festival like your mum and dad.'

'Is she a film star like Mummy?' Cindy whispered back.

'Gosh, no,' Tom said. 'She's too old. I think she helps make the films.'

Anna, smothering a smile, opened her eyes. 'Hello, Tom. Who's this?'

'This is my new friend, Cindy. Her mummy is an actress.'

'Hello, Cindy,' Anna said. 'That's a pretty name.'

'It's what Daddy calls me,' Cindy said. 'My real name is Lucinda, but he says I'm his little princess like Cinderella became when she lost her shoe and married the prince. And now everyone calls me it,' and Cindy gave a strangely resigned grown-up shrug as she smiled at Anna.

'Is your daddy an actor too?' Anna sat up as she spoke.

Cindy shook her head. 'No. I don't know what he does, but he's always very busy,' she said seriously. 'It's my birthday next week,' she said. 'Mummy says we might go on a boat and see the whales, but Daddy doesn't know yet if he can come.'

'How old will you be?' Anna asked.

'Six.'

'Tom. Cindy. Teatime. Leave Anna in peace,' Poppy called.

'Bye, Anna,' Tom and Cindy said together as they ran over to the cottage.

Anna pushed her sunglasses to the top of her head and watched the children disappearing into the cottage, before slowly making her way into the villa to prepare and eat a cheese baguette so she'd at least have some food inside her before the party in Super Californie she'd promised to attend with Rick.

Half an hour later, with Cindy between them holding their hands, Daisy and Nat walked down to the grand belle-époque villa where Teddy Wickham and his family were staying for the festival.

Nat pressed the security button, the gate swung open and Cindy skipped inside. Nat glanced at Daisy.

'I've got tickets for the cinema on the beach tomorrow evening, want to join me? Not sure what's showing – could be Tom and Jerry or a decent classic feature.'

'Hey, don't knock Tom and Jerry,' Daisy

laughed. 'I'm a big fan. Shall I see you by the Carlton beach after the evening's red carpet proceedings? I'll need to take a look at that first. Should be finished about eight o'clock.'

'Look forward to it. Thanks for this afternoon and tea,' Nat said, followed Cindy into the landscaped villa gardens and the gate closed behind them.

10

As Daisy cut through the back streets of Cannes and continued her way down to the Palais des Festivals via the old port, she thought about Nat. How nice he was. How kind he was. How different he was to Ben. As for those blue eyes of his... they were simply spellbinding, she decided. It would be fun spending time together and getting to know him better at the beach cinema tomorrow evening.

Several of the yachts moored alongside the quay were hosting parties and Daisy caught snippets of conversations in French, Italian and what she took to be Russian as she walked past a white hulled sailing yacht where a television crew were on board busily filming a bikini clad actress.

Dodging the crowds that were still swarming around the tents of the Village International, Daisy made her way to the front of the Palais des Festivals hoping to find Marcus there. He might have heard some more gossip regarding the rumours that were circulating about Philippe Cambone. The sudden end to the conversation she'd had with Bernard outside the Cambone's restaurant earlier was still puzzling her.

There was the usual scrum of paparazzi, busy snapping away at the stars arriving for the evening show. Daisy stood watching as five or six actors, all in a row with their arms linked, made their way along the red carpet towards the steps. Cameras flashed, smiles gleamed and jewellery sparkled. For a brief moment Daisy wondered what life must be like living in the spotlight. It wasn't something she'd enjoy that was for sure. It was several moments before she finally spotted Marcus photographing a leggy blonde getting into a Ferrari parked near the red carpet.

'You get my text?' he asked, turning to greet

Daisy, as the Ferrari engine revved noisily before taking off down the Croisette with its passenger, at an enforced sedate pace. 'Dinner tomorrow night?'

Daisy shook her head. 'Sorry. Nat's already asked me to go to the beach cinema with him.'

'Okay. We'll make it next Tuesday evening.' Marcus sighed when Daisy shook her head again.

'It's Anna's party at the villa and I've been invited.'

'Can I come?'

'I'll ask Anna,' Daisy promised, not wanting to say an outright no, but she doubted that Anna would invite him. 'We could have that dinner Bill is treating us to this evening if you like?' she suggested tentatively. 'I'm not dressed for anywhere too posh but—'

'Bernard's got me an invite to a swish party,' Marcus interrupted. 'In fact, it's time I showered and got into my evening suit. I'll see you around,' and he was gone.

Pensively, Daisy crossed the Croisette. Surely Marcus could have wangled an invite for her too?

Daisy wandered slowly along, looking at the

expensive boutiques. It was impossible to see much because of the crowds and in the end she gave up and made for a seat under a palm tree in the nearby gardens of the Hotel de Ville.

Pulling her laptop out of her bag she began to write up some notes ready for her next report.

As the sun sets, flashing lights and neon signs take over in the twilight, indicating that the glamorous nightlife of Cannes, which will continue into the early hours, is once again starting. The 'Welcome to the Cannes Film Festival' illuminated sign strung across the road reminds you, in case you forget, you're on the Cote d'Azur at the world-famous event.

Out in the bay, I can see lights on Roberto Cavalli's large purple yacht, where the crew are preparing for a big party on board tonight; among other celebrities, Naomi Campbell is rumoured to be a guest.

Earlier, limousines discharged their VIP passengers outside the Palais des Festivals, where they faced the usual barrage of flashlights and shouts of admiration from the waiting crowds before walking up the red carpet lined steps into the theatre. Some lucky fans managed to obtain the autograph of their favourite star and a few even managed to persuade their idols to stand alongside them for a once-in-a-lifetime photograph.

Music is pounding from cars as they move slowly along the Croisette, under the censorious gaze of stern-faced gendarmes. The weather tonight is perfect for the cinema on the beach. People are hurrying past me to claim a seat on the sand under the stars, ready to watch a movie in a truly romantic setting with the Mediterranean gently lapping at the shoreline and a balmy breeze providing the best air conditioning.'

Daisy closed the laptop, slipped it back into her bag and sat for a few moments people watching before getting up and walking back to the villa.

Poppy was sitting reading under the loggia.

'Tom in bed?' Daisy asked, joining her sister.

'Yep. I wasn't expecting you until later. Everything all right? I guess it's busy down town?' Poppy said.

'Mayhem. Poppy, can we talk? I haven't told you about the letter from Ben I received the day I flew out here. I hadn't forgotten about it, but festival things pushed it to the back of my mind.'

Poppy closed her book. 'Oh. What did he have to say for himself?'

Daisy took the letter out of her bag and handed it to her sister. 'Read it. I'm going to have a shower.'

A bottle of wine, glasses and a plate of sliced baguette and parma ham with melon was on the table alongside Ben's letter when she returned fifteen minutes later.

'Honestly, Poppy, I'm going to be so fat by the end of the festival. I always eat too much when I stay with you. Everything seems to revolve around drink and food down here.'

'Because it's France. It's the way they are – besides, you could do with a bit more on you,' Poppy said, helping herself to a slice of melon. 'So what are you going to do about Ben? Are you going to fly halfway around the world and run back into his arms as he suggests?'

'I don't know.' Daisy sighed as she poured two glasses of wine. 'Was hoping you'd help me decide.' When Poppy didn't answer, she continued, 'Part of me thinks, no way, but then another part says, why not?'

'Big decision. I know he says he misses you and "thinks" he's made a mistake, but really, Daisy, he could just be homesick. You could pack everything in at home, get out there and find it's you who's made the mistake.'

Daisy nodded. 'I know.' She took a sip of wine. 'I was thinking I could go for a holiday, say three weeks. Surely I'd know by the end of it whether I wanted to stay or not. Wouldn't I?'

'How much do you really miss Ben these days? I mean, really, really miss? You said you were enjoying being single.'

'I am. But you know how it is. It's lovely to have someone special in your life. Someone who honestly cares.'

'Which Ben clearly didn't, otherwise he wouldn't have broken it off with you and then buggered off to Australia in the first place, would he?' Poppy demanded.

Daisy looked at her sister. She had a definite point there. And Poppy so rarely swore, Daisy knew the whole idea of her sister jetting off to Australia and taking up with Ben again had upset her.

'I'm going indoors to phone Dan, I promised I'd call him tonight,' Poppy said, standing up. Daisy could tell from the set of her shoulders that Poppy was now in full big sister bossy mode. Her next words confirmed it.

'Only you can decide,' Poppy said. 'Personally, I think you'd be making a huge mistake in running after Ben. Unless of course it's true love on both your parts. I have to say, though, I somehow doubt that you've ever really been in love with Ben.'

Daisy stared at her sister's retreating back. Of course she'd loved Ben in the beginning – hadn't she?

11

Anna put the finishing touches to her make-up before making her way downstairs to wait for Rick and the taxi. She was already regretting agreeing to go to this party, but it was too late to back out now. These extravagant sponsored parties held by the likes of Chanel and Chopard were simply not her scene, she didn't even know who was holding tonight's extravaganza. Anna glanced at her watch. Just time to give Leo a quick ring before she left.

'Not sure what time I'll get back here from this party,' she said when he answered. 'So I thought I'd ring you first. How are you? And Alison?'

'Everything is fine this end. Can't wait for to-morrow,' Leo answered. 'Hope to be with you early afternoon. Have you booked us somewhere exotic for dinner?'

Before Anna could tell him her plans for an al fresco supper at the villa, a car horn sounded outside. 'Got to go. Rick's here early. Love you. See you tomorrow.'

The taxi took Anna and Rick quickly up through town and into the affluent area of Super Californie, where they caught glimpses of imposing villas hidden away behind large iron gates and towering cypress hedges.

'Have we had many acceptances yet for our party on Tuesday?' Anna asked.

'Fifteen definites, eight refusals so far and fifteen still to answer,' Rick said.

'So we're on course to end up with the thirty-five or so guests we'd hoped for?' Anna said thoughtfully. 'Including us, Leo, Daisy and Poppy.' She hoped she hadn't put too much pressure on Poppy by asking her to help with the catering. Maybe she should have gone for professional outside caterers for such a large number of guests.

The taxi slowed and joined a queue of taxis and limos edging their way between intricate wrought-iron gates onto a gravelled driveway that finally ended in front of an impressive flight of steps leading to a grand column-dominated entrance.

'This place is something else, isn't it?' Rick said as they walked into the huge marbled entrance hall, with its four overhead chandeliers casting their palatial glow over everything.

An elaborately carved four foot high gold fountain, decorated with naked nymphs and grapes, was gently tinkling water into its two basins, from where it flowed over into a marble-lined base, where goldfish could be seen swimming under water lily leaves.

Liveried footmen holding silver trays full of crystal flutes filled with pink champagne moved effortlessly through the crowd. Rick took two, handed one to Anna and said, 'Cheers.'

'Cheers,' Anna replied, looking around at the paintings and tapestries hanging on the walls under elaborate gold friezes. 'I've been in some luxurious places over the years,' she said. 'But this is amazing. Are those original Picassos and Renoirs? Who does this place belong to?'

Rick shrugged. 'Some Arab prince or other, so I'd guess, yes, they'll be originals. The main event is in the marquee on the terrace. Shall we?'

Anna followed him as he made his way out through open French doors leading onto the terrace and acres of landscaped gardens.

'Just spotted Rosa Cruft. Come on, I'll introduce you,' Rick said.

Rosa, talking animatedly to a man who had his back to them as they approached, smiled in welcome.

'Hi there, Ricky. Great to meet you at last, Anna. You guys know Bernard?'

As the American made the introductions and Bernard shook her hand, Anna found herself face to face with the man she'd seen earlier in the day with Jacques Cambone. She caught her breath and shook the man's hand without looking him directly in the eye.

'Anna, nice to meet you. Have we met before? Are you in the business?'

Anna didn't answer his first question, saying,

'Yes, I am in the film industry. Rick and I are business partners. You?'

'I'm in finance. You sure we haven't met? Something very familiar about your face. We must get together sometime and discuss our pasts,' Bernard said, smiling at her.

'Maybe,' Anna said lightly, before turning to face Rosa. 'Rosa, I do hope you can make our party next week. We can chat more then. Now, if you will excuse me, I need to find the cloakroom. Back in a few moments,' and Anna made her way back into the mansion.

One of the liveried footmen pointed her in the direction of the ladies' cloakroom. To her relief, it was empty and Anna stood in front of the large gilded mirror above a marble sink with gold taps and tried to reapply her lipstick with a shaking hand. She'd finally remembered who Bernard was – Philippe's best friend.

So why hadn't she admitted to him that, yes, they had met before? Because it had been a long time ago when Philippe had introduced her to his best mate – whose name she was sure hadn't been Bernard in those days. She seemed to remember it had been... Brian. That was it. Idly, she wondered when and why he'd changed his name. People changed their names for all sorts of reasons, she knew. Usually to hide from someone or to keep a secret. What would his reaction be if she went back out there and told him the truth about herself? That yes, he had met her before, at an infamous festival long ago – when she'd been with Philippe. Should she do it?

She pushed the lid back onto her lipstick. No. Not here tonight. Not ever. What would be the point? Philippe was dead. Bernard/Brian and her were unlikely to see each other ever again after the festival finished – why would they? Just because he'd been close to a man she'd once known years ago didn't mean they too, would be friends in the present.

She glanced at her watch. How soon before she could decently leave? Quarter of an hour – or longer? She sighed before resolutely returning to the marquee and regarding the party scene for several moments.

Disco music with a loud beat was filling the air and people were dancing. Anna saw Rick and

Rosa Cruft had moved and were now in the middle of a large crowd to one side of the tent. Should she join them? She looked across to where Bernard was listening attentively to something a younger man at his side, his arm around the shoulders of a blonde girl, was saying.

As she watched, Bernard turned his head un-expectedly and looked directly at her. Anna sensed, as his intense gaze caught her own look from across the room, that he'd realised who she was. The younger man turned too and looked across at her, before leaning and muttering some-thing to Bernard. Smiling, Bernard slowly raised his arm in greeting and beckoned her to join them.

In a daze, Anna acknowledged the greeting before turning away to make for the exit. She'd make her apologies to Rosa Cruft when they met up next week, but there was no way she could face returning to Bernard tonight and all the questions he was sure to level at her.

To her relief, a doorman was able to immedi-ately summon her a waiting taxi and she sank down gratefully on to its upholstered seats. She would go back to the Villa Flora and dream about Leo and her future – not dwell on the past.

* * *

The next morning, Anna, sleep having eluded her for most of the night as images of herself and Philippe from the past kept floating into her mind, made herself a strong cafetière of coffee, hoping the caffeine would jolt her into the day. She was sitting on the terrace, starting to feel more human after her second cup when her mobile rang. Rick.

'How are you this morning?' he asked.

'Fine. I'm sorry I ran out on you last night,' Anna said apologetically.

'Not a problem,' Rick answered. 'I know those sorts of dos aren't your thing. Anyway, that's not what I'm ringing about. Thing is, a courier has just arrived here with a package for you marked "Private and Confidential". Shall I send him up to the villa or do you want to come into the office and collect it?'

'Any idea who it's from?' Anna asked.

'No. There isn't a company name or anything on the envelope. It is marked urgent though.'

'You'd better send it up here then,' Anna said. 'I hadn't planned to come down to the office today. Thanks.'

By the time the motorbike courier arrived fifteen minutes later, Anna had given up trying to second guess who the package was from and what it contained.

Wandering back into the villa holding the packet, she stood in the sitting room examining the envelope for clues before slowly opening it. Inside, a sheet of writing paper was folded around a photocopy of a black and white photograph.

Two young people, arms entwined around each other, smiled happily at the camera. Anna bit her lip, recognising herself and Philippe in the photograph. In the white space at the bottom Anna could just read the words that had been scrawled across the bottom of the original photograph: 'One Life. One Love.'

Standing there holding the old photograph of herself and Philippe, Anna felt all the emotions of her teenage love flooding through her body.

She remembered being so happy the evening this photograph was taken. They'd taken a boat across to Sainte-Marguerite with a group of Philippe's friends and spent the day lazing on the beach and swimming. She and Philippe had slipped away from the group for a couple of hours when Philippe had taken her to see an empty cottage with wonderful views across the bay.

'It belongs to my family,' he'd said. 'I shall restore it and we will live the simple life here. Our children will have a childhood to remember.'

Laughingly, Anna had protested, 'We've only known each other five days and you've already got us married.'

Philippe had taken her in his arms then. 'But, already, I know you're the only one for me. I want to spend the rest of my life making love to you. I hope you're ready to be the wife of a famous film director because that's what I intend to be. And you will be a wonderful mother to our children.'

Anna had laughingly poked him in the chest. 'And I hope you, Monsieur Cambone, are ready to be the husband of a famous set designer, because

I intend to have a career as well as being a wonderful mother to our family.'

A barbecue on the beach later that evening had been the perfect end to a wonderful day for Anna. As they'd sat side by side in the boat on the return journey, Philippe, his arm around her shoulders holding her tight, had whispered repeatedly, 'Je t'aime. I love you,' and Anna had thought she would explode with happiness.

Now, as she stared blurry-eyed at the photograph, the question was, who had sent her the print?

Apprehensively, as the tears finally began to flow down her cheeks, Anna unfolded the writing paper and read the message it contained.

Please, I beg you, have lunch with me today –
1.p.m. The Auberge, Cannes. I need to talk to you
about Philippe Cambone.

The message was signed simply,

Bernard.

Sinking down onto the settee, Anna gazed un-seeingly out of the window, questions spinning around in her head. How had Bernard come by the photo?

Thoughtfully, Anna brushed the tears away. She'd come to Cannes this year determined to talk to Philippe Cambone and put the past to rest, only to have his unexpected death put paid to her plans in that respect. Could Bernard answer some of the questions she'd planned to ask Philippe? Could she talk to him as she'd planned to talk with Philippe? Should she?

Resolutely she stood up. Yes. She would have lunch with Bernard and listen to what he had to say. Then, when Leo got here later this afternoon, she'd talk to him truthfully about the past and they would decide together how to deal with it as she finally put it behind her.

Picking up the phone, she booked a taxi to col-lect her at quarter to one. She'd spend the rest of the morning swimming and relaxing by the pool, and try not to think about the past too much. Or about why Bernard wanted to talk to her after all these years.

12

Anna dressed carefully for her lunch appointment with Bernard and was ready and waiting when the taxi arrived. Fighting a sudden inclination to tell the driver to go away, she'd changed her mind and didn't need a taxi, she climbed into the back and hoped he knew where The Auberge in Cannes was.

The streets were busy with the midday rush hour traffic and Anna was five minutes late arriving at the restaurant in one of the quieter streets on the outskirts of town. The maître d'hôtel came forward to greet her as the doorman ushered her in.

'Mon ami, Monsieur Bernard...' she started to say, before realising she didn't remember, possibly had never known, Bernard's last name. Anna hesitated, looking around her hoping to spot Bernard.

The maitre d' glanced at a list of reservations, 'Madame Carson for Monsieur Audibert, Bernard?' When Anna gave a relieved nod, he said, 'This way, s'il vous plaît,' and he led Anna through the full restaurant and out into a wisteria covered courtyard, where Bernard was waiting for her at a secluded table in the corner.

'I'm sorry I'm late,' Anna apologised. 'I'd forgotten how busy the traffic is at this time of day.'

'I was afraid you'd decided against coming,' Bernard said.

'I almost did,' Anna confessed. 'I don't normally accept lunch invitations from...' she hesitated. 'Strangers.'

'But I'm not a complete stranger,' Bernard said. 'I think you know I'm an old acquaintance you lost touch with. Shall we order?'

Anna took the menu from the waiter. 'I'm not really hungry. I'll just have a salad.'

Bernard sighed and she glanced sharply at him.

'Anna, this is one of the finest restaurants in town, it would be a crime not to enjoy your meal here. So order something you like, then, if we fall out and never speak to each other again, at least you will have had an enjoyable meal to remember.'

In spite of herself, Anna smiled. 'Okay. Do you recommend anything in particular?'

'For starters, I'm going to have roasted figs with goat's cheese, followed by the sea bass baked in a salt crust, speciality of the house. If I've got any room left, I shall then indulge in the chef's splendid chocolate truffle cake.'

'Sounds delicious – I'll have the same,' Anna said.

'In which case I'll order us a bottle of white wine,' Bernard said and smiled at her.

As the wine waiter uncorked Bernard's choice and offered it for his inspection, Anna studied the man sitting opposite her. Was he really the person she'd known as Brian? Watching him as he lifted the glass to his lips to taste the wine, she noticed the middle finger of his left hand was a deformed stump. That was all the confirmation she needed. Years ago that deformed hand had been a huge source of embarrassment to Philippe's friend.

Bernard nodded at the wine waiter and waited as he poured two glasses before raising his and saying softly, 'Here's to Philippe. Rest in peace.'

Silently Anna held her glass aloft in acknowledgement and took a sip, before saying quietly, 'You were Brian, weren't you?'

He smiled and nodded.

'So you know who I am?' she said, putting her glass on the table.

'Yes. The love of Philippe's life.'

Anna caught her breath at his words before managing to answer. 'I'm surprised you recognised me after all these years.'

'I didn't totally at first,' Bernard said. 'There was just something about your face that seemed hauntingly familiar. It wasn't until a photographer friend told me last evening that he'd photographed you leaving a flower in tribute to

Philippe, that I knew the impossible had finally happened. Albeit too late for Philippe to know.' He glanced at her. 'I'd seen your message with the flower. "One Life. One Love. Farewell." Philippe's mantra for the rest of his life after he met – and lost – you. To know you were somewhere in Cannes, that you'd finally returned—' He regarded her over the rim of his glass and took a sip before saying, 'But then you ran away again before I could talk to you.'

Bernard took another photo out of his wallet.

'You and Philippe only had eyes for each other back then, but this is one of the three of us,' and he handed Anna the photograph.

'Oh, I remember the day this was taken,' Anna exclaimed. 'You had a questionable taste in fluorescent pink socks and trainers in those days,' she laughed.

'Guilty as charged.' Bernard stuck an elegantly shod foot out for her inspection. 'The name and the socks went a long time ago. Look, my taste is all grown-up sophistication now.'

Anna laughed. 'I can see that.' She took a sip

of her own wine before asking. 'Did you ever marry?'

'I was married for a year or two, and I have a son. Philippe is— was, Justin's godfather. Sadly my marriage didn't work.' Bernard took a mouthful of wine before sighing. 'I like to believe that it wasn't entirely my fault it failed as my ex-wife is currently on her third husband.'

'You've never met anyone else?'

'No. Once bitten twice shy as the old saying goes. Enough about me. Today we need to talk about you and Philippe.'

The waiter arrived at that moment with their starters, and Bernard was silent until he'd gone.

'Philippe's love for you didn't disappear over the years. He was a man who once his word was given, never changed his mind,' Bernard said, a serious look on his face. 'He always loved you and wanted you in his life. You broke his heart, you know,' he added, looking at her.

'I'm sorry about that,' Anna said softly, 'Mine was also fractured irreparably.'

'Why didn't you return later that summer like you said you would?'

Anna bit her lip. 'I wrote Philippe a letter explaining, but he never replied to it, so I assumed he'd changed his mind.'

'Wrong,' Bernard said. 'He did answer it. I know because I posted it for him. But it was returned, marked "unknown at this address", a week or two later. He went to England looking for you that year too,' Bernard continued quietly. 'Didn't your parents tell you he visited, pleading with them to tell him where you were? He wanted to marry you. Take care of you.'

'I never saw that letter.' Anna gazed at him, appalled and fighting back the tears that threatened at the knowledge that Philippe had come for her and her parents had sent him away. 'My parents, especially my father, were very controlling. Always acting in my best interest, according to them. I was never told about the letter,' her voice trembled. 'Or that Philippe came looking.'

'I can believe that. They were apparently less than friendly to Philippe.'

'I'm afraid I was a big disappointment to them,' Anna said. 'They expected me to marry well – a doctor or a lawyer would have been ideal

– although in reality no one would have been good enough.' She shook her head. 'The fact that I was arty and wanted to work in the film industry – well, they simply couldn't get their heads around that.' She smothered a sigh. 'They virtually disowned me in the end.'

'Philippe would never have disowned you. He never forgot you. Oh, he had relationships down the years – he was only human. But nothing serious. No one ever got as close to him as you. He tried to find you for years. I can't believe you both worked in the film business and your paths never crossed again,' Bernard said, shaking his head in disbelief.

'That was a deliberate ploy on my part,' Anna said softly. 'I knew Philippe's work took him to the States more and more, so I made sure I stayed very firmly this side of the pond, in a part of the industry far removed from his, and...' Anna hesitated before looking at Bernard and saying, 'Let's just say I took a couple of extra precautions to make sure I remained incognito. And out of sight of the man who I thought had rejected me.'

'Did you ever marry? Have a family? Meet another special person?' Bernard asked gently.

Anna shook her head. 'No. I've never married. But I've recently met a man who makes me happy, like Philippe did all those years ago.' She twirled the wine in her glass before saying reflectively, 'I've spent my whole adult life regretting my teenage love. It's so cruel that the year I decide to come back to Cannes and make my peace with Philippe, it's too late to talk to him.' She swallowed hard, knowing that once again tears were perilously close.

Bernard handed her a napkin as she fought to control the tears from falling.

'I did love him, you know, totally,' she said. 'I would have done anything he asked me to do.'

'I believe you,' Bernard said quietly.

Anna jumped as her mobile phone rang in the silence that followed his words.

'Excuse me,' she said, pressing the answer button. 'Leo, darling. Everything all right?'

'My flight was early. I'm about fifteen minutes away from the villa – are you there?'

'No. I'm in Cannes having lunch with... with

an old friend,' Anna said, smiling at Bernard. 'I'll meet you at the villa in about twenty minutes.'

Ending the call, Anna turned to Bernard.

'I'm so sorry, but I'll have to skip dessert, Leo has arrived early. Listen, why don't you come to the party I'm giving on Tuesday night? Bring a guest if you like. I'll get Rick to send you an invite with the details, shall I? We can finish our talk then. Thank you for a lovely lunch,' and Anna stood up to go.

'I'm sorry you have to rush off,' Bernard said, also standing up. 'We still have a lot of catching up to do. But, yes, I would like to come to your party next week.'

'Good,' Anna said. 'I look forward to introducing you to Leo.'

A serious look crossed Bernard's face as he studied her before saying, 'Anna, before you go, was there something in particular you were hoping to talk to Philippe about? Or was it just a question of ending a forty year silence?'

Anna hesitated, torn between telling Bernard the truth now and wanting to tell Leo first.

Bernard, sensing her hesitation, stretched his

hand out to hold and squeeze Anna's in a conciliatory gesture. 'I feel I must warn you about something that is likely to come to a head in the next few days. Something, as you were once so close to Philippe, you might find upsetting.'

Anna looked at him and waited for him to continue.

'The Cambone family are investigating a couple of letters that Philippe received in the weeks before he died. Letters relating to his past. Apparently the person who wrote them is here in Cannes for the festival and has asked to meet with Jacques urgently.' As Anna stared at him, Bernard continued, 'It seems Philippe's legacy and integrity are about to be questioned.'

'His legacy? To the film word? He made some wonderful films. I know. I saw them all.'

Bernard shook his head. 'Not his professional legacy. His personal one. Rumours are flying around and people are jumping on the publicity bandwagon.'

'Are you talking about this actor Sean someone or other claiming to be Philippe's son?'

'Yes. He was a fraud, but the letters Philippe

received in a similar vein do appear to be genuine.'

Anna's heart skipped a beat. She took a deep breath. 'Thank you for the warning, Bernard. I sincerely hope for the Cambones' sake this person, whoever it is, isn't intent on making trouble for the family. Or besmirching Philippe's name.'

13

'Right, I'm off,' Daisy said. 'Not sure what time I'll be back, so don't wait up.'

'Not wearing jeans tonight then?' Poppy said. 'That dress suits you, by the way.'

Daisy looked down self-consciously at herself and shrugged.

'Fancied a change. Oh, is this Anna's partner coming over?' Daisy said, looking past her sister towards the villa garden.

Poppy turned. 'Oh dear, I hope nothing is wrong,' she added anxiously, moving towards the kitchen door to greet Leo.

'I'm sorry to disturb you, Poppy,' Leo said. 'I

was wondering if you had an ice bucket? I've bought some champagne for this evening and need something to keep it cool on the table.'

'No problem,' Poppy answered, taking a silver ice bucket from one of the cupboards and handing it to Leo. 'This is my sister, Daisy, by the way.'

'Good to meet you, Daisy,' Leo said.

'You too,' Daisy answered.

'Would you like some extra ice as well?' Poppy asked.

Leo shook his head. 'No. I think I've got enough. Thanks for this,' and he turned to go back to the villa.

'Wonder if he's planning to celebrate something in particular,' Daisy said.

'Probably just celebrating being together down here,' Poppy replied. 'You'll be late for the stars arriving at the screening if you don't get going. Enjoy the film with Nat.'

* * *

As usual, Cannes port was busy and Daisy had to

dodge the crowds as she made her way to the front of the Palais des Festivals to watch the stars arriving for the evening screening.

A friendly gendarme allowed her to squeeze through the barrier when she showed him her press pass and she stood on her tiptoes in the middle of the Croisette, trying to see over the crowds and record notes on her phone to jog her memory later.

The usual herd of paparazzi were busy snapping away, strident voices urging the stars to, 'Look this way.' 'Turn your head, love.' 'Regardez moi.' 'Stand still,' while the precious jewels they wore dazzled under a barrage of flashlights that sought to capture every detail.

The film showing that evening was a popular 'boy's own adventure' and the appearance of the ruggedly handsome male star was greeted with delight by the crowd. Mentally, Daisy made a note of his co-star's glamorous evening gown – an off-the-shoulder white affair with a sequinned bodice that clung to her body – and the stunning ruby necklace she was wearing.

As the stars made their way slowly up the red

carpet towards the entrance, Daisy scrutinised the paparazzi for a glimpse of Marcus but couldn't see him. A limousine, the French flag flying on the bonnet, drew up at the foot of the steps, discharging a government minister and his wife, in whom nobody was really interested; their progress up the steps, flanked by security men, was quick and over in minutes.

Guessing that all the 'A list' celebrities were now in the Palais waiting for the screening to begin, Daisy began to make her way towards the beach cinema and Nat.

A happy party atmosphere pervaded the length of the Croisette as the lights began to shine in the twilight; entertainers were still juggling and singing to the crowds.

Nat was waiting for her by the entrance to the beach cinema, a small black rucksack on his back.

'Hi. Sorry if I'm late,' Daisy said. 'I had to do some star watching for my next report.'

'No problem,' Nat said, giving her two cheek kisses. Kisses that were somehow totally different to the ones that Marcus had been insisting on giving her that were far too close to her lips for comfort. 'Come on. Let's find somewhere to sit,' and taking her by the hand, he led the way down onto the beach.

Once they'd settled themselves, Nat slipped the rucksack off his shoulders and began to open the straps. He glanced up at her.

'Have you seen Marcus today?'

'No. I expected to see him tonight outside the Palais, but he wasn't there. Why?'

Nat looked at Daisy seriously before asking, 'Are you two an item away from work? Marcus seems a bit... proprietorial is the word, I think, over you.' He paused before continuing, 'I don't want to step on anyone's toes. I'm kind of old-fashioned like that.'

Daisy smiled and shook her head as Nat looked at her anxiously. So he had got the wrong idea from all those French-style cheek kisses he'd witnessed Marcus giving her. Next time she saw him she'd make sure to tell him to stop with the kisses and to back off. She wasn't interested in him.

'Nat, I'm single. Marcus and I are colleagues working together this week, that's all. In fact, we barely know one another, we've seen each from time to time in the office, but this is the first time we've ever worked together. Besides, Jack the Lads really aren't my type.'

'You sure?'

Daisy nodded. 'Positive.'

'I saw Marcus earlier. Getting up close and personal with one of the stylists working for Dior. They're having dinner together tonight at the Palm Beach.'

Daisy shrugged. 'Nat, I really couldn't care less what Marcus gets up to – or who he's seen with.'

'Right, now we've cleared that up, let's have a drink.'

Daisy watched as Nat pulled a bottle of champagne and two glasses out of his rucksack. Should she tell Nat about Ben and Australia? Him wanting her to join him out there? Not tonight, she decided. It was too soon. When she knew him better. Besides, Ben was in the past and too far away to worry about.

Nat handed her the glasses. 'You look lovely tonight by the way.'

'Thank you,' Daisy said, smiling. 'Any news on your script?'

Nat shook his head. 'Not yet. Teddy Wickham has been too busy to do anything yet but keeps promising he will when he gets "a window in his schedule" sometime next week.' Nat shrugged resignedly. 'In the meantime, I'm trying to make a few contacts of my own.'

He eased the cork out of the bottle and Daisy held the glasses out as Nat carefully poured the champagne.

'Hey, want to come to Anna's party next week? She's on the production side of things, so who knows who might be there. I'm pretty certain I can wangle you an invite. It's Tuesday night. Can you get another evening off?'

'Not a problem. I can always bribe Jasmine the housekeeper with a box of chocolates to babysit again,' Nat said. 'You sure Anna won't mind?'

'Ninety-nine point nine per cent certain,' Daisy said. 'I'll check with her tomorrow and let you know. Can I ask you a personal question?'

'Yes, of course.'

'How did you become a nanny? I know these

days anyone can do anything they want, but you must admit it's still quite unusual to find male nannies.'

'Well, firstly, I'm not just a nanny. I'm a Montessori-trained nursery teacher. I knew I'd have to do something to earn a living while I tried to sell my scripts and I love kids – particularly three to seven year olds; they're fun to be around. Before you ask, the job of looking after Cindy for the festival came about via a friend of a friend. Normally I freelance in the UK through an agency, which leaves me time to write in between jobs. Cheers,' and the two of them clinked glasses.

'Sounds like freelancing is working for you,' Daisy said thoughtfully before taking a sip of her drink and changing the subject.

'Do you know what the classic film is tonight?' she asked.

'Well, it's not Tom and Jerry, that's for sure. It's *Dirty Harry* – if you don't like gangster films, we don't have to stay.' Nat glanced at her. 'We can always leave and find a quiet spot to drink this and just watch the sea.'

'What, and miss Clint Eastwood uttering those

immortal words: "Make my day"?' Daisy laughed. 'He's here at the festival this year, isn't he?'

Nat nodded. 'Yes, he's got a film showing and he's...' Nat's voice trailed away as he looked beyond Daisy. 'He's actually walking towards the screen. He's going to make a speech about the film by the look of things.'

They both listened as Clint talked about his 1971 film. His remark, 'If you have trouble recognising me, I'm the one with the brown hair and lots of it,' said with a self-deprecating smile, delighted the crowd and earned him a round of applause as the film began and he left.

Sitting on the beach next to Nat, Daisy found it hard to concentrate on the film. If she were honest *Dirty Harry* wasn't really her kind of film – she was more a *Sleepless in Seattle* type of girl. Sitting companionably at Nat's side, she let not only the rolling sound of the Mediterranean as it lapped at the beach wash over her, but also much of the film's dialogue and action as she thought about the future and Ben's letter.

Thinking he'd made a mistake wasn't the same as knowing and regretting, was it? He hadn't mentioned loving her in the letter, just that he was missing her. And did he seriously expect her to go halfway around the world on a whim of his? Probably, she decided. Ben had always been the one to decide what they would do as a couple and she'd tended to follow meekly in his wake.

She'd quite enjoyed her independence of the last few months – particularly once she'd got over the shock of Ben dumping her – and rediscovered some of her own dreams. So much that she'd wanted to do had been pushed to one side while she was with Ben. Like going freelance.

'No security in being a freelance,' Ben had said when she'd suggested it. 'You need a regular monthly cheque.'

Now she was alone, was she brave enough to do it? Give up the security of a regular salary. Unlike Nat, she didn't have any other training to fall back on. She did have some savings though. Enough to live on for at least nine months, she reckoned, if the freelance work didn't take off straight away. If she took voluntary redundancy, there would be a couple of months' pay to add to her savings as well.

When the cooling night air made her shiver and Nat placed an arm protectively around her shoulders, she snuggled in against him. Right now, she realised, she was happier than she'd been in years.

As the credits rolled, Nat asked, 'Taxi or shall we walk back?'

'Let's walk along the bord de mer,' Daisy answered. 'It's such a lovely evening.'

Late though it was, the restaurants along the bord de mer were still busy – there were even a few brave souls going for a late-night dip. Strolling along with her arm around Nat's waist and his arm around her shoulders felt comfortable and natural. As did the goodnight kiss he gave her as she pressed the security number into the electric gate on the villa's drive. A delicious tingling feeling flooded through her body.

'Goodnight, Daisy. See you tomorrow. Thank you for a lovely evening.'

As Daisy watched him go with a smile on her face, she realised, with that kiss, Nat had just 'made her day'.

14

Anna, putting the finishing touches to the special dinner she'd prepared, glanced out of the kitchen window to where Leo was busy organising things around the pool. He didn't seem disappointed that they were eating at the villa tonight instead of finding an expensive restaurant, as he'd initially suggested.

'A romantic dinner with just the two of us here will actually be perfect,' he'd said. 'So long as it's not too much trouble for you.'

'I love having someone special to cook for,' Anna had told him. Not adding that the lack of that special someone for most of her life made their relationship unimitated, unique and extraordinarily wonderful.

Watching Leo light the candles on the table and adjust the chairs, Anna felt a wave of love wash over her. She was so lucky to have met Leo.

Picking up their smoked salmon starters, she took them outside and placed them on the table. Standing there with the candles and the solar garden lights flickering into life and the occasional bat flitting through the twilight, Anna took a deep breath, looked at Leo, and said softly, 'I need to talk to you.'

Moving to her side, Leo took her in his arms. 'I want to talk to you too, but ladies first,' and he looked at her expectantly.

Anna was quiet for several seconds before saying quietly, 'You're the first person in nearly forty years I've ever told what I'm about to tell you.' She took a deep breath before looking at Leo and continuing, 'The truth is, when I was seventeen, I had Philippe Cambone's baby. Then I was made to give him away. Unfortunately, my late parents turn out to be the villains in all this. I keep telling myself it was a different era, but even that doesn't excuse their behaviour.'

Leo leant forward and gently wiped away the tears that were starting to fall down Anna's cheeks.

'Oh, my darling, that must have been so hard for you.'

Anna nodded, unable to speak as she tried to stem the tears.

'I'd sort of guessed there was more to your relationship with Philippe than you'd told me,' Leo said. 'But you having a baby and having to give it up didn't cross my mind.' He pulled her close and held her tight for several seconds before she spoke again.

'When my parents realised "my condition", all hell broke loose. I told my parents that Philippe loved me and we'd get married. They didn't believe me. Said that he'd had his fun and wouldn't want to pay the price. They also called me names and said I was a disgrace to them. When I didn't receive a reply from Philippe to my letter telling him I was pregnant, I believed he'd changed his mind about me. That he didn't love me like he said. That he had no interest in the baby or being a father. I waited and waited, hoping to hear from him, but nothing. My parents had been proved right.' She bit her lip. 'So I gave in and did what they told me. I wish I could challenge them about their actions now. I should have suspected at the time that they were behind Philippe's rejection of me. Only he didn't reject me. They refused to let him contact me.' Anna sighed. 'I'd like to think that they were acting in the belief they were doing the right thing for me at the time, but sadly, I think they were just plain mean and vindictive.'

'The swinging sixties didn't embrace everyone, did they?' Leo said.

'Certainly not my parents, or me really, in the end. I was bundled off to a home for wayward girls and told if I kept the baby I was never to darken their doors again,' Anna said. 'Seems un-believable now in the twenty-first century, doesn't it?' She shook her head. 'Bernard told me today that not only did Philippe reply to my letter, but he came to the UK to find me and take care of me.' Anna gulped. 'My parents sent him away and never told me.' Anna paused, her voice trembling. 'Anyway, when Jean-Philippe – that's what I called my son – was twenty-four hours old, I had to say goodbye and hand him over for adoption.' Anna bit her lip at the memory of that moment. 'I've had no contact with him from that day to this. I had hoped when the adoption privacy laws changed a few years ago, he would try get in touch, but...' she shrugged her shoulders despondently. 'I guess he's happy without me in his life, the mother who gave him away.'

'I'm sure that's not true. I'm sure Jean-Philippe would want to know both his parents if he traced you. ' Leo shook his head. 'I can't believe you both worked in the film industry for so many years and that you and Philippe didn't bump into each other. That all this hasn't come out before.'

Anna shrugged. 'Bernard said the same. It's such a vast industry and I made sure I was in a totally different section of it. Besides, Philippe worked mostly in the States and I took a conscious decision to stay this side of the Atlantic.' She glanced at Leo. 'I did follow his career for years. In the beginning, I couldn't help myself. I had to know what he was doing. The year he won his Oscar, I cheered for him. I even went to a lecture he gave one year at the Film Institute in London, just to be close to him. It was torture and I never did it again.'

Anna was silent for a moment, remembering the afternoon that could have changed her life if only she'd had the courage to approach Philippe and say hello. The determination to speak to him, to demand answers, that had accompanied her on the journey and into the room had vanished the moment he'd walked onto the podium to begin his lecture.

Being in the same room as him, albeit with a couple of hundred other people, had been both wonderful, and unbearable. However he felt about her, she'd known without a doubt that she still loved him. The thought of him rejecting her again, only this time to her face, was too much to bear. Instead, she'd drank in the sight of him, the sound of his voice, his remembered mannerisms, before taking one last look and slipping quietly out of the room after he finished his lecture. Thankfully there hadn't been time for him to notice and maybe recognise her.

Anna's body trembled as she let out a distraught sigh. A silent Leo handed her a handkerchief and she wiped her cheeks with it before twisting it into knots as she looked at him, her eyes glistening with tears.

'There's something else that Bernard told me too. A week or so ago, Philippe received a letter from someone asking to meet him during the festival as they believe they are related. Philippe had agreed to a meeting but no firm date was arranged. The Cambones are worried now there may be an unexpected, unwanted claim against Philippe's estate. Or even a smear campaign.' Anna bit her lip as she looked at Leo. 'Do you think this person who wanted to meet him could be my son?'

'Oh, Anna, my darling, anything is possible, but don't get your hopes up too high. Did Bernard give you a name or anything? Indicate what the relationship was? Who'd written the letter?'

'No. I left before I could ask him any questions,' Anna said. 'To think I'd almost come to terms with the fact that I would never see Philippe again or meet my son,' Anna said. 'But now, suddenly, I've got hope that maybe my son is here in Cannes...' her voice trailed away.

Leo sighed as he gently stroked her hand. 'Don't raise your hopes too high for Jean-Philippe, my darling,' he said quietly. 'Yes, it could be Philippe's child seeking to establish his roots, but it doesn't necessarily mean that it will be your child. Philippe could have had a relationship with anybody during the last forty years.'

'I know, I know,' Anna said, before whispering, 'But wouldn't it be wonderful if it was my Jean-Philippe after all these years?'

She wouldn't think about the other, awful, possibility that even if it were her son, he might hold the fact that she'd given him away as a baby against her and refuse to acknowledge her as his mother. If that happened, she would simply have to find a way to deal with it.

It was only later as they prepared for bed that

she realised Leo hadn't said what he wanted to talk about.

'I'm sorry I forgot – what was it you wanted to talk about.'

'No worries. It'll keep for a few more days,' Leo said.

15

After a restless night, Anna woke on Sunday morning to the sound of rain splattering against the windows. Quickly, she pushed the covers back and swung her legs out of bed. This was the South of France, it shouldn't be raining, especially not today, with the premiere of *Future Promises* tonight. The one thing she didn't need was a walk up the red carpet in the rain.

The smell of coffee was wafting upstairs and she could hear Leo in the kitchen whistling happily. Shrugging herself into her silk dressing gown, Anna made her way downstairs.

Leo turned as she entered the kitchen. 'Good morning, my darling. Coffee?'

'Please. I can't believe it's raining,' Anna said.

'Forecast is for it to clear by midday,' Leo said reassuringly. 'Now, what's our timetable for to-day?' he asked, handing her a mug of coffee.

'Hairdresser for me this morning. There is some jewellery being delivered here this after-noon at about five o'clock, then a limo arrives at seven to takes us to town.'

'So, nothing major for me to get involved with?' Leo asked.

Anna shook her head. 'No. Is there something you'd like to do? We could have lunch in town after my hairdo is finished if you like. The Auberge restaurant in Cannes where I met Bernard yesterday was very good, but you choose.'

'Okay. I'll book us a table somewhere.'

'Talking of Bernard,' Anna hesitated, not sure how Leo would react to her next words. 'I'm going to ring and ask him to tell me the name of this person who has contacted the Cambones – if he knows it.'

'Oh, Anna, d'you think that's wise? Why not

wait until after the premiere at least. After this evening, you'll be able to relax and deal with... well, deal with whatever the remaining week of the festival throws at you.'

'I just want to know the name,' Anna said. 'But you're right. I'll wait until after the premiere. We'll enjoy the party tonight.'

'Does Bernard know about the true depth of your relationship with Philippe?' Leo asked.

'You're the first person I've ever told about the baby since I gave him away. But from the way he was talking yesterday, I'd say Bernard definitely knows. Philippe obviously talked to him about me – he knew about the letter and the visit. They were best mates after all.'

They both turned as there was a gentle knock on the door. When Anna opened it, Daisy was standing there looking apprehensive.

'Anna, Leo, I'm sorry to bother you so early, but I wanted to ask you a couple of things.'

Anna looked at her warily. 'Go on.'

'First, your party on Tuesday. Could my friend, Nat, possibly come? He's a scriptwriter trying to make some contacts. At the moment he's had to resort to taking a nanny job – oh, I think you met Cindy the other day, didn't you? She's Verity Raymond's daughter and Nat's looking after her while her parents are at the festival; her father's on the jury.'

'Of course Nat may come. He should be able to make a few contacts, if nothing else. I'll try to introduce him to as many people as I can,' Anna said generously. 'What was the other thing?' She found herself hoping against hope that it wasn't the guided tour of Cannes.

Daisy hesitated. 'My editor emailed me this morning. He's heard that Bill Nighy and Judi Dench are both in town because they're signing up to make a film about older people changing their lives. I think the title is *The Best Exotic Marigold Hotel* and it's going to be set in India. Anyway, he wants me to try and get a personal interview with one of them. As if!' Daisy shook her head. 'They're A-list celebrities – they're not going to talk to me.' She sighed and looked at Anna. 'But he's definitely putting the pressure on for me to come up with something, so I was wondering if you'd thought any more about walking around

Cannes with me and giving me the before and after picture?' Daisy looked hopefully at Anna. 'I know you weren't keen, but I thought I'd ask again. I know you value your privacy.'

'Oh Daisy, I really don't know,' Anna said, sighing.

'Any reason why I shouldn't tag along?' Leo asked unexpectedly. 'I'd be interested in hearing your reminiscences first-hand. Would you mind?' he asked, turning to Daisy.

'No, I don't mind,' Daisy answered. 'Especially if it would make Anna feel better about doing it?' and she looked at Anna questioningly.

'Okay,' Anna sighed. She remembered how hard it had been to make a name for herself in the film industry and suspected it was the same in journalism, 'I give in. But anonymously. And I'm still not sure that I'm going to remember anything of importance – or even of interest. It was all so long ago.'

'Thank you so much, Anna. I really appreciate it,' Daisy said. 'Twelve o'clock outside the Palais des Festivals tomorrow morning all right for you?'

It was Leo who answered. 'Twelve o'clock will

be fine for us,' he said. 'I'm looking forward to it.' He took hold of Anna's hand and squeezed it.

'Enjoy the premiere tonight. Really hope the rain clears up for you. Thank you so much again, Anna.'

As Daisy left them, Anna turned to Leo. 'I knew coming here would be a trip down memory lane but I didn't realise it would involve a guided tour.'

* * *

The weather forecast was right. The rain did stop and by the evening, as Anna and Leo prepared for their appearance on the red carpet, it was dry, even if the breeze was on the chilly side.

Anna handed the diamond and sapphire necklace that had been delivered to the villa late that afternoon to Leo. 'Could you do the catch, please? I'm terrified I won't do it up properly and I'll lose it. I dread to think how much it's worth.'

'It's rather lovely, isn't it?' Leo said as he carefully did up the clasp and double-checked it. 'The sapphires match your dress perfectly.'

'Does my dress look all right?' Anna asked anxiously. 'I wasn't sure when I bought it whether it was too fitted for me. And these sandals,' she glanced down at the silver strappy shoes with their five inch heels. 'They're not too high, are they?'

'Anna, Anna,' Leo said as he turned her round to face him and gently kissed her. 'You look beautiful tonight, my darling. Your dress, your hair, your shoes – everything is perfect. Now, relax and try to enjoy the evening.'

Standing in the circle of his arms, Anna smiled. 'I'll try. Having you here makes it very special. Have I told you how handsome you're looking tonight?'

Leo shook his head. 'We make such a perfect couple!' he said, laughing, and delicately traced the outline of her face with his fingers before gently kissing her again.

As a brisk toot of a car horn sounded outside, Leo placed Anna's white fake fur shrug around her shoulders, before picking up and handing her the small beaded clutch handbag she'd decided to use and taking her by the arm.

'The red carpet awaits – let's go.'

Sitting next to Leo as the limousine made its way towards the Palais des Festivals, Anna checked the contents of her bag: lipstick, comb, tissue and her locket. It was the first time in years that the gold locket wasn't around her neck, but the diamond and sapphire necklace had to take precedence tonight.

'Relax and enjoy the evening,' Leo whispered as the limousine came to a halt at the foot of the famous steps. A burly security man opened the car door and together Anna and Leo stepped onto the red carpet.

Nothing had prepared Anna for the noise and the exuberance of the large crowds lining the Croisette and along the front of the Palais. Four or five deep in places behind the barriers, she could see people standing on stools, several strategically placed ladders, all hoping for a better view of the stars as they arrived. Now, standing on the actual red carpet in the open air, the noise was amplified several times.

Leo took her hand as numerous flashlights went off.

'Who do they think we are?' Anna whispered to Leo.

'Someone very famous, obviously – you're looking so glamorous tonight,' Leo said, pulling her towards him and kissing her, to the delight of the crowd.

Rick was waiting for them on the red carpet, standing slightly to one side of the stairs. 'Anna, you look stunning. Nice to see you, Leo. Helen and Rupert should be here in a moment,' he said. 'Then it will be our turn to walk the walk and face the paparazzi.'

'The atmosphere is amazing,' Anna said, looking around.

To her left a couple of television reporters were facing cameramen and talking rapidly into microphones, detailing the scene before them, announcing the names of the famous stars as they arrived and describing the sumptuous gowns and jewellery.

Further up the steps, Anna caught a glimpse of Bernard being approached by another reporter with a cameraman in tow. She'd forgotten he'd become a big name down here and his thoughts on the festival would obviously be sought after by the media.

The gentle pressure of Leo's hand in hers brought her attention back to their own group and she smiled apologetically at Leo.

'Sorry,' she whispered. 'That's Bernard up there.'

Leo followed her gaze.

'I wonder what he's talking about to the TV reporter,' Anna said. 'Ah, here are Rupert and Helen,' she added, as a silver limousine drew up.

Watching the two young stars of *Future Promises* arrive on the red carpet, Anna felt a surge of affection for both of them. A couple of people in the crowd, realising who they were, called out their names, 'Rupert, Helen love, can we have your autographs?'

Smiling happily, the two went over and graciously signed the offered magazines, books and cards.

Finally they all linked arms and began to make their way up the paparazzi-lined flight of steps through a barrage of flashlight. As they drew level with Bernard on the last of the red carpeted stairs and went to enter the Palais itself, Anna couldn't help overhearing the interviewer say.

'Finally, Bernard, can you give us any information about this latest development in the Philippe Cambone saga? I know you two were very close. Were you aware of this secret family he had in the States?'

Anna gasped involuntarily as she heard the question and would have fallen if Leo's grip on her arm hadn't tightened and saved her as she stumbled, trying unsuccessfully to hear Bernard's reply.

Leo looked at her, concerned. 'Anna, are you okay? They're waiting to show us to our seats.'

'I'm fine,' Anna said, gripping Leo's hand tightly. 'Lead on.'

16

It was nearly 2 a.m. when Anna and Leo got back to the Villa Flora after the party. Anna felt completely exhausted but strangely exhilarated at the same time. The two of them sat for a few moments in the moonlight out on the terrace, listening to the frogs and winding down.

'That was quite a party,' Leo said, standing up and taking her hand to pull her onto her feet. 'Never let it be said that I'm getting old, but I honestly don't know how people cope with partying every night during the festival.'

'Neither do I,' Anna said.

'Come on, let's go to bed.'

Hand in hand, they made their way indoors and up to the bedroom. Leo carefully unhooked the expensive necklace from Anna's neck and replaced it in the box.

'I'll put it somewhere safe until we return it later today,' he said.

Anna smiled her thanks as she slipped her beloved pendant over her head and back around her neck. 'As beautiful as that necklace is, I'm more comfortable wearing my lowly gold pendant.'

Leo smiled in understanding.

Anna, too tired to do more than remove her make-up and clean her teeth, climbed into bed, gave Leo a quick kiss and was asleep within minutes, her dreams filled with memories of the party.

So many people, so many congratulations, so much champagne. The general consensus of the evening had been that *Future Promises* was about to be a big hit at the box office and would earn worldwide recognition for its young stars. Consequently, Helen and Rupert had been the toast of

Cannes. Anna, delighted for them, had enjoyed basking in the reflected glory.

The theme of the after-screening party – 'Future Promises – What's Yours?' – had proved to be a major hit. The venue, draped and decorated like a mystical sheikh's tent, with zodiac signs, huge silver moons and stars hanging from the pleated ceiling and large golden suns shining from the walls, had been a perfect setting for a fun evening of make-believe and fortune telling.

There was a wheel of fortune, origami fortune tellers, fortune sticks, Chinese fortune cookies, astrology readings and even a Romany gypsy, complete with bunches of lavender and a crystal ball, in a curtained booth for those that fancied a personal consultation.

Partygoers eagerly entered into the spirit of things as a king's fool and jester cavorted around making mischief and encouraging everyone to join in the fun. Music had been provided, disco-style, by a young DJ and the whole evening had been, as Leo said later in the limousine going home, 'a night to remember for all the right reasons'.

Anna had seen the gypsy fortune teller early in the evening and had been tempted to have her gaze into the crystal ball on her behalf then, but the number of people already waiting had put her off. It was gone one o'clock in the morning as she and Leo swayed to a last smoochy dance tune when she saw 'Cassandra' sitting alone in her booth.

'I know it's silly,' she'd said, glancing at Leo. 'But shall we? Just for fun.'

Smiling, Leo had led her by the hand over to the booth. 'You go in and see what she has to say. I'm going to organise our car home.'

Cassandra had looked up as Anna hesitated at the entrance to the booth, suddenly not sure that she wanted to do this.

'I'm sorry – am I too late?'

Cassandra had smiled, shaking her head as she beckoned her in. 'Please, sit.'

Anna had sat down in front of the round table with its scarlet velvet covering and watched apprehensively as Cassandra had gazed trance-like at her crystal ball before starting to speak.

'Although something from the past is making

waves in your life at the moment, you are entering a very happy period. I see a man who loves you and wants to take care of you in the future. Through him, the family life you've always dreamed of will be yours, I see grandchildren – a little girl holding a toddler by the hand – families coming together. A journey of some sort. The past embracing the future.' Cassandra had paused and looked up at Anna before adding quietly, 'Do not mourn the past, nor worry about the future, live the present moment wisely and earnestly.'

* * *

The next morning, as she slowly came to after a few hours' sleep, the exciting events of the previous night's party floated through Anna's mind. Followed swiftly by the scene with Cassandra and her words about not mourning the past.

Anna knew the gypsy had told her mostly things that she already knew. She knew she loved Leo as much as she hoped he loved her and knew they could be happy together, that his family could become hers, his grandchildren hers. But 'the past embracing the future' – what did that mean?

As the picture of Cassandra in her booth faded from her mind, and knowing she wouldn't go back to sleep, Anna slipped out of bed. Pulling on her dressing gown, she tiptoed out of the room and went downstairs.

Her mobile phone was on the kitchen work surface and she picked it up before unlocking the door and stepping out onto the terrace. Sitting in one of the cane chairs Poppy had placed out there, Anna opened her phone and scrolled down until she found the number she wanted and pressed the dial button.

As the connection was being processed, Anna tensed, her whole body rigid with expectation, her fingers playing with the locket chain that was again around her neck.

'Bonjour.'

'Bernard, it's Anna,' she said quickly. 'I need to talk to you.'

'I'm listening.'

'You didn't tell me Philippe had a secret family in the States.'

'That's because he didn't,' Bernard said.

'That reporter last night, at the Palais?'

Anna could hear Bernard's deep sigh down the telephone.

'The press, as usual, have got hold of the wrong end of the stick, Anna. They've heard about the possibility of a claim against the estate and have jumped to conclusions. Philippe did *not* have a family he kept secret. I told you, not having a family was the biggest regret of his life. He would have adored having children.'

'Bernard?' Anna hesitated. 'Will you tell me the name of the person who wrote to Philippe please?'

There was a pause before Bernard answered.

'Oh, Anna. I don't think I can without getting permission from the Cambones. Not sure they'd want the name made public.'

'Okay. If I put it another way, maybe you can answer me.' Anna took a deep breath before continuing. 'Does the signature on the letters contain the name Jean-Philippe? Is that name mentioned in the letter anywhere?'

'I'm sorry, Anna, that name is not a part of the

signature on the letters Jacques showed me. Neither is it in the letters,' Bernard said gently. 'I can tell you the letters were from a woman,' he added quietly. 'Not a man.'

Anna, unable to bear the message concealed behind his words, twisted her fingers round and round in her locket chain until it was cutting into her. As, sad and frustrated, she pulled at the chain trying to untangle it, the chain broke and the locket fell to the floor.

'Thank you, Bernard,' Anna managed to whisper as she pressed the off button on the phone before beginning to sob uncontrollably as she scrabbled on the floor to find and pick up her locket.

She was still crying when Leo found her ten minutes later, her face red and blotched, the locket and its broken chain clutched in her hand.

'I'm sorry,' she sobbed as Leo took her in his arms to comfort her. 'I'd pinned my hopes on it being Jean-Philippe who had contacted Philippe. Bernard has just told me it's a woman. Which means it's not my son who wrote to him. And now I've broken my locket chain.'

17

'Good morning, Poppy,' Daisy said, running downstairs into the kitchen on Monday morning. 'You look busy.'

Her sister was sat at the kitchen table surrounded by pieces of paper, recipe books and a cold mug of tea. Poppy groaned as she looked up from the shopping list she was writing.

'You'll definitely be around to help me tomorrow, won't you? This party is getting out of hand. I'm terrified of forgetting something important and ruining things.'

'I promised I'd help, didn't I?' Daisy said, helping herself to a banana from the fruit bowl on the table and glancing quickly at the various lists on the table. 'What's the problem anyway?'

'Everything! I'm spending the rest of the morning cooking the savoury stuff I can't buy in the market tomorrow – I'll do the sweet stuff this afternoon. There's still so much to organise, I'm beginning to panic. Oh, and Leo wants me to arrange a cake as well as an official photographer – at a day's notice,' her voiced faded away.

'What kind of cake?' Daisy asked curiously.

Poppy shrugged. 'Just a good cream-filled gooey cake was all he said,'

'Doesn't sound like the normal finger food that festival parties offer,' Daisy said thoughtfully. 'Anyway, calm down. Finding a photographer is not a problem. Marcus has already asked if he can come, so now he can – officially. As for a cake, this is France, remember. Every patisserie on every street corner has wonderful cakes, not to mention the supermarkets. We'll buy a cream-laden cake from one. Okay? I'm seeing Marcus this morning, so I'll tell him he can come, and then I'm meeting up with Anna and Leo at midday. Anna has kindly agreed to help me with my "Then and Now" feature,' she explained, sensing Polly's unspoken question. 'But I'll definitely be back mid-afternoon and we'll make a start on getting everything sorted. Okay? I'll order the cake while I'm in town and then tomorrow morning I'll come to the market with you for all the fresh stuff and we can collect the cake. Sorted,' and Daisy threw her banana skin in the bin before smiling at her sister.

Later, walking down into Cannes, Daisy thought about the feature she planned to write with the help of Anna's memories about the twenty-first festival. She'd already found a few archive photos of Cannes back in the 1960s to go alongside some of Marcus's modern-day shots. Hopefully, Anna would have some nostalgic anecdotes about her first visit to the festival. If not, Daisy decided, she'd make it more of a photo feature, with just a few words comparing the old and new pictures.

Before starting to look for Marcus in the Village International on the quay, Daisy found an empty seat in the gardens near the Hotel de Ville, took her laptop out of her tote and began to type.

The rain clouds have gone and once again the sky is the usual clear azure blue. It's hard to believe that it's Monday already and the festival is entering its final week. The days have simply flown by, but people are still busy partying and networking in the cafés and bars. Along the Croisette people are desperately strutting their stuff knowing that time is running out.

The presenting of the Palme d'Or on Sunday is looming closer, but still the hype continues. Will it be like the year when the very last film to be premiered won the coveted award? Maybe we've already seen the winner?

Daisy glanced up as she heard clapping and watched a fire-eater entertain a small crowd for a few moments before returning her attention to the laptop.

Today is the private funeral of Philippe Cambone, the famous film director, born in Cannes, who died suddenly last week. Flags are expected to fly at half mast this morning, but industry VIPs and the public will have to wait to pay their respects at a memorial service to be held after the festival ends.'

Thoughtfully, Daisy saved her notes and switched off her laptop.

She'd get another report emailed to the paper today, write up her 'Then and Now' feature tonight and then tomorrow she'd help Poppy all day and enjoy the party in the evening. Now to find Marcus. She needed to make sure he still wanted to come to Anna's party tomorrow and that he was available – didn't have a hot date with a blonde.

'Great. I'll definitely be there,' he said, when Daisy tracked him down in the American marquee in the Village International.

'Enjoy your dinner at the Palm Beach the other night?' Daisy enquired casually.

'Yes, thank you. You and Nat have a good evening?' Marcus returned equally casually.

Daisy nodded. 'Marcus, I think we're going to have to forget that dinner on Bill's expenses. I'm running out of evenings. Things are so hectic down here. Like you said. There's always so much going on. Besides, I think it's better if we keep things on a strict work basis. Okay? Friends?'

'Nothing to do with you and Nat then?'

Daisy shook her head. 'Nat and I are just friends.' She had no intention of placing Nat in a difficult position with Marcus while they were here – what happened after the festival was another matter altogether. 'I've heard from Ben,' she said quietly. 'He wants me to join him in Sydney and I'm thinking about it.'

There, that should be enough to stop Marcus speculating about her and Nat.

* * *

Anna tried to marshal her thoughts as she floated lazily on her back in the villa swimming pool before preparing to go indoors to shower and meet Daisy in town.

Tired after the premiere and the party and emotionally drained after her conversation with Bernard, she desperately wanted to be able to concentrate on the present and her future with

Leo. To make plans. He hadn't said yet what he wanted to talk about, but she knew he was a great organiser, so it was probably about some family events with Alison over the summer that needed to go in her diary.

But shaking off thoughts about what was currently going on in Cannes with the Cambone family was proving impossible. She might have successfully buried the past deep in the recess of her mind, but by coming to Cannes this year the jack in the box had jumped out and was now snapping at her heels.

The fragile emotional dam she'd built around herself over the years had been breached and unleashed a veritable flood of evocative thoughts and feelings. If only Philippe hadn't died and she'd been able to make her peace with him face to face as she'd planned, she would have been able to make plans for her future with Leo with more composure? Wouldn't she?

Or was it possible the opposite would have been true? Would she have found her lifelong love for Philippe was greater than that for Leo? That was a hypothetical question too far and

Anna turned on to her front and began to swim slowly towards the poolside steps. All these 'ifs'. And just then a new major 'if' popped uninvited into her thoughts. If she wasn't careful her dead past could drive a wedge between her and Leo. And that possibility didn't bear thinking about.

Climbing out of the pool, Anna slipped into her towelling robe, resolutely tying the belt around her waist. The past was over and done with; the sooner she accepted that Philippe was dead and that Jean-Philippe would never be a part of her life, however much she wished for it, the better.

She'd treat today's walk around Cannes as a cathartic exercise – dig as deep as she could into her memories, expose them to scrutiny and finally exorcise them. Then she'd get on with the rest of her life with Leo. Push Philippe and the whole Cambone family back deep into the past where they belonged. They certainly had no part to play in her current life.

* * *

The Croisette was crowded with sightseers when Anna and Leo arrived and it took them several moments to find Daisy, who was talking to Marcus near the foot of the Palais steps.

'Hi. This is Marcus – he's agreed to be your official photographer on Tuesday,' Daisy said, introducing them.

'Official photographer?' Anna said, surprised. 'I don't think we need one.'

'I asked Poppy to find us one,' Leo explained quickly. 'I'm sure Rick and the rest of the office would like some mementos of the party too. Could be useful PR.'

'See you Tuesday then,' Marcus said. 'Just had a tip-off that Madonna is coming ashore at the Palm Beach, so I need to get down there ASAP.'

As Marcus left, Anna turned to Daisy and quietly asked, 'Now, where shall we start this trip down memory lane?'

'Other side of the road outside the hotel that stands on the old Palais site and make our way along inwards to the centre of town?' Daisy suggested.

As they dodged past cars, scooters and an

open-top bus to cross the road, Anna, trying to get into the spirit of things, said, 'There was less traffic around in those days, that's for sure. The crowds are different too.'

'How?'

'Older and more middle-class. In '68 there were lots of students – of which I was one. It was not nearly so colourful then either,' Anna said, looking at a particularly garish gold and silver window display. 'I found it all rather intimidating, particularly as news of the Paris riots filtered down and there were demonstrations. Philippe wanted to get involved – did get involved – but I was too scared, particularly after I nearly got trampled.'

'Philippe? Trampled?' Daisy asked.

Anna took a deep breath and began to explain. 'My job at the festival was to act as general dogsbody and messenger between the various companies and film studios who were down here,' Anna said. 'One morning when I was trying to deliver some reels of film, I got caught up in a student protest. Actually, it was just along here, past the Carlton. I slipped off the pavement, twisted my ankle and fell over as the students broke through the barriers the police had erected and surged forward towards the Palais. Philippe left the crowd when he saw me sitting on the pavement nursing my leg and helped me move to safety. Refused to leave me.' Anna smiled.

'Philippe, as in Philippe Cambone?' Daisy asked slowly.

'Yes,' Anna said. 'I'm sorry, Daisy. I didn't lie to you when you asked if I'd ever worked with him – I hadn't. But I should have been honest and told you I did know him back then.' Anna gave a slight shake of her head before continuing.

'Meeting Philippe changed my life. For ten days, he showed me another world. Growing up in a quiet Devonshire village, I'd never experienced a place like Cannes. Never realised how different other people's lives could be,' Anna said.

She glanced at Leo. Her memories of Cannes in the late sixties were joined together in a complicated knot involving Philippe. No way was she going to upset Leo by talking about another man. But the expression on his face was one of interest, so she continued.

'Philippe was very French in his support of the students and took me to several meetings, wanting me to get involved.' She shrugged. 'How could I? I didn't speak the language for a start, and secondly, I was going home at the end of the festival. Back to my parents, art college and a different life.'

A couple of council workers were preparing to erect some temporary barriers across the road and gesticulated to them to walk through quickly.

'Despite the unrest and the protests, it was a lot easier to get close to people in those days. Security was very low key, virtually non-existent. I saw – and in some cases even met – people like Ringo Starr and George Harrison. Philippe introduced me to several up and coming stars too. Bridget Bardot was here that year and Orson Welles.'

Anna paused as a group of Japanese tourists threatened to run them down in their eagerness to pass along the street before the barriers were in place.

'It was when somebody high up in Paris tried to sack the popular Henri Langois, head of Cinématèque Française, that the festival itself erupted into disarray. Suddenly everyone was protesting and boycotting things, jury members were resigning, and there were calls for the festival to close – which, of course, it did.'

'I found an archive photo of Geraldine Chaplin pulling the curtain across at a screening,' Daisy said. 'Was that the end of the festival that year?'

Anna nodded. 'End of the festival, yes, but the national strikes made it impossible for people to get away. I couldn't leave for another four days.'

'What did you do?'

'Spent most of the time with Philippe. We talked for hours, planning our careers, our lives for the next few years.' Anna was quiet for a moment, remembering the intensity of those days.

Anna gave Leo another quick glance.

'The words "Life without Limits" was the phrase on everyone's lips that year. Philippe and I promised ourselves that would be the way we'd live our lives together.'

'Together?' Daisy said.

Anna gave her a sad smile.

'It didn't happen. Philippe was already under contract to work in America for a year. Once the strikes were over, I went back to England and lived another life. A life that has been good to me on the whole and one that has now given me Leo,' Anna said, catching hold of Leo's hand and squeezing it. Telling Leo about the baby had been the right thing to do but it was too soon to tell anyone else the secret she'd kept all these years – especially after the events of the last few days.

'The future is looking good,' Leo said, drawing her towards him and, oblivious of the sudden crowd of people entering the street, kissing her gently.

'Shall we try to make our way to rue d'Antibes? They seem to have closed this road completely for some reason. Can't think why. It's not really anything to do with the festival,' Daisy said, trying not to envy them their closeness and still thinking about the implications of that word 'together'.

'Think maybe that's your answer,' Leo said quietly, moving closer to Anna and watching as a large black hearse drew up behind the barrier in front of the ornate entrance to a church. He tightened his hold of Anna's hand as he felt her tremble.

'Philippe's funeral cortège,' Anna whispered. 'I'd forgotten it was taking place this morning.'

'We'll go this way,' Leo said decisively and led them into a small alleyway. 'Hopefully we'll come out by the station and we can carry on with our tour.'

18

'Look what I've got for us,' Daisy said, emptying a carrier bag onto the kitchen table in front of Poppy. 'I had a quick mooch around the shops and the market after I left Anna and Leo this morning. See what I found for us to wear to-morrow evening. What d'you think?' she said, slipping a velvet and pearl headband around her head. 'Very 1920s? I thought you'd look great in this hanky-hem dress,' she said, shaking it out and handing it to Poppy. 'I offered to buy Anna and Leo lunch, but they said they had some shop-ping to do and then planned on having a sand-wich in the garden. Are they back yet?' Daisy asked, glancing out across the garden towards the villa.

'About half an hour ago. Anna went straight indoors and Leo is down by the pool sunbathing,' Poppy answered, holding the dress against herself. 'This is so pretty, thank you. Did Anna remember anything useful?'

Daisy nodded. 'Enough, but it came to an abrupt end shortly after we saw Philippe Cambone's funeral cortège. Anna couldn't seem to concentrate after that.' Daisy slipped a black beaded jacket over her shoulders. 'I love this.' She glanced at Poppy. 'You remember Anna saying she couldn't help me with reminiscences about Philippe Cambone? Well, this morning she admitted she did know him and I'm convinced that there was more to their relationship than she's saying publicly. You should have seen how white she went when we saw the funeral cars. Leo was so protective.'

'I have to go across later to finalise some of the arrangements for tomorrow.' Poppy said. 'Hope she's all right. I like Anna.' She glanced at her sister. 'But first there is something I have to tell you.'

Poppy hesitated. 'I'm afraid when Nat came to collect Tom to play with Cindy, Ben came up in the conversation.'

'How?' Daisy took the jacket off and looked at her sister.

'Oh, Nat said something about you being a journalist and I flippantly said yes, if she doesn't jack it all in to join Ben in Australia. Which seemed to throw him. I take it you haven't mentioned Ben to him?'

'No. It never seemed to be the right moment somehow. *Oh, by the way I've got an ex-boyfriend in Sydney who unexpectedly wants me to join him* isn't easy to drop into the conversation.'

'Doesn't sound that difficult to me if you like someone. Telling them the truth from the beginning is the best policy,' Poppy said.

'Yes, well. It's not a big deal. I'll tell him soon. Promise.' Daisy folded the jacket and put it in the bag. It was one thing giving Marcus the wrong idea, but Nat was different, she really liked him. 'I'll take this lot upstairs and then I'm going to do some work on my laptop, after that I'll be free to help you with things. Okay if I work under the loggia? Don't want to be in your way.'

'I'm going to start doing a few table decorations and the flowers before Tom gets back,' Poppy said. 'Could do with a hand when you've finished. Oh, what about the cake?'

'I've ordered one from the supermarché near the market. We can collect it in the morning,' Daisy said. 'So no worries there.'

* * *

Daisy emailed her report and put the finishing touches to her 'Then and Now' feature before taking a deep breath and writing another email to Bill, her editor. She quickly pressed send before going down to join Poppy in the kitchen.

'Well, that's that then. I've just sent an email to the office saying I'd like to accept voluntary redundancy. I'm going freelance. Things are definitely on the slippery slope at the paper, so better to get out whilst the going is good. Hope you meant that about me renting the cottage?'

Poppy glanced up from the table decoration she was making. 'Of course I did.'

When Nat returned with Tom and an excited Cindy, the two sisters were busy assembling the last of the table decorations for the following evening.

'Tom's coming to my birthday tea on Wednesday and on Saturday Nat's promised he'll take us both to see the whales, he says Daisy might come too,' Cindy told Poppy excitedly.

'The festival will have wound down by then with everyone really just waiting for the winner of the Palme d'Or to be announced,' Nat said. 'So you don't have to worry about missing anything.'

'I'm not worried,' Daisy said. 'You are coming to the party tomorrow night, aren't you? I've cleared it with Anna. She's said she'll introduce you to a couple of people.'

'Great. Teddy Wickham has finally read one of my scripts too and wants a producer friend to read it.'

'Nat, that's wonderful,' Daisy said.

'Might mean disappearing to America for a

few days or even weeks if they like it,' Nat said. 'Fancy coming with me?' he asked, staring at her.

'Aren't you rather rushing things here, Nat?' Daisy said, smiling.

'I'm sure you'd find plenty to write home about from Los Angeles. Unless you've got other plans? Poppy – and Marcus – seemed to think you might.'

'Ah. Can we talk about this another time?' Daisy said, realising there was an edge to Nat's voice. An edge she'd not heard before.

'Tonight? Meet me for a drink later?'

'Oh, I said I'd be at Poppy's beck and call tonight and tomorrow to help with party preparations,' Daisy replied. 'I don't know if—'

'We're well ahead here now,' Poppy said. 'Don't worry on my account.'

'In that case, I'll pick you up about eight thirty. Nowhere dressy,' Nat said. 'Come on, Cindy. Time we went back to the villa.'

Poppy looked at Daisy as the door closed behind them. 'Nat's a good bloke.'

'I know. I really like him, but we've only just met. I can't believe that—'

'I knew Dan was the one for me within twenty-four hours of meeting him,' Poppy interrupted. 'Trust your instincts for once.'

Daisy sighed. She remembered how Poppy had returned home after her first date with Dan positively glowing with happiness and absolutely knowing how she felt about him. But Ben running away like he did had shaken Daisy's faith in her own judgement. For months she'd thought Ben was the one for her – true, she didn't think she'd glowed with happiness like Poppy had with Dan, but she'd felt they fitted together well. Nat needed to hear about Ben from her. It was her own fault that something that finished months ago was being blown up out of all proportion and threatened to spoil her burgeoning relationship with him. Because she did like Nat, and she'd realised instinctively without Poppy putting it into words, that he was special.

* * *

Leo and Anna were sitting on the terrace in the late afternoon when Leo reached into his pocket and placed a small package on the table. 'Before I forget. I got you something in town earlier,' he said. 'Where's your locket?'

'Upstairs in my purse,' Anna replied, opening the tissue wrapped package to find a gold chain nestling within its folds. 'Oh, thank you. I'll get the locket.'

Returning a few moments later clutching the locket, Anna was surprised to find Leo talking on her mobile phone which she'd left on the table.

'Here she is, Bernard, I'll hand you over,' Leo said.

'Hi,' Anna said. 'How did it go this morning? We saw the cars,' she added.

'It was a beautiful service, but I still can't believe that Philippe has gone,' Bernard answered. He hesitated before continuing. 'I told Jacques you were in town for the festival and he wants me to take you to see him tomorrow morning.'

'Why?'

'He would like to meet you again.'

'I can't really see the point,' Anna said.

'Please, Anna. I think you should find the time. He says there is something he needs to give you. It's important to Jacques – and for you. Ten o'clock at the Cambones', okay?'

'I've still got things to do for tomorrow night's party,' Anna protested. 'I'm not sure I can spare the time. Wednesday would be better for me.'

'Sorry, Anna, Jacques is going to Paris on Wednesday. It shouldn't take more than half an hour. I can organise a car to collect and return you if that helps?'

Anna sighed before reluctantly agreeing and saying goodbye. She turned to look at Leo.

'Jacques Cambone wants a meeting with Bernard and me tomorrow morning. Will you come too?'

Leo shook his head. 'No.'

Anna stared at him, shocked by the determination in his voice.

He held out his hand. 'Give me the locket and I'll put it on the chain.' Leo concentrated on threading the chain through the small loop at the top of the locket, before looking up at Anna. 'It's your past – only you can deal with it. We'll face the future together, but we both have to deal with the baggage from our previous lives ourselves. Of

course I'll support you in any way I can, but ulti-
mately you have to face certain things alone. May
I open the locket?'

Anna nodded. Leo was silent as he looked at
the faded picture of Anna and Philippe and gently
fingered the few fine strands of hair that were
curled around the inside of the locket.

'Jean-Philippe's?'

Anna nodded, unable to speak as her eyes
filled with unexpected tears. 'I always longed to
update the contents.'

'Come here,' Leo said, closing the locket and
holding it out to place around Anna's neck. 'I'll do
it up for you.'

Pushing the clasp tightly closed, he bent his
head and brushed her cheeks with his lips.

'I love you so much, Anna, but you must rele-
gate these ghosts to your past where they belong.
Hopefully meeting Jacques tomorrow will help
you to do that.'

'I can't imagine why Jacques wants to meet me
again,' Anna said. 'I only met him briefly before.
Perhaps he too wants to close the door on
Philippe and the past.'

19

Daisy pulled on her best pair of skinny white jeans and a pale blue sweatshirt, and topped it off with Poppy's leather jacket she'd found hanging in the wardrobe. She and Poppy had always borrowed each other's clothes, so she knew it wouldn't be a problem.

Nat might have instructed her not to dress up, but she still wanted to look good. Idly she wondered where they would go for a drink. Be difficult to find somewhere quiet in Cannes this Monday evening, that was for sure.

Nat was talking to Poppy in the kitchen when she went downstairs.

'Hi. So where are we going?' Daisy asked.

'Just along the coast road to Juan-les-Pins,' Nat said. 'If you're happy with the transport, that is,' and he handed her a crash helmet.

Daisy laughed when she saw the Vespa scooter outside. 'Nat, you're full of surprises.'

'I've got a Harley at home, but these seem to be the in thing for nipping around on down here.'

Sitting behind Nat, arms clasped tightly around him, Daisy enjoyed the ride along the coast road as Nat expertly weaved his way through the traffic. The main Juan-les-Pins streets, when they arrived, although less crowded than Cannes, were bustling with locals and holidaymakers enjoying themselves. Parking the scooter near the marina, Nat held Daisy's hand as they strolled back towards the town centre.

Passing the derelict Hotel de Provence currently concealed behind scaffolding and tarpaulin, Nat said, 'I love that place. I'd love to be able to put the clock back and see it in its heyday with the Fitzgeralds, the Murphys, Cole Porter et al. It must have been really something. Great to see it being restored – even if it's being converted into yet more apartments.'

'When you're a rich and famous Hollywood scriptwriter you can buy one and pretend you're a reincarnation of Scott Fitzgerald,' Daisy teased.

Nat shook his head. 'No. I want to live in the country. I don't like towns that much. A farm up in the back country here would suit me fine. Peace and quiet for being creative. How about you? Are you a real townie?'

'I grew up on the edge of a town, with fields and a wood at the end of the garden. Poppy and I were always disappearing and building dens and having adventures. So I guess I like a mixture of both town and country, but I definitely prefer old houses to modern. I'd love to do what Poppy and Dan have done. Restore something.' Daisy glanced at Nat. 'That is what apparently freaked Ben out – that and having to make a commitment.'

'So, tell me about Ben,' Nat said. 'Marcus told me you were going to join him in Australia.'

Daisy sighed. 'That's probably my fault. Marcus was starting to come on to me, nothing wildly out of the way, just annoying things, like constantly kissing me on the cheek, putting his arm around my shoulders.' Daisy shrugged. 'You know the kind of thing. I wanted to get the message over that I wasn't interested in him, so I inferred Ben and I were probably getting back together simply to get him off my back – and also to stop him realising how friendly you and I were becoming. I didn't want him making innuendos about you and me. But it's backfired on me a bit.'

'I know what Marcus is like,' Nat said, squeezing her hand. 'How long were you and Ben together?'

'Nearly eighteen months when we came down here for a holiday with Poppy and Dan. The night before we went home, I joked about how we could follow their example and find a property to renovate together. That simple remark was apparently enough to trigger a commitment phobia in Ben.'

Nat let go of her hand as a group of holiday-makers monopolised the pavement. Minutes later, as they approached the shops and restaurants that lined the coast road of Juan-les-Pins, the crowded pavements narrowed and they were forced to walk in the road for a while. Nat's arm around her shoulders made Daisy feel protected – unlike the occasions when Marcus had done the same. Once they were on the wider pavement above the beach and could walk easily, Nat kept his arm around her as Daisy began to speak.

'We'd been home a week when Ben announced our relationship was crowding in on him. He wasn't ready for any kind of commitment. What he really wanted was space. Turned out to be Australian space.' Daisy went quiet. 'That was six months ago. I had my first letter from him last week, suggesting if I was missing him as much as he missed me, I could join him out there.'

'Are you going to? Marcus gave me the impression you couldn't wait to book your ticket.'

'Like I said, I deliberately misled Marcus,' Daisy said. 'I did think about going out for a holiday. See Australia and finally decide how I feel about Ben when I saw him face to face, but I've realised I don't need to do that.' Daisy smiled at Nat. 'Ben is definitely in the past. I'm sorry I didn't tell you about him before.'

'Why didn't you?'

Daisy bit her lip. Why hadn't she told him? Was it simply a question of the right moment not showing up? Or was it because she was still flirting with the idea of her and Ben getting it together again? No, definitely not that.

'I didn't really know how to. I felt a bit self-conscious telling you about an ex-boyfriend when you and I had only just met. I knew I liked you a lot, but I didn't know how serious you were about me.'

'Oh, I'm serious about you,' Nat said. 'Have been from day one.'

'Oh,' Daisy said. 'That's nice.' And immediately felt silly for using such an inadequate, ordinary word. It was more than nice. 'Seriously nice,' she added as Nat looked at her, laughing.

'Come on, let's try one of these Italian glacés. They look "seriously nice" too!' Nat said.

Sitting at the brasserie on the beach, spoon feeding each other with tastes of their different delicious ice creams, Daisy knew that her feelings for Nat went far, far beyond what she'd felt for Ben. Feelings that were confirmed when, four hours later after a visit to a jazz club in the hills behind Cannes, Nat took her home and kissed her goodnight when he left.

Daisy trembled. There it was again. That delicious tingling feeling that only Nat aroused in her. But what would happen when the festival ended and they went their separate ways?

20

Bernard was waiting outside the 'Chez Cambone' restaurant when the car dropped Anna off on Tuesday morning. The window blinds were still lowered, making it impossible to see inside. The heap of floral tributes lying in the restaurant entrance had been carefully placed to one side.

The door was ajar and as Bernard pushed it open, a bell jangled. 'Jacques, nous sommes arrivés,' he called out, closing the door securely behind him.

'J'arrive,' and Jacques Cambone materialised out of the gloom of the bar area. 'Bonjour, Anna,' he said gravely, taking her by the hand.

Anna, steeling herself for the usual cheek kissing from this man who reminded her so much of Philippe, felt her hand shake in his.

'Thank you for coming. Please sit.' Jacques gestured towards three chairs around a table with a pot of coffee and a plate of biscuits.

Anna regarded Jacques intently as he poured coffee. Identical twins they might have been, but she'd never mistake him for Philippe. For her, there had been something about Philippe's charisma that had simply outshone his brother's.

Now, though, she found herself wondering whether Jacques was still the mirror image of Philippe. Had Philippe's hair greyed at the temples like Jacques? Had he needed reading glasses like the ones Jacques had placed on a folder in front of him? Had his eyes still crinkled when he smiled?

Of course she'd seen photos of Philippe at various festivals over the years, but these days so many were photoshopped, keeping up the pretence of youth for both women and men.

The stress of the last week was clearly etched

across Jacques' face as he pushed a coffee across the table to Anna.

'I'm sorry we meet again under such sad circumstances,' he said quietly. 'It is a pity you did not return to Cannes before. Philippe would have loved to have met up with you again.'

Anna accepted the rebuke and the coffee silently, willing him to tell her what the meeting was all about, wishing Leo had felt able to come with her, and wishing she was anywhere but here.

'I've found something amongst my brother's possessions that I think by rights belongs to you. Also,' Jacques paused, 'Philippe left you some papers.'

Anna stared at him as he reached into the folder and pulled out two envelopes. One, small and brown around the edges and bearing an old-fashioned stamp, was clearly old. Anna recognised her father's writing scrawled over the crossed out address: *Gone Away. Return to Sender.* She fought back the tears as she realised it was Philippe's reply to the news of her pregnancy all those years ago. The envelope had never been opened. The other, larger envelope was new, unstamped and bare, except for her name written across it.

Anna's fingers trembled as she stretched out her hand to take the two envelopes.

'Philippe started to write the letters and the other things you'll find in there after he received the first letter from his... his possible relation,' Jacques said.

Anna bit her lip and tried to stop the tears flowing down her cheeks. Gratefully, she accepted the handkerchief Bernard handed her.

'I'm sorry,' she said. 'This is all so unexpected.' She looked at Jacques. 'What is happening? Can you tell me who has been in touch? Bernard did tell me it was a woman.'

She glanced at Bernard, hoping that Jacques knowing she and Bernard had talked about who it was wouldn't make things difficult for Bernard.

'A Felicity Howell wrote on behalf of her husband, who believes he is Philippe's son. She is telephoning me this afternoon,' Jacques said. 'I hope to learn more from her then.'

Anna tensed. 'Did the letter mention her husband's name? His mother?'

Jacques shook his head. 'No. It simply said her husband had been adopted at birth and had never known either of his real parents. When I speak with her, I will of course try to extract as much information as I can. Anna,' Jacques said gently, 'there is more. Philippe's lawyer wants a meeting with you. He suggests eleven o'clock tomorrow morning if that is convenient for you? A couple of months ago, Bernard and I witnessed Philippe's will – you were to be a beneficiary if you could be found at the time of his death.'

Anna stared at him. 'Me? A beneficiary?'

Jacques nodded. 'Yes. The lawyer will explain when you meet him tomorrow. Why don't you take the envelopes and read Philippe's letters in private and we can meet again later in the week, when I should have more information – and more time,' Jacques suggested, standing up. 'I'm afraid I have to leave soon.'

'It was good to meet you again.' Anna stood up and held out her hand. 'Thank you for these,' she said, indicating the envelopes.

'I'll ring for the car,' Bernard said, reaching for his mobile phone.

Anna stopped him. 'Not for me, Bernard. I think I'd like to take a walk. Clear my head.' It was all becoming rather surreal. Lawyers. Jacques. Beneficiary. Felicity Howell.

'May I walk a little way with you?' Bernard asked. Taking her agreement for granted, he held the door open for her and ushered her through.

Both were quiet for several minutes, lost in their own thoughts as they made their way through Cannes. It was Bernard who broke the silence.

'The letter you wrote Philippe telling him you were pregnant? He gave it to me to read the day he received it. He was absolutely thrilled and could hardly contain his excitement at the news.' Bernard turned and looked at her. 'I have to ask you a question – one I think I already know the answer to – but I need to hear the truth from you,' Bernard said, taking a deep breath. 'Did you go ahead and have the baby or—'

Anna stopped, shocked. 'Did I abort the baby? Oh, Bernard, how can you even ask me a question like that. I loved Philippe with all my heart. There was no way I would ever do that. So, to answer your question, yes, I had Philippe's baby. I named him Jean-Philippe before I was made to give him away. The possibility that this Felicity Howell's husband could be...' her voice trailed away.

'I was certain that was going to be your answer,' Bernard said. 'Oh Anna. I don't know what to say.'

'It was a long time ago, so there's nothing left to say really,' Anna said sadly. 'Other than for me to say I'm so sorry Philippe never got a chance to meet his son, either as a baby or as a grown man.'

'Yes, he would have welcomed that,' Bernard agreed as he glanced at her. 'There's something else I need to say to you. You have to understand Philippe never forgot you, never truly stopped loving you, never had a committed relationship with another woman, but he never lived the life of a monk. There is a chance that whoever this man is – he's not necessarily your son.'

Anna smiled ruefully. 'I realise that. Leo has also pointed it out. But I can't take the risk of not finding out. I have to know.'

'So long as you realise it is a risk however it turns out,' Bernard said as they crossed the

Croisette and began walking in the direction of the harbour. 'Now, has the fresh air cleared your head? I have to leave you here, I'm afraid. I have a meeting in ten minutes.'

'I'm fine,' Anna said. 'Honestly,' she added, seeing the worried look on Bernard's face. 'I'd quite like some time on my own before I meet up with Leo. I'll see you tonight at the party.' She reached up and kissed him gently on the cheek. 'Thanks, Bernard.'

After Bernard left her, Anna pushed her way through the crowds loitering around the harbour and began making her way along Quai Saint Pierre with just a single thought in her mind. She had to get away from all these people. Try to get things into perspective.

A poster for the ferryboats that operated between Cannes and the Iles de Lérins caught her eye. Running the length of Quai Laubeuf, she bought a ticket for the next sailing and was the last person to board the crowded boat.

Twenty minutes later, Anna followed her fellow passengers up the quay to the small traffic-free road that circled the Ile Saint-Honorat.

Watching as everyone else took the clockwise route, Anna deliberately turned in the opposite direction and began making her way along the coastal track towards an almost deserted beach.

Perched on a small rock, Anna finally opened the letter Philippe had sent her nearly forty years ago.

> My darling,
>
> What wonderful news! Where shall we get married – France or England? Where shall we live while the island cottage is being done up? What shall we call the baby? Will you come to America with me? (I promise we'll be back in time for 'it' to be born in France – or England, whatever you decide.) I can barely believe we're going to be a family so quickly. I promise to take the greatest care of you both.
>
> All my love, Philippe.

Underneath his signature the words 'One Life, One Love' were followed by a string of kisses.

Anna gazed out unseeingly across the Mediterranean towards Cannes, tears spilling from her eyes. Why hadn't she believed in their love more? Whatever her parents had thought and said all those years ago about it being a 'holiday romance' with Philippe taking advantage of her naivety had been so wrong. Philippe had wanted her and Jean-Philippe. The fault was all hers for not believing in him and allowing her parents to bully her into doing what they wanted and considered to be the right thing.

A family running down to chase and splash each other on the edge of the sea a few yards away from her jolted Anna out of the trance-like state she'd slipped into. She watched them for a few moments, envying their easy familiarity with each other, before pulling the contents of the second envelope out with shaking fingers.

Hesitantly, Anna flipped through the pages of the spiral-bound notebook dislodging a piece of folded paper that fluttered down to the shingle at her feet. Picking it up, she began to read:

Ma Chérie, this is a letter I hope to give you when we are together again.

I can't tell you how excited I am by the

arrival of a letter from the wife of a man who could turn out to be our child. To think, after all these years, I could be about to meet my son and through him, hopefully, you, again.

I intend to keep a journal record as things unfold so that when we all finally meet you will be able to see how everything happened. I fervently pray that this is not a false alarm and we will be able to finally welcome our son into his family.

I appreciate how different your life must be after all these years and you may find it upsetting as the past makes its presence known in the present, but if nothing else, I hope we can meet as friends and share a part of our lives in the future.

A simple 'Philippe' signature this time at the bottom of the page. No quotation. No kisses.

Anna refolded the piece of paper and carefully slipped it in towards the back of the notebook as she opened it. Philippe had started his journal six weeks earlier, carefully dating the first page – the day he'd received the first letter.

Reading Philippe's journal and his obvious delight in the possibility of meeting his son, Anna could again hear the voice of the boy she'd loved. The pages were full of his thoughts and hopes for the future – and questions about how she, Anna, would be.

Will I recognise you – you, me? I was so angry with you when you disappeared. The one thing I wanted was to find you and care for you. For years I tried to find you. Hoped you'd get in touch with me. I saw you once in the audience at the Film Institute in London, but you'd left the building before I could get to you. I saw you getting into a taxi and vanishing out of my life again. The years and life took on their own momentum and suddenly thirty years had passed. I realised even if I did find you, it was too late for us to be that happy family, but I couldn't – and didn't – stop looking for you. But you vanished very effectively.

The last entry started:

Today Jacques and I had words about me meeting my son. He is very sceptical about things working out, but I believe they will. I feel in my heart of hearts that the time has finally come for me to be able to right wrongs done so many years ago. I'm off to America tomorrow, when I return, the Cannes Film Festival will be in full swing – who knows, by the time it finishes, I may have definite news about our family. 'Our family.' Oh, how I love that phrase.

Anna, unable to control her sobbing, searched frantically for a tissue in her bag, aware that the family playing nearby were watching her, trying to hide their concern. She forced a smile in their direction, praying they wouldn't approach her, and tried to stop herself shaking. The blue 'missed message' light on her mobile in the bottom of her bag was flashing. Leo.

With shaking fingers, she pressed the redial button and waited for Leo to pick up.

'Anna, where are you? I've been frantic with

worry. When I rang Bernard, he told me you left him over an hour ago.'

'I'm on Saint-Honorat. Leo darling, I'm so sorry. I just had to be by myself for a while.'

'Are you okay?' Leo asked anxiously. 'Bernard said it was an emotional meeting with Jacques.'

'It was. I'll be back soon. I promise I'll catch the next boat back. There's one coming across the bay now. Leo, we need to talk when I get back,' Anna said, her voice trembling.

'We'll talk as much as you want to,' Leo said firmly. 'There are things I need to say as well.'

Thoughtfully, Anna pressed the off button on her phone. Carefully, she placed the two envelopes with their revealing contents in her bag. She had all the proof she'd ever needed that Philippe Cambone had truly loved her – had probably still loved her at the time of his death.

Anna pressed her hands against her eyes and rubbed hard, trying yet again to stem the tears. She knew she had only herself to blame for the mess she'd made of things. How was she going to live with herself now, knowing how much she'd hurt Philippe with her selfish act of giving their son away? Not that she could have done anything else at the time and really and truly it had been forced on her by parents who had acted in the most despicable and selfish manner all those years ago.

21

Daisy had offered to take Tom to school Tuesday morning, an offer Poppy had gratefully accepted. When Daisy returned, Poppy was sitting at the table scribbling a shopping list.

'Time for a quick coffee?' Daisy asked.

Poppy nodded absently as she added something else to her list. 'The pianist is coming this afternoon to check the piano over. I just hope the weather stays okay for this evening. I've got extra candles to put around the place, and lots of floating ones for the pool. Oh! Nobody is going to want to swim, are they?' She looked up at Daisy anxiously.

'Not when they're all dressed up in their glad rags,' Daisy answered reassuringly. 'Although some of the tales I've heard about parties down here, with people jumping in fully clothed, you never know. Floating candles should put them off though,' she added, seeing a worry frown appear on Poppy's face.

'D'you think I've hired enough glasses? People do hang on to their glass don't they, rather than taking a fresh one each time?'

'Of course you've organised enough glasses. Now stop worrying for goodness' sake and let's hit Forville market for the fresh stuff and pick up the cake,' Daisy said.

They were strolling around the market when Poppy asked, 'I almost forgot. How was your evening with Nat? Heard you come in at two.'

'Oh, hope I didn't wake you.'

'I couldn't sleep,' Poppy said briefly. 'Did you tell Nat about Ben?'

'Yes. It was a great night. Nat and I seem to be on the same wavelength over lots of things. He took me to a jazz club he knew up in Valbonne, out in the country behind Cannes. He actually likes Jamie Callum as well. Remember how Ben always used to moan at me for listening to him? And yes, I did tell him all about Ben.' Daisy looked at her sister. 'Can you believe Marcus had also poked his oar in? Gave Nat the impression that I couldn't wait to jet off to be reunited with him. At least you didn't do that when you mentioned Ben. Two dozen eggs enough?'

'Plenty. Cheese stall next. How did he react?'

'He was fine – told me all about Julia, the love of his life in primary school,' Daisy laughed.

She'd really enjoyed last night. Nat was so good to be around. And honest about his own past. He thought her plans for the future – going freelance and moving into the cottage – were great.

As Poppy stood by the cheese stall agonising over how big a brie to buy and whether gorgonzola was a popular choice, Daisy wandered over to the flower section to look at several vases filled with one of her favourites – vibrant, happy sunflowers. Just what she needed – a visual reminder of the happy mood she was in.

Her mobile trilled its text alert as she selected three sunflowers and paid for them.

'Seen any reasonably priced asparagus anywhere?' Poppy asked, joining her.

'That stall over there and the next one for the olives and the tapenade you wanted. Think that's everything on the list then. No, we still need some smoked salmon. And then the cake.'

Walking back to the car with Poppy carefully carrying the large cake box, Daisy took a quick look to see who the text was from. She didn't recognise the international number and it wasn't until they'd stowed the shopping in the car and were driving home that she clicked on the message.

srry hve bn fool. rtrning to uk nxt wk 2 marry u. lv u. ben.

Daisy hit her knees with her fist clenched. 'I don't believe this,' she said, reading the message out to Poppy. 'Now what do I do?'

'You should have replied to his letter, telling him it was too late, days ago,' Poppy said, with a typical bossy big sister tone to her voice. 'You'll have to text him back and tell him, no way.'

'It's just typical of Ben, though, to assume I've nothing better to do than hang around waiting for him.' Daisy threw the phone in her bag.

'Aren't you going to text him right away?' Poppy asked.

'No. I'll email him the minute we get back,' Daisy said. 'I'm not that keen on texts. All those abbreviated words can lead to misunderstandings. I'm going to have to spell it out in full. Make sure he gets the message. Can't you drive a bit faster? I need to get this over and done with.'

'No, it's a thirty speed limit along here. I don't want a speeding ticket and points on my licence, thank you very much. What are you going to say Ben?'

'That if he thinks he can just waltz back into my life and nothing will have changed, then he's not only wrong but stupid. Besides, I'm not sure I'll even be back in the UK next week. I was thinking I might stay down here longer with you.'

Once back at the cottage, sitting in front of her laptop, Daisy clicked on Ben's email address.

Thank God she hadn't deleted it from her address book in a fit of pique. Now, how to be polite and firm but kind?

Dear Ben, re your recent text. Marriage is not on, I'm afraid, so suggest you stay where you are. Not sure I'll be in the UK next week. Have a good life. Daisy.

Thoughtfully, she looked at what she'd written. Too short? Too cruel? What else was there to say? She didn't want him harbouring any false hopes of a reconciliation. This last week, since she'd met Nat, had convinced her there was absolutely no way she wanted Ben back in her life. Ben was in the past – his choice. Nat was the future – her choice.

P.S. I hope you meet someone special soon. I have and I'm very happy.

There, that should get the message across.

Daisy pressed the send button before she could change her mind. Her computer pinged. Incoming mail – one from the paper, two from journalist friends. Daisy read them in a daze before closing her laptop. That was all she needed.

Poppy glanced at her as she walked into the sitting room. 'Told him? You all right? You look a bit shell-shocked.'

'The chief reporter has been sacked from the paper. Two of my friends who were on short contracts have been told they won't be renewed. One has gone already and rumour has it at least ten per cent of the staff face the chop. Thank God I said I'd take voluntary redundancy when I did.' Daisy looked at Poppy, a rueful smile on her face. 'At least, hopefully, I'll receive some redundancy money to help kick-start my freelancing with. Think I might be living down here sooner than I expected.'

'Fine by me,' Poppy said. 'Now, can we get on with the party preparations? I wish Anna was here. Leo said she had an important meeting in town and she'd be back later.'

22

Anna could see Leo waiting for her on the quay as the ferryboat pulled alongside the pontoon. The last to step ashore, Anna ran towards him, a feeling of relief washing over her as he put his arms around her and held her tightly for several seconds without speaking.

'Are you all right?' he asked finally, holding her at arm's length and studying her face. 'I was so worried when you didn't return.'

'I'm sorry, Leo. I just needed to be on my own to read the papers Jacques gave me and to think about what he'd said. To have a good think about everything really.'

Leo looked at Anna questioningly as he noticed the envelopes sticking out of her bag for the
first time.

'I'll tell you what happened this morning as
we walk back to the villa,' Anna said. She tucked
her hand into Leo's. 'Preparations going okay for
the party?'

Leo nodded. 'Think Poppy is getting stressed
having to take decisions she feels you should be
making, but other than that, things are on
schedule for this evening.'

'I do feel guilty for not being around this
morning.' Anna answered. 'Although I've never
felt less like a party in my life,' she added quietly.
Walking along the bord de mer, Anna told Leo the
name of the woman who had contacted Philippe.
'Felicity Howell. Which means nothing to
Jacques, Bernard or me.'

She told him too about the long-lost letter
from Philippe and the journal that Jacques had
given her.

'I wish I'd come back to Cannes years ago and
found Philippe. Told him the truth. My life could

have been so different. So much better.' She sighed. 'Still it's too late now.'

Leo was silent and Anna glanced at him, concerned. She'd clearly upset him today, first by disappearing and now by inferring how much better her life would have been if she'd married Philippe all those years ago. Anna bit her lip. The last thing she wanted to do was hurt Leo. She loved him too much. Before she could say anything, Leo started to speak.

'I don't think you coming to Cannes this year was a very good idea,' Leo said slowly. 'You seem to have jumped on to an emotional roller coaster that is in danger of running you over. I dread to think what would have happened if Philippe had been here in person.' Leo indicated an empty bench overlooking the beach and the Mediterranean. 'Let's sit down for a few moments. I need to say something to you. I don't think it can wait until after the party like I hoped, after all.'

Obediently, Anna followed Leo across to the bench and sat down. As Leo took her hand in his, he gently played with her fingers before starting to speak.

'I'm beginning to wonder if Philippe hadn't died and the two of you had met up again this week, whether you and I would still be together.' He was silent for a moment, gazing out to sea before turning to face her. 'This pining for something that might have been has to stop, Anna, if we are to have any sort of future.' His hand holding hers squeezed so hard, Anna thought her fingers would drop off. 'We are both old enough to know, and accept, that nothing is ever simply black or white – particularly with the baggage we all collect as we go through life. By the time we get to our age,' Leo shrugged. 'Well, there's usually lots of it. I have baggage of my own.'

He was silent for a second or two before continuing.

'Anna, we have to be totally honest with each other before our relationship can go any further. I love you with all my heart – I feel we're soulmates. But I'm scared I'm only second best for you after Philippe. I'm worried too that there is always going to be a dead third presence hovering between us. A presence that won't allow me to get as close to you as I want to. I truly couldn't bear that.'

Anna stared out across the bay, knowing that whatever she said to Leo in the future, nothing would ever be more important than the words she said right now.

'Leo, you must never ever think again you're second best in my life. These months since I've known you have been the happiest of my adult life. I didn't expect to ever love and be loved in return – I thought it was far too late. I do love you, Leo, and I can't imagine my life without you in it.' Anna paused. 'What you said about us being soulmates is true. I'm sorry about inflicting my pain over the past and Philippe on to you. I don't want a dead presence coming between us any more than you do. But it's Philippe's legacy that is at stake here.' Her hand still rested in Leo's, clenched into a fist. 'It's the possibility of finally meeting my son, Jean-Philippe, that is really beginning to tear me apart in all this.'

Anna turned to face Leo, her voice taking on a desperate note. 'You've got children. Imagine if you no longer had any contact with Alison. Or your Luke? If there was a possibility you would never see your grandchild when it's born. How would you feel? I know the whole sorry business is my fault – I was the one who denied Philippe his rights as a father when I gave Jean-Philippe away – but now if there's just a chance I can explain things, make amends in some way, then I have to try. Please help me to get through this, Leo.'

'Anna, I promise I'll give you all the help I can but when will all this torment stop? When we leave here at the end of the week or will you carry on punishing yourself for the past? Beating yourself up with guilt? It's impossible to know what Philippe's true feelings were for you all those years ago, or whether things would have worked out if you and he had stayed together. As for Jean-Philippe,' Leo shook his head. 'Who knows what kind of effect finding him will have on your – on our – lives?'

Anna handed him the letter Philippe had written. 'No, it's not impossible to know what Philippe's true feelings were. Read this and then tell me I shouldn't feel guilty about things.'

She stared at Leo's impassive face as he read

the letter, trying to gauge his reaction to the emotions expressed by Philippe so long ago.

'Now do you see why I can't give up this emotional roller coaster, as you called it, until I have some sort of closure?' she asked quietly as Leo handed back the letter.

He nodded. 'I still think you're wrong to take one hundred per cent of the blame on your shoulders. There were other people involved too.'

'I know,' Anna said. 'But I'm the last one left who can try to right the mistakes that were made.'

Leo sighed. 'L.P. Hartley was damn right when he said the past is a foreign country. It's certainly not a place I'm keen to visit for long. I just want us to get back on track to enjoying the rest of our lives together.'

'We will, I promise. I'm looking forward to the future with you so much,' Anna said. 'There's something else you have to know. Something that never ever occurred to me was a possibility.'

Leo looked at her warily and waited for her to continue.

'Philippe has named me as a beneficiary in his will. I have to meet his lawyers tomorrow morning for them to tell me what that means exactly. Will you come with me this time please, Leo?'

'Yes, but I need you to promise me one thing, Anna. Whatever happens, please don't let it come between us and destroy what we have now in the present.'

'I promise,' Anna said and, oblivious to passers-by, leant forward and kissed Leo passionately.

23

'I picked up a sparkling candle too,' Daisy said as she and Poppy admired the decorated gateau with its swirls of cream and chocolate hearts that they'd collected from the patisserie. 'Just in case.'

'Just in case of what?' Poppy asked.

Daisy shrugged. 'Don't know really, but sparkling candles on a cake is always festive. I thought it would go well... here,' and she carefully pushed it into the centre of the cake. 'We can light it just before the official toasts.'

'Better put the cake back in the fridge,' Poppy said. 'Don't want the cream going off before we serve it.'

'Right,' Daisy said. 'Now where's that list? What else have we got left to do?'

Poppy looked at her clipboard. 'Think we're done. We just have to put the food out on the table, what, quarter of an hour before people are due?' she said, glancing at her watch. 'We'll have to light the candles and float them on the pool, but that's not until later as well. Nat will be bringing Tom back soon. Shall we eat something with him or wait for food this evening?'

'Oh, let's eat something light with Tom. Shouldn't drink champagne on an empty stomach,' Daisy said. 'Anna and Leo look as if they are still putting the world to rights,' Daisy added, looking across to the villa, where Anna and Leo were sitting by the pool. 'Anna's looking so miserable. I wonder what's upset her? Tonight's supposed to be a happy occasion.'

'I thought she looked as if she'd been crying when they got back here earlier,' Poppy said. 'She was very subdued when I went across to finalise a few things.' She turned as Nat opened the garden gate. 'Ah, Tom and Cindy are back. I'll organise some food. Would you and Cindy like to stay?' she asked Nat.

'Thanks. Not sure how hungry these two will be. Lots of candy floss and other delicacies on offer today on the Croisette – along with balloons,' he said, catching hold of Cindy's pink helium-filled balloon as it threatened to slip out of the little girl's hand and float away from her.

Daisy helped Tom tie his blue one to the back of a chair before following Poppy into the kitchen to help with the food.

'How's your day been then?' Nat asked as Daisy put some slices of melon on the table for the children to snack on.

'Well, I no longer have a job to return to, but my voluntary redundancy package will be waiting for me,' she explained as Nat looked at her. 'So I'm going to be freelance sooner rather than later.'

'Which you can do from anywhere in the world,' Nat said thoughtfully.

'True, but first I'll need to do some serious networking to let people know I'm available. Poppy's already agreed I can have the cottage while I look around for something down here.'

'A new start in all sorts of ways,' Nat said. 'Exciting.'

'Yep,' Daisy replied, deciding not to mention the other event in her day – Ben's marriage proposal. She'd tell him later, of course, when they could laugh about it together.

'Cindy, Tom, when you've finished your quiche and salads, I'll make you a small chocolate milkshake each. Okay?' Poppy called from the kitchen.

Half an hour later the children finished their tea and Nat pushed his chair back. 'Time to go, Cindy,' he said.

As they said their goodbyes and untied Cindy's balloon, Anna walked through the villa garden towards the cottage.

'Hello, Tom and Cindy. Love your balloons.'

'Are you having balloons for your party?' Cindy asked.

'No, we completely forgot about ordering balloons,' Anna said.

'That's sad,' Cindy replied solemnly. 'You can borrow mine if you like,' she offered, holding it out to Anna. 'Not to keep. Just for your party.'

'Thank you, Cindy. That's very kind of you,' Anna said. 'It's your birthday soon, isn't it?' she asked. 'You'll need your balloon for your tea party then, so you'd better take it home with you now.'

'Okay,' Cindy said. 'Is my mummy coming to your party?'

'She's welcome to come, but I expect she's busy with festival things. I think Nat's coming,' Anna said, glancing across at him.

'Mummy's not busy. I heard her telling Daddy she didn't have anything to do tonight.'

'Well, you tell her if she wants to come with Nat, she'll be very welcome,' Anna said. 'I would love to meet her.'

'Come on, Cindy, let's go,' Nat said. 'I'll see you all later.'

'Bye, Cindy, have a lovely birthday. Such a sweet little girl,' Anna said before turning to Poppy. 'How's it going? It all looks very organised.'

'I think we've got everything covered,' Poppy said. 'We'll light the floating candles before everyone gets here and then the others during the evening as it gets darker, if that's okay? And, of course, the solar lights will be on.'

'Sounds perfect,' Anna replied. 'Leo suggests about quarter to nine for the official champagne toast. Everyone should be here by then and afterwards we can just party.'

'Okay, Daisy and I will bring the champagne out then,' Poppy said. 'And now we'd all better think about getting ready.'

* * *

Anna, returning to the villa, saw Leo nervously pacing up and down on the terrace by the swimming pool, and she hurried to his side.

'Has something happened? You look worried? Is Alison all right? Luke?'

'There's nothing wrong. I just need to talk to you again before the party. To ask you something,' Leo said quietly, catching hold of her hand. 'It's just I'm no longer confident about how you'll respond.'

Anna stilled and waited. She thought their talk earlier had cleared up lots of misconceptions, but she'd never seen Leo so unsure of himself.

'Anna, my darling, I love you so much. I know

I should really get down on bended knee to ask this, so forgive me that, but I'm hoping tonight will be more than a festival party. I'm hoping it will be remembered as the night you agreed to be my wife. Please say you'll marry me?'

Although she'd been longing to hear Leo ask her that question for weeks now, she hadn't expected him to choose this particular evening to voice it and Anna looked at him in wonder before answering quietly, 'Oh Leo, I'm so sorry I've given you cause to doubt me – I love you too so much. There's nothing I want more in the world than to marry you. So, yes, I'll marry you.' She hoped the radiant smile she gave him would convey exactly how happy she was at the thought of becoming Mrs Leo Hunter.

Leo took a small box out of his pocket; the ruby and diamond ring he slipped on her finger was a perfect fit and Anna gazed at it in wonder.

'Thank you for such a beautiful ring,' she said as Leo took her in his arms.

'Beautiful, like my wife to be,' he said, before sealing their engagement with a kiss.

24

The sun had set over the Esterel Mountains to the right of the villa as Daisy lit the floating candles and pushed them out on to the gently moving water of the swimming pool. Dan had phoned earlier to talk to Tom and Poppy and now Tom was tucked up in bed in the cottage with a new Dr Seuss book that Daisy had bought him.

The gentle strains of a Cole Porter song as the pianist began his warm-up medley were drifting around the garden, competing with the noise of the resident frogs.

Anna, standing with Leo's arm around her shoulders and a glass of champagne in her hand, smiled happily. The pool with its floating candles looked so pretty and some of the solar lights in the villa garden were starting to glow. She knew Leo was looking forward to announcing their engagement later. She glanced at the ring on her hand. So beautiful. Despite the uncertainty shrouding her past, life at this moment was good and promising to get even better with Leo at her side permanently from now on. The future was what truly mattered, not the secrets of the past.

'Oh, here come the first guests,' she said. 'Time to party.'

Daisy finished lighting the pool candles and made her way over to Poppy, who was standing by the drinks table handing out glasses of champagne.

'Marcus has arrived,' Daisy said. 'With a friend. I'll be back to help in a moment. Need to have a word,' and she made her way over to Marcus as his blonde companion went to look at the buffet table. 'What's she doing here? Anna didn't invite her.'

'Everybody gatecrashes parties down here.

You should have security checking tickets if you want to avoid unwanted guests.'

'It's not that sort of party,' Daisy said. 'Besides, you're not a guest – you're the official photographer.'

'So, she's my assistant.' Marcus shrugged.

'Go and take some photos then and make sure your "assistant" doesn't get in the way,' Daisy said. 'I'm going to go and apologise to Anna about her uninvited guest.'

Several other people arrived at that moment and Daisy, seeing Anna busy making introductions, decided to leave her apology until later and made her way instead back over to Poppy, who was counting glasses on the drinks table.

'I hope we don't run out of glasses,' Poppy said. 'D'you think everyone is here yet?'

'Anna said she expected about thirty-five, didn't she?' Daisy said, looking around and trying to do a rough head count. 'So, yes, I think most people are here. Nat isn't though. Hope he gets here before the food disappears.' Daisy helped herself to a plate of appetisers from the buffet. 'Seen any one famous yet?' she asked, offering

Poppy a smoked salmon blini. 'Try one. I know the chef. They're delicious.'

'Thanks. No, I don't recognise a single face. No, I lie,' Poppy said. 'The handsome man who's just arrived with a blonde and another man looks very much like your Nat. Don't know who the couple are though.'

Daisy turned to look down the driveway. 'Poppy, how can you not recognise Verity Raymond? Cindy obviously told her what Anna said about her being welcome to come. The guy with her is Bernard. A big shot in the film world on the money side of things.'

The two watched as Anna greeted Bernard like an old friend and then welcomed Verity to the party, before introducing them both to Leo.

'That's interesting,' Daisy said quietly. 'Bernard was a great friend of Philippe Cambone. I wonder if Anna knew him as well back in the past. I must ask her.'

Poppy looked at her sister anxiously. 'Please, don't start asking questions tonight. Let Anna enjoy her party. I think the last few days have been very hard on her for some reason. She's brighter tonight, but the last few times I've seen her she's been very subdued.'

'Poppy, what d'you take me for? Of course I won't bother Anna tonight. Might have a word with Bernard though,' Daisy said mischievously, ignoring Poppy's sharp intake of breath and smiling at Nat making his way towards them. 'Nat. You're late. Everything okay?' Daisy asked as Nat hugged and kissed her.

'Think so. Verity and Teddy had a major fallout earlier. That's why we're late. To be honest, I'm surprised Verity still wanted to come, but she said she needed to get out of the villa. Also, she wanted to meet Anna. Thanks,' he said, accepting a glass of champagne from Daisy. 'Love your headband. Very flapperish. You look lovely,' he said, gently kissing Daisy again and placing an arm around her shoulders. 'Dance with me later?'

'Of course. Not sure I'm up to the Charleston though,' Daisy said, watching a couple by the pool giving it their best as the pianist romped through 'Ain't She Sweet'. 'It always looks so complicated to me. All that leg swinging and knee holding.'

'Don't worry. It's one of the dances I can do,'

Nat said. 'In fact, I'm a bit of an expert. My gran was a great ragtime dancer and taught me everything she knew.'

'First the Harley and now a Charleston expert – you're full of surprises, Nat.' Daisy laughed.

'I think Leo is about to make the announcement,' Poppy interrupted. 'We'd better get the cake and have the extra champagne at the ready.'

'Back in five,' Daisy said, handing Nat her champagne glass. 'Ready for the toast.'

'I'll keep this short,' Leo said, calling for everyone's attention. 'Welcome everyone. We have two reasons for celebration tonight. *Future Promises* was well received at the festival and we raise our glasses to Helen and Rupert – stars of the future.'

He paused as Helen and Rupert acknowledged the cheers and the applause.

'The other, personal, reason for celebration,' Leo continued, 'is that Anna has done me the honour of agreeing to become my wife.'

'So that's what the cake was for,' Poppy muttered, sotto voce, to Daisy.

'See – I knew that candle would come in useful!'

As everyone shouted congratulations, Daisy fetched the cake and carried it out carefully with its sparkling candle.

Leo took Anna into his arms. 'All I want to say, Anna my darling, is that I love you and will do my utmost to make you happy for the rest of our lives.'

The gentle strains of 'Come Fly With Me' floated on the evening air as the happy couple swayed gently together and everyone raised their glasses. 'Anna and Leo.'

25

An hour or so later when the party was in full swing, and Leo and Rick were deep in discussion about the woes of both the publishing and film worlds, Anna slipped away for a few moments by herself.

So many people here wishing her and Leo well; some she knew as friends, others she knew as business acquaintances, others she had no idea who they were. She could see Bernard on the terrace, standing apart from everyone and taking a call on his mobile. She hoped she'd get the opportunity to talk to him before the evening finished. See if he had any idea what Philippe had written in his will before she went to the lawyers tomorrow.

There was somebody sitting on the uphol-stered swing seat hidden away in a quiet corner at the top of the garden. Not wanting company, Anna was about to turn and leave when she heard the sound of sobbing. Moving closer, she asked quietly, 'Are you all right? Can I help? Or would you rather be left alone?'

The tear stained face that Verity Raymond turned towards her made Anna hurry forward, and sitting alongside her, she gently placed an arm around Verity's shoulders and waited for the younger woman to compose herself.

'Teddy is furious with me,' Verity said, strug-gling to control her sobs. 'He thought I'd given up on something, but today when I told him some exciting news, he realised I hadn't. He's even ac-cused me of trying to get my own way by going behind his back. He was still on about it this evening and we had another major row.' Verity wiped her face with the back of her hand. 'All I want is for him to be happy and for us to have an-other baby. He adores Cindy and I'm sure he'd feel the same about another child, but now he just refuses to discuss it.'

'Cindy is a delightful child,' Anna said. 'You must be so proud of her.'

'Yes, I am, but I do worry that she is being spoilt as an only child. I had been hoping she would have some brothers or sisters before now but...' Verity shook her head. 'Anyway, I mustn't bore you with my personal problems. What are you doing up here? It's your party. You should be down there living it up.'

'Oh, I just needed some time out,' Anna said. 'You know how it is.'

Verity nodded her agreement. 'Maybe this is the wrong moment, but I was hoping to talk to you sometime about your new film project. Would there be a part for me in the film?'

Anna looked at her, astonished. 'It's a period drama. Not your sort of thing, surely?'

'My very first role in rep was Rosalie, the maid in *Lady Windermere's Fan*. I've had a soft spot for costume drama ever since. The contemporary stuff I do now is great fun, but I'd love a chance to wear long skirts for a change!'

'Well, I'll tell the casting director about your interest, but I can't promise anything,' Anna said. Verity Raymond in the already star-studded cast would certainly be a plus. 'You know shooting is going to start this autumn in the UK? Don't you live in the States these days?'

'We're buying a place near my parents in Gloucestershire. Cindy needs to be settled in school for the next few years,' Verity said. 'At least Teddy and I are agreed on that, and that it will be in England.'

'Well, when you're settled in Gloucestershire, we'll meet up. Leo is quite close, in the Cotswolds, and when we're married, I'll be moving there. You must come for lunch and we'll get to know each other properly.'

'I'd like that. Thank you, Anna.'

'Ah, this is where you're hiding,' Leo said, suddenly appearing at the top of the path. 'Anna darling, Bernard has been looking for you. He wanted to talk to you before he left. You may just catch him if you're quick. If not, you're to phone him tomorrow.'

'I was hoping to have a word with him too. Excuse me, Verity. I'll see you later.'

Anna made her way back down into the garden and onto the driveway, where she could see Bernard standing by the villa gates, clearly waiting for a taxi.

'Bernard, you're not leaving already? Leo says you were looking for me?'

'Yes. I wanted to congratulate you on your engagement. I sincerely hope you'll be happy with Leo.' He paused and looked at her, a serious look on his face. 'And I have something to tell you.'

'Something about Philippe?'

'Jacques phoned just now to tell me about the telephone conversations he's had with Felicity Howell.' Bernard looked at Anna before saying quietly, 'Jacques has also been putting two and two together by the way. He asked Felicity if she knew the name of her husband's mother. She said yes, it was on the copy of the original birth certificate they'd managed to obtain, but that it was proving impossible to trace her.' Bernard glanced at Anna. 'Rightly or wrongly, when she told him the name,

Harriet Ann Carstairs, Jacques said he'd known a woman with that name a long time ago and that she was in town for the festival for the first time in years. Felicity immediately begged him to arrange a private meeting for her and her husband.'

Anna gasped. She could hardly believe what she was hearing. 'What did Jacques say?'

'That it wasn't his decision, but he would see if he could arrange a meeting. He's asked me to talk to you first because it now appears not to be as straightforward as a simple meeting,' Bernard paused. 'Her husband has had second thoughts about this whole business of tracing his roots. Because Philippe died before they could meet up, he has decided not to continue the search for his mother.' Bernard was silent for a moment. 'I'm sorry to be the bearer of bad news, but it's basically because he's very bitter about the fact that his mother gave him up. So, even if you agree to a meeting, there's no guarantee that he will come. It could turn out to be just you and this Felicity Howell.'

'Is her husband in town for the festival too? Do we know what he does?' Anna asked.

'Yes, he's in town and he has some sort of connection with the film industry. Felicity was vague on the subject – deliberately, Jacques felt. Will you let Jacques arrange a meeting?'

'I don't know,' Anna said with a sigh. 'Is there any point if my son has decided he doesn't want to see me? Doesn't want to have any contact because I abandoned him?'

'Wouldn't you like to know about his life? Learn how he's turned out? There are all sorts of things his wife could tell you. Maybe even persuade her husband to meet after all.'

'Have you met this Felicity woman? What is she like?'

Bernard shook his head. 'I don't know. Like Jacques, I haven't met her, but she sounds genuine enough. Jacques says she's desperate to help her husband come to terms with his adoption. Philippe dying so close to their planned first meeting has really shaken him. He had so many questions he wanted to ask him. Questions only you can answer now. If you do meet Felicity, it might be the start of getting him to change his mind over you,' Bernard added gently.

'So you think I should agree to meet this woman?'

Bernard sighed. 'Anna, it has to be your decision and yours alone. No one is going to pressurise you into doing something you're not comfortable with.'

'I told Leo earlier that I had to continue trying to trace Jean-Philippe, but I also promised him that I would stop beating myself up with guilt. That the future was more important to me now than the past,' Anna said slowly. 'To be so close to meeting Jean-Philippe, only to learn that he despises me...' her voice trailed away. 'I don't think I could cope with him saying that to my face. Maybe it would be better just to leave things the way they are, go home after the festival finishes and get on with my life with Leo.'

'It's your decision, Anna,' Bernard said. 'Don't decide anything you might regret while you're so emotional. Talk it over with Leo. Sleep on it. Give me a ring when you know what you want to do. Ah, here's my taxi – and here's Leo to claim his fiancée for the last dance of the party. Goodnight, Anna.'

'What did Bernard want?'

Anna, tense in Leo's arms as they danced slowly together as the notes of 'Begin the Beguine' drifted around the garden, stumbled over her own feet at his question and Leo's arms tightened around her.

'Are you okay?'

Anna shook her head. 'Not really. Can we find a quiet spot and talk?'

Wordlessly, Leo led her to a deserted corner of the garden out of sight of the remaining partygoers. 'Now tell me.'

'Felicity Howell wants to meet me, even though her husband has decided he doesn't want to continue the search for his real mother.'

'Why and how does this woman know about you?' Leo demanded. 'Did Jacques tell her who you were?'

'No. It was only after Felicity told him the name on the birth certificate they'd seen was Harriet Ann Carstairs, that he said he used to know someone of that name, and that he believed she was in town for the festival.'

'Your name isn't Harriet Ann Carstairs...' Leo's

voice died away. 'Of course. Changing your name was one of those precautions you took to ensure you disappeared, wasn't it?'

'Yes. I did it all legally, but my parents insisted that Harriet Ann Carstairs died the day I gave Jean-Philippe up for adoption. "Put the father's name on the certificate – he can deal with it if the boy wants to trace him in the future," they said, "but you, afterwards you change yours and disappear." Those were the instructions from my parents. They couldn't cope with the shame of a daughter who'd "gone bad", to quote their words. As for acknowledging an illegitimate grandson...' Anna was silent for a moment before continuing. 'So, I became Anna Carsons; new name, new beginning, but same old memories,' she said, biting her bottom lip and starting to shake.

Leo held her close and waited.

'But now, the worst part is, this Felicity says her husband despises his mother for giving him up and has decided against continuing to try and find her. Says knowing who his father was will be enough.'

'So, right now, we're talking about the possibility of you learning your son's identity, meeting his wife but not getting to meet Jean-Philippe face to face,' Leo said slowly.

Anna nodded. 'I've got to decide whether to meet Felicity and hope her husband comes with her. Or whether to walk away – and this time it really would be forever.' She sighed. 'I don't know what to do. Bernard said I shouldn't rush into a decision, that I should sleep on it and talk it over with you.'

'I agree with Bernard. Sleep on it and to-morrow we'll decide what's the best thing for you to do,' Leo said gently. 'Right now, I think we should find Poppy and Daisy and say goodnight. Our guests all seem to have left.'

Poppy and Daisy were at the table on the vil-la's terrace, enjoying a last glass of champagne and some of the leftover party food. Nat, who'd been wandering around the garden making sure all the candles were safely out, had just joined them.

'Hi,' Daisy said. 'It was a great party, wasn't it? Are you going to join us for a late snack too?' And she pointed to the leftover food. 'Congratulations to you two by the way. May I see the ring?'

Anna held out her hand and smiled happily.

'Oh, that's so beautiful,' Daisy said.

'Have you set a date for the wedding?' Poppy asked, admiring the ring too.

'Not yet,' Leo answered. 'I'm trying to persuade Anna sooner rather than later. I have hopes of a summer wedding.'

Anna laughed. 'Leo doesn't realise just how much organising even a quiet wedding takes,' she explained. 'I think October is probably the earliest, but we shall see. We really came to say thank you for all your hard work and to say goodnight, but I'd love an extra slice of quiche,' Anna said, suddenly feeling hungry. 'Need something to soak up all the champagne.'

'I can't resist another slice of this wonderful gateau,' Leo said. 'Thanks, Poppy, Daisy. We'll always remember the evening we got engaged, won't we, Anna?'

Anna smiled. 'Definitely. Everybody seemed to enjoy themselves. Must say, you do a good Charleston, Nat.'

'Thanks. Bernard's rock and roll routine was spectacular too, wasn't it?'

'He's certainly perfected it from his original attempts,' Anna laughed.

'You've known Bernard a long time then?' Daisy said, ignoring the warning look Poppy threw at her.

'Yes, we go way back, but we hadn't met for years until this week,' Anna said. 'As Philippe Cambone's lifelong friend, he's trying to help the family sort out Philippe's affairs. His unexpected death has created several problems.' She paused slightly before continuing. 'The main one concerns his estate. Right now, Bernard's involved in trying to untangle something complicated with a woman called Felicity Howell.'

'Felicity Howell?' Nat repeated, turning to look at Anna.

'Yes, do you know her?' Anna asked. 'She's written to the Cambones saying she believes her husband is Philippe's illegitimate child.'

'You mean there really is an illegitimate son around? It wasn't just a publicity stunt dreamt up by that actor Sean somebody or other,' Daisy said.

'Yes, there really is a son and heir,' Anna said, but before she could say any more, Leo stood up.

'Come on, Anna, soon to be Mrs Hunter, I think it's time we said goodnight.'

'I'm going too,' Nat said, pushing his plate away and standing up. 'Thanks for a great party, Anna – and the introductions.'

'I'll come and open the gate for you,' Daisy offered.

'Nat, before you go, you didn't say whether you knew this Felicity Howell,' Anna said.

Nat looked at Anna and hesitated slightly before nodding and saying, 'Yes, I know a Felicity Howell.'

'Really? Could you introduce me if I asked you to?'

'You've already met her.'

Anna gave him a surprised look. 'I have?'

'Yes. She was here this evening.'

Anna looked at Nat in open-mouthed astonishment. 'She was?'

Nat nodded. 'Maybe it's just a coincidence, someone with the same name contacting the Cambones about Philippe, I don't know,' Nat shook his head. 'But what I do know is this: I'm working for Verity Raymond which is a stage name for Felicity Wickham – née Howell.'

Leo was just in time to catch Anna and save her from hitting the ground as she fainted.

26

Last night, I went to a private party that could have come straight out of a nostalgic 1920s film being shown here at the festival.

Picture the idyllic setting: the candlelit garden of a belle-époque villa, piano jazz drifting on the night air, the champagne flowing into crystal glasses, handsome men flirting with elegant, beautiful women.

An engagement is announced, people are dancing, then somebody's real name, as opposed to their stage name, is mentioned and the newly engaged heroine of the story faints. Throw in an illegitimate child, an unhappy

mother, a dead father and you have a storyline
fit for the next blockbuster.

Daisy pressed the save button and sat back in her
chair under the loggia. Waking early, she'd crept
downstairs with her laptop to start writing her
daily report.

The table was still littered with debris from
the previous evening: screwed-up paper napkins,
discarded cocktail sticks, paper plates. Making a
space for her laptop, Daisy had glanced across at
the villa. The bedroom curtains were still drawn
and downstairs the kitchen blind was pulled.

As Anna had regained consciousness after
fainting last night, Leo had taken charge, saying, 'I
think the best thing for Anna is bed,' and wishing
everyone goodnight, he'd gently led Anna into the
villa and closed the door behind them.

'Oh dear,' Poppy had said. 'I do hope Anna is
okay. Hasn't got food poisoning or anything. I'd
hate to think I was responsible for making anyone
ill.'

'You are such an old worrier, sis,' Daisy said. 'I
think Anna just had a shock, that's all.'

Afterwards, when Nat had left, Daisy had helped Poppy to take the leftover food into the kitchen before they went to bed.

'Leave everything else,' Poppy had said, smothering a yawn. 'I'll throw all the rubbish into a bin bag tomorrow.'

'Morning, Daisy,' Poppy said now, appearing with two mugs of coffee and a plate of croissants, 'Couldn't you sleep either?'

'No. Thought I'd try to get ahead with today's report. I've promised Nat I'll meet up with him later in Cannes, so I need to get organised.'

'No sign of life over there yet,' Poppy said, looking across at the villa. 'Wonder how Anna is this morning? I'll go across later and see if Leo thinks she needs a doctor to check her over. Fainting like that for no reason,' Poppy shook her head.

'Come on, sis,' Daisy said. 'Even you must be starting to put two and two together about Anna's past.'

'What d'you mean?'

Daisy tapped her fingers. 'One: Anna comes to the festival for the first time in years. Two:

Philippe Cambone, an international film director whom she initially denies knowing, dies unexpectedly. Three: there's a rumour circulating of an illegitimate heir making a claim against the film director's estate. Four: A woman using an alias to contact the Cambones about the said illegitimate heir turns out to be married to the up and coming director, Teddy Wickham. Five—'

'Stop,' Polly said. 'So are you suggesting Anna is somehow involved in all this?'

'I think she's right at the centre of things. I'm ninety-nine point nine per cent certain she'll turn out to be Teddy Wickham's mother,' Daisy said.

* * *

Anna pulled her croissant apart and pushed the pile of crumbs around her plate.

'You were meant to eat that, not play with it,' Leo said.

'Not really hungry,' Anna replied. 'Sorry.' She glanced across at Leo. 'What time are we going down into Cannes today? I can't remember.'

'Your appointment with the lawyer is for eleven,' Leo answered.

'I want to get Cindy a birthday present,' Anna said. 'A proper present from her unknown grandmother.'

A short silence followed her words before Leo sighed. 'Oh, Anna darling. You don't think you're leaping to conclusions too soon here? You haven't got one hundred per cent confirmation yet that Teddy Wickham is going to turn out to be your Jean-Philippe.'

'I know, I know, but the more I think about it, the more certain I am that he is my Jean-Philippe. Anyway, I'm going to buy Cindy something special for her birthday,' Anna said stubbornly. 'From a friend. She did offer me her pink balloon for the party. It's the least I can do.'

'What about Teddy and Verity? Are you going to meet them now? Discuss the possibility of your relationship? Tell them who you were, rather than who you are now?'

Anna shook her head. 'Tell them I was Harriet Ann Carstairs in another life? No. If Teddy is really going to give up searching for his mother, there is no point at the moment. I shall keep in touch with Verity and Cindy though – as me, Anna Carson.' She looked at Leo, anticipating his reaction. 'Did you know they are planning to move to England? To Gloucestershire. We'll virtually be neighbours when we're married. We can meet up with them as Mr and Mrs Hunter.'

'Let me get this straight. You're planning to become friends with Verity and her family without telling them the truth about your relationship to Teddy and Cindy? Why?'

'Because if Teddy hates his mother that much for giving him away and he learns my true identity, he could stop Verity and Cindy from seeing me,' Anna said. 'I'll become a good friend to them all before I think about telling them the truth.'

'Oh, so you do plan to tell them someday?'

'Yes, when Teddy knows and trusts me.'

'He'd never trust you again, if you do this, believe me.' Leo ran his hands through his hair. 'Anna, this is so not a good thing to do. Please think about it.'

'I can't stop thinking about it, Leo,' Anna said.

'How else can I stay in touch with Cindy? Watch her grow up?'

'I don't know,' Leo said. 'But I do know that by getting the truth out into the open and not compounding past mistakes with silence, you stand a far better chance of living happily in the future.'

Anna slumped down into her chair. 'Leo, I'm frightened telling the truth will make everything go wrong again and I'll never get to know Teddy or Cindy – my grandchild – properly.'

Leo took her left hand in his and squeezed it. 'Anna, even if you're terrified about the outcome, I really urge you to tell Verity and Teddy who you are. You could write a letter if you don't want to tell them face to face, but I feel having come this far, you need to see things through to the truthful end.'

Anna bit her lip as Leo continued.

'Think about it, Anna. You didn't come to Cannes this year looking for your long-lost son. You came simply hoping to finally tell Philippe the truth. To tell him that somewhere in the world was a son he'd never met. The fact that Philippe died before you could make your confession has just complicated things.'

'What do you mean?'

'Instead of telling Philippe about his son, you have to tell the son about his father.' Thoughtfully, Leo brushed her face with a finger. 'Teddy deserves to know the truth about his birth and adoption, and about how much you loved his father. Meet Verity, tell her your story, please. She can at least talk to Teddy and he can then decide whether he wants to acknowledge you or not.' His lips touched hers gently before he spoke again. 'I suppose what I'm really saying, Anna, is this: you've lived all your adult life without either Philippe or your son. You know you can survive with neither of them in your life, but the truth still needs to be told. Then you and I can get on with the rest of our lives together.' There was a serious look in his eyes as he said, 'Promise me you'll think seriously about whether to meet Verity or not.'

Before she could answer, Anna's mobile phone rang and Leo watched as she quickly snatched it up.

'Oh, hello.' Anna listened for a moment. 'I'll mention it to Leo, but I doubt we'll come, Bernard. I think I've had enough of parties for a while. Thanks for calling. Speak later,' and she ended the call. 'Another Cannes party,' Anna said. 'Boat ride over to the islands and then a party on the beach on Sainte-Marguerite.'

'Sounds fun,' Leo said. 'When is it?'

'Thursday evening. I didn't really take in the details as I didn't think we'd be going,' Anna said.

'I'd quite like to see one, if not both, of the islands,' Leo said.

'Oh Leo, I'm sorry, I should have asked you first, not just assumed we wouldn't be going.' Anna looked at Leo aghast as a sudden thought struck her. 'Do you think Bernard already knows who Felicity really is? Has done more than speak to her on the telephone? Surely he would have told me if he had?'

'You'll have to ask him,' Leo said. 'He did arrive with Verity and Nat last night, but I think that was coincidence. I'm sure he'd have told you immediately if he knew her true identity. He seems very fond and protective of you. Anna, about what we were discussing?'

'Okay, I promise I'll think about whether a meeting with Verity is a good idea, and decide before the end of the festival,' Anna said. 'Now, can we go down early to Cannes? I think I know the present I'd like to get Cindy, but I might have to try a few shops.'

'Go and shower. I'll book a taxi for an hour's time,' Leo said. 'That should give us plenty of time to go shopping before your lawyer's appointment. But, Anna, promise me you'll do more than just think about meeting Verity. The time for secrets has long gone. If you do decide to meet her, you have to tell her the truth.'

27

Anna tried very hard to concentrate on what the lawyer was saying, but her gaze kept straying to the small carrier bag she was holding on her lap. She'd found the perfect present in only the second shop they'd tried. A delicate gold rope necklace with gold letters hanging from it spelling out the name Cindy. Now gift wrapped and secure in the bag, Anna was trying to decide how to get it to Cindy. She really wanted to give it to her today, her actual birthday, but that would mean calling in at the villa where the Wickhams were staying. What if Verity – or even Teddy – was there?

'Ms Carson?'

Anna looked at the lawyer, startled, 'I'm sorry. You were saying?'

'Philippe Cambone's will. He altered it recently in your favour, but there are certain unusual clauses I have to make you aware of.'

'Unusual clauses?' Anna asked.

The lawyer nodded. 'To put it briefly, Philippe has bequeathed a large sum of money, the cottage, the boat "One Life, One Love" and the boathouse on the island to you.' He paused and looked at the paper in his hands. 'You are free to do what you wish with the boat, although Philippe did express the wish that if you decided not to keep it, you would first offer it to his long-time friend, Bernard Audibert.'

Again the lawyer hesitated.

'The cottage is slightly more complicated. Legally, it will be yours for your lifetime, but you are not allowed to sell it. On your death, it will revert to the Cambone family and not be passed on to any other family you may have. Unless – and on this rather delicate point Philippe Cambone was insistent – before your death, it is proven that you and he had a child together. In which case the child will be recognised as his heir and, under French law, you will be required to bequeath the cottage to him.'

As Anna tried to take in the enormity of what he was saying, the lawyer pushed a bunch of keys across the desk to her.

'Perhaps you'd like to take a look at your new possessions and then come back to see me with any questions you may have. There will, of course, be the usual French bureaucracy to deal with and paperwork to sign in due course.'

Dazed, Anna picked up the keys and put them in her handbag, before standing and thanking the lawyer for his time. As she and Leo left the building and made their way to the nearby taxi rank, she said quietly, 'Philippe clearly hoped his unknown son was about to enter his life.'

Leo took her hand and squeezed it. 'Yes.'

'I don't need a boat. Do you think Bernard will? As for the cottage. We're never going to live there, are we? Shall I just refuse it? Let it go straight to the Cambones? Let them sort things out with the lawyer?'

'Anna, Anna, calm down,' Leo said. 'Why don't

we go across to the island and take a look at things before you decide?'

'Bernard's party tomorrow tonight,' Anna said impulsively. 'We can slip away and have a quick look around then.'

'You wouldn't rather go alone? Without having a crowd of people around?'

'Maybe we'll go across at the weekend on our own as well. I need to talk to Bernard too,' Anna said. 'I just want to see the cottage – and the boat.' The boat with the name that summed up her and Philippe's relationship so long ago.

'Let's go back to the villa then,' Leo said, as a taxi drew up alongside. 'We can phone Bernard and get the details.'

* * *

Poppy was working in the garden, deadheading some roses when they arrived back at the villa. Leaving Leo to make the phone call to Bernard, Anna took her carrier bag and walked across to see Poppy.

'Hi, no nasty lasting after effects from the party then?' Poppy asked, looking at Anna.

'No. I'm fine,' Anna assured her. 'Is Tom still going for a birthday tea with Cindy this afternoon? She's such a sweet child, I've bought her a little present. Could Tom deliver it for me please?'

'No problem,' Poppy said, wiping her hands before carefully taking and holding the bag by its handles. 'I'll take it indoors and put it with the present I've bought for him to give her.'

* * *

Nat had Cindy with him when Daisy arrived at the café they'd arranged to meet in at the top of rue Saint Antoine, away from the majority of the festival crowds.

Cindy was already tucking into a large dish filled with multicoloured glacé balls, swirled with cream and chocolate crumbs and topped with two crunchy fan wafers.

'Happy birthday, Cindy. That looks yummy,' Daisy said.

'Glad you like the look of it, 'cause I've ordered

us one each by way of celebration,' Nat said, pulling her close and kissing her before releasing her and nodding at the hovering waiter. 'Ready for our ice creams s'il vous plaît.'

'Celebration?' Daisy said. 'Cindy's birthday. Anything else?'

'My script is going to be auctioned,' Nat said. 'Teddy has shown it to another couple of producers who both like it. He says the most important thing now is for me to get a top-notch agent who can handle things. He's given my name to a leading London agency who are keen to sign me up. I've already had an email asking me to contact them and arrange a meeting for early next week.'

Daisy threw her arms around him, 'Nat, that's wonderful. Congratulations.' Daisy spooned a mouthful of ice cream. 'I could get addicted to this stuff,' she said, before looking up at Nat. 'I've decided I'll get the festival out of the way and then next week, start to plan the future.'

'Which will I hope, include me,' Nat said, squeezing her hand. 'You can always come to the States with me.'

Daisy nodded. 'I could.' She smiled at Nat.' If you really want me to.'

'I really, really want you to,' Nat said. 'In fact I—'

'Mummy says we're going to live in England soon,' Cindy interrupted. 'How will you look after me then, Nat?'

'You won't need me, you'll be at school,' Nat said. 'I promise to come and visit you though.'

'Will you bring Daisy?'

Nat and Daisy laughed as they both said, 'Yes' at the same time.

'We promise,' Nat said. 'Now eat your ice cream.'

Daisy looked at Nat. 'What were you going to say?'

'I know we've only just met, but like I told you the other evening, I can't imagine my future life without you in it. I can't bear the thought of us going our separate ways when the festival ends. Being on different continents is a definite no-no. I want us to be together. To love each other,' he added quietly, looking at her intently as he spoke.

'Oh Nat. Are you sure...'

He leant across and silenced her with a gentle kiss. 'Very sure.'

'Ugh, you two are soppy,' Cindy said.

Later as they strolled hand in hand down through the crowded streets towards the Croisette, Daisy asked Nat, 'How are things at your place today?'

'Back to normal,' Nat said, with a glance at Cindy, who was holding Daisy's other hand, before mouthing quietly, 'Tell you more later. How's Anna today?'

'Haven't seen her. Poppy was going to go and see if she needed a doctor but...' Daisy shrugged.

'Is Anna ill?' Cindy asked. 'I like Anna. She's really nice. Did she eat too much at her party?'

'I think perhaps she did,' Daisy said. 'Now, Cindy, I saw a pink bag in a shop earlier. Would you like me to buy it for your birthday?'

'Ooh pleeease. Pink's my favourite colour and I need a bag for school,' an excited Cindy said when she saw the bag with its silver stars and letters spelling out the word 'Cannes'.

'Not sure it qualifies as a schoolbag,' Daisy laughed. 'But Mummy can decide about that.'

A short time later, as an excited Cindy handed Daisy her precious bag to look after and clambered on board the carousel, Daisy asked Nat, 'So how are things with the Wickhams then? Last night's problems forgotten?'

'If not forgotten, at least not being argued about loudly. Verity is definitely the Felicity Howell who contacted the Cambones. I overheard Teddy telling her there is no way he intends to pursue the search for his mother now that Philippe is dead and he made Verity promise to stop trying to arrange a meeting between him, the Cambones and this unknown woman who could turn out to be his mother.'

'Poppy doesn't believe me, but things are starting to add up in my mind,' Daisy said. 'I think Teddy Wickham's mother is—'

'Anna,' Nat said quietly.

'You think the same?'

Nat nodded. 'The way she fainted last night when she heard who Felicity Howell really is makes me think it could be.'

'The thing is – do we tell Verity about our suspicions?' Daisy asked. 'Or wait and see what happens?'

'I don't really think we have any choice but to keep quiet,' Nat said. 'It's none of our business for a start and, secondly, we don't have any proof. Besides, these things always seem to have a way of working themselves out for the best.'

Daisy sighed. 'I do so want a happy ending – especially for Anna. I really like her.'

When they returned to the villa to collect Tom for Cindy's birthday tea, Poppy gave Cindy the present Anna had left for her.

'May I open it now?' Cindy asked.

'Don't see why not,' Nat said.

Cindy squealed with delight as she saw the gold necklace with her name hanging from it and insisted on putting it on straight away.

'Is Anna in?' Nat asked Poppy. 'Because if she is, I think you should go and say thank you straight away, Cindy, for such a lovely present.'

'I'll come with you,' Tom said, and the two children raced across the garden towards the villa.

Left alone, the three adults looked at each other.

'That's a lovely present for a child you barely know,' Daisy said. 'It's something you'd buy a very special child.'

'Mmm. I wonder what Teddy and Verity will make of it,' Nat said thoughtfully.

'Oh, come on, you two,' Poppy said. 'This is beginning to sound like some sort of conspiracy theory to me. It's simply a nice present from someone who can afford it for a child she likes.'

Daisy looked at her sister. 'Just you wait and see.'

28

Cannes was still in party mode as Anna and Leo walked along the bord du mer towards the quay on Thursday evening.

The paparazzi were gathered, as usual, at the foot of the Palais steps; restaurants and bars were full; glamorous women in impossibly high-heeled shoes were stepping into limousines to be chauffeured away to some upmarket establishment along the coast to be wined and dined. International TV crews were everywhere filming, their reporters talking earnestly to cameras, trying to convey the frenzied atmosphere around them to audiences on different continents.

Bernard, casual in chinos and a black polo shirt, welcomed them aboard the large yacht he'd chartered for the evening as the stewardess offered them glasses of champagne.

'Anna. Leo. So glad you changed your minds. Should be a fun evening.' He hesitated as he looked at Anna. 'Leo told me what happened last night after I left. Are you all right? I'm struggling to accept it, but with that wonderful thing called hindsight, I can definitely see a resemblance between Teddy Wickham and Philippe – and to you too.' Bernard paused. 'Verity and Teddy are hoping to join us later.'

Anna could feel the panic rising. 'You haven't said anything to Verity about me, have you? Or told her you know she's Felicity Howell?'

'No, of course not. It's a bit late, but would you like me to ask them not to come?' Bernard asked.

'What reason can you possibly give them, Bernard? But I'm not ready for a confrontation with Teddy Wickham yet, so Leo and I will endeavour to stay out of the way. Once on the island we'll... we'll do our own thing and miss the barbecue. I'm not hungry anyway.'

'If you're sure,' Bernard said. 'I'll try and make sure Teddy and Verity are kept occupied on the yacht.'

'Thanks.' Anna hesitated. 'Are you going to say anything to Teddy about Philippe? About how close you both were?'

Bernard shook his head. 'Not directly, no. After all, Teddy isn't aware that anybody knows his true identity and without breaking several confidences, I can't tell him. But I may talk in a loud voice when he is within earshot about how friendly Philippe and I were. See if he picks up on it.' Bernard swished the champagne around in his glass before taking a sip and looking at Anna seriously. 'You're probably the only one who can approach the subject with him – if you choose to do so.'

Anna grimaced. 'From what Verity is saying, there seems very little point, so I'm thinking the best thing is to leave it. Although Philippe's will has complicated things,' she sighed.

'We went to the lawyers this morning,' Leo explained. 'Anna is about to become not only a

French householder but also the proud owner of a boat.'

'Philippe left you "One Life, One Love"? As well as the cottage?' Bernard looked at her.

'With certain clauses attached,' Anna said. 'One of which I need to talk to you about sometime, but not tonight. I've brought the keys to the cottage with me. Leo and I are hoping to have a quick look around tonight.'

'Philippe invested a huge amount of money in that cottage over the years – he always hoped to eventually live in it full-time. He loved it over there.'

Anna nodded. 'I know he did. He told me what his dreams were for the place the one time he took me there.' She glanced at Bernard. 'Did you not know the contents of the will?'

'No. As a witness, I just had to sign along the dotted line. Once I'd done that, the lawyers, as appointed executors, whisked it away for safekeeping.'

More guests began to come aboard and Bernard went to greet them, leaving Anna and Leo to make their way along the deck to hide themselves in amongst the crowd of people. Teddy and Verity were the last to arrive and Anna caught her breath as she saw them walking up the gangplank, barely able to keep her gaze away from the man whom she now knew was her son. Leo, realising, moved in front of her, shook his head and, without a word, blocked the view. A few minutes later, the hum of the engines could be heard as the yacht began to manoeuvre off the mooring and make its way towards the island.

Bernard had instructed the skipper to take the yacht around the bay, 'Give everyone a chance to enjoy the champagne and nibbles,' and it was an hour before the yacht drew up alongside the island's public pontoon and people disembarked. Anna and Leo hung back and waited until they'd seen Teddy help Verity off the yacht and join a group making their way to the beach.

The caterers had the barbecue, a few hundred yards along the beach, well under control as everybody arrived and people were soon tucking into the tuna steaks, lamb seasoned with herbs de Provence and pork chops that were on offer.

Across on the mainland, lights were beginning

to shine as twilight drew in.

'Time to go and find the cottage, while everyone is busy eating,' Leo said. 'Don't want to be stumbling around in the dark. Do you remember where it is or do we need to ask Bernard the way?'

'We need to find the lane that goes around the island and it's one of the few houses along there that has a boathouse,' Anna answered. The location of the cottage had been embedded in her mind ever since that magical evening she'd spent there with Philippe.

The gate to the cottage, when they found it ten minutes later, opened easily and together they walked down the path towards the front door. Leo waited as Anna pushed the key into the lock and turned it before he put his hand on her arm and stopped her.

'I think I'll go and take a look in the boathouse. Have a look at your boat, if that's all right with you? Give you five minutes on your own with your memories. Love you,' and Leo kissed her cheek gently, before leaving her to push the door open and enter the cottage.

Inside, Anna pressed a light switch and ceiling spotlights threw a seductive golden ambience over the hall and the sitting room it opened onto. The room, with its Provençal colour scheme and traditional furniture, felt warm and inviting. Original paintings lined the wall. Silver-framed photographs stood on the piano in the corner. An Oscar stood on the mantelpiece.

Anna could almost sense Philippe's physical presence in this room: standing in front of the French doors, watching the yachts out in the bay; playing the piano for his friends; pulling a log from the basket standing at the side of the granite fireplace and throwing it on the fire; turning to smile at her before pouring a glass of wine from the table in the corner; sitting on the comfy sofa reading to a child.

Stairs from the hallway led both up and down. Trying to rid herself of images of Philippe in the sitting room, Anna went upstairs. Three bedrooms, a modern bathroom. A small box room, its walls decorated with faded nursery characters, empty, save for the old-fashioned wooden cradle in the corner.

Stifling a sob, Anna turned and closed the door, before running back downstairs to the hallway and on down again to the kitchen that occupied the entire ground floor of the cottage.

Taking a glass from the dresser, Anna filled it with tap water and sipped it slowly, trying to regain her composure. The house was beautiful, Philippe had done a brilliant job in restoring it, but could she ever live in it – even for brief holidays – with Leo? Wouldn't the memory of Philippe and what might have been, infiltrate everything they did together?

Footsteps sounded upstairs in the hallway. Would Leo like the cottage?

'I'm down in the kitchen. Just coming up,' she called in response to the muffled 'Coo-ee' from upstairs.

Anna rinsed the glass and replaced it on the dresser.

'Did you like the boat?' Anna asked as she climbed the stairs to the hallway. 'What sort of boat is it? Oh!'

For a moment she thought she was hallucinating as she looked at the man standing in front of her. A stranger, yet achingly familiar in so many ways.

'I'm sorry to intrude, but I saw the lights were on and I couldn't resist asking if I might have a look around?'

Speechless, Anna gestured towards the sitting room and the man smiled his thanks as he held his hand out.

'I guess I should introduce myself, I'm—'

'You're Teddy Wickham,' Anna said. 'I recognise you from... from the TV coverage of the festival,' she added wildly. 'Why do you want to look around?'

'It's just that... that I was a great fan of Philippe Cambone's work and wanted to pay my respects. Are you his caretaker?'

'Sort of,' Anna said, realising that he was being as economical with the truth as she was.

Suddenly Leo's advice that getting the truth out into the open was the only way to go came into her mind. Lying at this first meeting with Teddy Wickham was the wrong thing to do. Before she could say anything, Teddy spoke again.

'It's a lovely place. Sensational views. It would

make a wonderful family home,' he said, strolling towards the window. 'Do you know what will happen to it now that Philippe is dead?'

Anna shook her head. 'The details still have to be sorted out.' That at least wasn't a lie. 'Would you like to see upstairs?'

'Please.'

Her heart thudding in her chest, Anna led the way upstairs.

'This is the largest of the bedrooms, so I suppose you'd call it the master bedroom,' she said. 'The last time I saw it, it definitely didn't look like this. There was only...' she stopped, realising she had been about to say that the only furniture the room contained years ago had been a double bed. Too much information too soon. Ignoring Teddy's puzzled look, she opened the door of the box room. 'This appears to be the only room Philippe hasn't redecorated,' she said. 'Maybe it was next on the list.'

'Hey, I love these old nursery characters,' Teddy answered, peering at the faded pictures on the wall. 'Looks like a Winnie-the-Pooh theme. As for this cot, it's beautiful.' He fell silent as he carefully pushed the curved rail and it began to gently rock on its runners.

Anna, watching him, felt the huge lump in her throat and swallowed hard. She knew she was standing within three feet of the man who, as a baby, should have occupied that cradle, of that there was no doubt in her mind. If ever there was a time to speak out it had to be now, surely?

'Actually, I'm not the caretaker,' she said, faltering as Teddy turned to look at her. How would he react if she told him the truth right now?

'Oh?'

'I'm... Philippe was an old friend.'

'I was due to meet him for the first time last week,' Teddy said, a sad expression on his face. 'Sadly, I left it too late. Everybody I talk to say he was one of life's gentlemen – in every sense of the word.'

'Yes, he was,' Anna said quietly. She took a deep breath before continuing. 'I've met your daughter, Cindy, at the villa where I'm staying. She's a lovely child. You must be very proud. Your wife too – Verity – she came to my party recently.'

'Hang on. Are you Anna Carson? The woman

who gave Cindy that lovely necklace as a birthday present?'

Anna nodded. 'Yes. She offered to lend me her balloon, the helium one, for my party.'

Teddy looked at her incredulously. 'And because of that you bought her a gold necklace for her birthday?'

Anna shrank beneath the intensity of his gaze. 'No, not just because of the balloon. I wanted to give her something special – she's such a sweet child and...' She took another deep breath as she came to a decision. 'And because in another life, my name was Harriet Ann Carstairs – and yours was Jean-Philippe – and in all probability Philippe Cambone had intended that cradle to be yours.'

In the silence that followed her words, Anna clutched the pendant around her neck tightly, praying that she had chosen the right moment to speak out. That she had done the right thing. That Teddy would respond favourably to her.

But Teddy had taken a step backwards, away from her. His face void of any expression, he said, 'You're Harriet Ann Carstairs?'

Anna gave him a tentative smile, her whole

body taut with anticipation as she waited for her son to acknowledge her.

'So, that makes you the mother who gave me away and deprived me of knowing my natural father.'

Anna nodded slowly, as anxiety gripped her body. His response to her words was all wrong. She didn't want him looking at her like that with pure disdain in his eyes. Eyes that just a moment ago had reminded her of his father. She wanted to explain and for him to understand, even if forgiveness was impossible.

Several seconds passed before Teddy spoke again. 'As far as I'm concerned, you have no right to call yourself my mother and my daughter already has a grandmother. She doesn't need or want another one.'

He turned away and left her standing alone in the room that should have been his nursery. Anna listened to his footsteps echoing through the cottage as he ran down the stairs and out into the lane, slamming the door behind him.

29

'Thanks,' Anna said, wrapping herself in the towel Leo handed her as she climbed out of the pool early on Friday morning. 'Are you going to have a swim?'

'Not right now. I've made us some coffee,' Leo answered, indicating the cafetière and cups on the patio table. 'We need to talk.'

Ignoring his last words, Anna moved towards the table. 'I've been thinking, how d'you feel about doing some sightseeing over the next few days? I was thinking we could go to Monaco today and have a mooch around. Maybe Antibes tomorrow? There's so much to see down here, we'd be silly not to do some exploring while we're in the area. We could even go over the border to Italy. San Remo maybe? I've never been to southern Italy. What d'you think?'

'I think you're trying to avoid the subject, but, yes, we could do some sightseeing if that's what you want – after we've talked.'

Anna sighed, knowing what Leo wanted to talk about: last night – or rather the consequences of last night. The memory of that meeting with Teddy Wickham in the cottage would remain with her forever. Talking would not erase it from her conscience or alter its effect on her life.

'I meant what I said on the boat coming back, Leo. Teddy Wickham has made up my mind for me,' Anna said quietly. 'The matter is closed. No more soul-searching. No more hoping for any sort of reconciliation.' She could feel her heart breaking even as she uttered the words and her hands shook as she accepted the cup of coffee Leo had poured for her. 'Like you've been saying all week, I have to move on. Let my past mistakes go. Get on with my – our – life together.'

'You're not even going to fight to see Cindy then?' Leo asked.

Anna bit her lip. 'No.'

'I know I've been saying leave the past behind, but all the same I can't help feeling you should try again to get Teddy to listen to the truth,' Leo said. 'Then you will at least know you've done all you could to do the right thing as far as your Jean-Philippe is concerned. As well as for Philippe and yourself,' he added gently.

Leo placed his coffee cup on the table and took Anna's from her before taking hold of her hands.

'I love you and know the kind of person you are – caring, kind and compassionate. Teddy has this picture of you as the hard-hearted woman who didn't care about him from the beginning. A picture that I know is simply not true,' Leo paused. 'Verity is clearly on your side. Go and see her. Get her to talk to Teddy. I think he should at least be presented with the evidence that the fault was not all on your side. I can't bear the thought of anybody thinking so badly of the woman I love.'

'Leo, you didn't see the look in Teddy's eyes when he told me I didn't have the right to call myself a mother. He didn't need to tell me how much he hates me – it was all there in his expression.' Anna was silent for several seconds before adding, 'I don't think there is any way through that kind of anger. I don't think I have the courage to even try.'

Just then, the entrance phone for the villa gate buzzed. Leo answered it, turning to look at Anna, before he pressed the button to open the gate and replaced the phone.

'It's Verity. She wants to talk to you.'

'I can't see her now. I'm going to take a shower and get dressed,' Anna exclaimed. 'I'm sorry. You'll have to talk to her. Get rid of her,' and Anna ran into the villa, leaving Leo to deal with their unexpected visitor.

Upstairs, Anna took her time, soaking in the bath rather than having a shower, deciding what to wear and then applying her make-up. As she turned to go downstairs to Leo, she saw her laptop on the bedside table and impulsively opened it up. Now she knew the name of her son, even though he refused to acknowledge her, she could look him up and at least learn about his career and maybe a little about his personal life.

It was over an hour before she went back downstairs, relieved not to hear voices.

'Leo darling, I'm sorry I took so long,' she said, walking out through the kitchen to the terrace. 'I'm ready now. Where shall we go...' her voice trailed away as she saw Verity sitting with Leo. She turned to go back upstairs.

'Anna, please listen to what Verity has come to say,' Leo said, standing up and putting his hand on her arm. 'I'll leave you two alone to talk.'

'Leo, please stay,' Anna said, taking hold of his hand before turning to face Verity. 'Do I call you Verity or Felicity? Did Teddy send you?'

'Most people these days call me Verity and, no,' Verity shook her head, 'Teddy didn't send me. He doesn't know I'm here. He's told me that I'm to sever all contact with you.'

'So why are you here?' Anna asked.

'Because I like you, Cindy likes you and I know if he'd only give himself the chance to get to know you, Teddy would come to like you too.'

'He told you about our meeting in the cottage

last night? Told you what he said? How he made it clear that he wanted nothing to do with me when I told him who I was.'

Verity nodded. 'He told me. He's also saying knowing his father's family will be enough, but I know it won't. Deep down he's desperate to know the whole truth about his past, to know what both his biological parents were like, to see any family likenesses that have come down through the generations. To know who he truly is.'

Anna gave a wry smile. 'That desire certainly wasn't showing last night. Anyway, how do you propose getting him to change his mind about me?'

Verity shook her head. 'Not me. You. I want you to talk to him.'

'No.'

'Meet him tomorrow morning and tell him your side of the story,' Verity pleaded. 'He'll be at the villa alone – Nat is taking Cindy out and I've promised myself some last minute retail therapy in the rue d'Antibes. You can explain things. I'm sure he'll respond.'

'No,' Anna repeated.

'Anna,' Leo said. 'Don't you think—'

Anna shook her head. 'However much you two want me to see him, I can't.' Her voice broke as she struggled to explain. 'Teddy would only be meeting me under sufferance and I, the guilty one – and make no mistake I am as guilty in my own eyes as I am in his – would have to try to persuade him to listen. Then, to forgive me for something I find as unforgivable as he does.'

Both Verity and Leo looked at her in silence.

'Sorry, but I've finally made up my mind to let the past go and to make the most of the present and the future. Of course, I would like nothing more than to get to know Teddy and I long to tell Cindy I am her grandmother, but I can't inflict a grandmother on her who her father detests. It would do nothing but create tension between them, and I'd hate to be the cause of that. I've caused enough unhappiness as it is.'

'Please, Anna,' Verity pleaded. 'Try again with Teddy. I know he will eventually respond. As for Cindy, she already adores you.'

Anna shook her head. 'No. Any approach now has to come from Teddy. He has to be ready to listen. I will make you a promise though. If at any time in the future Teddy decides to contact me, I will see him and answer his questions as best I can. Maybe over the next few months you can use your powers of persuasion to change his mind?' She gave Verity a sad smile.

Verity sighed. 'I intend to. Maybe when we're living in England, he'll listen to sense.' She glanced at Anna. 'Are we still going to meet up occasionally? Have lunch?'

'I'd like to,' Anna said. 'Though I'm not sure it would be wise. A complete break might be better. Besides, I thought Teddy had told you to sever all contact with me?'

'We don't have to tell him, do we?' Verity said with a smile. 'Anyway, in a few months' time, things might have changed. He could want us all to be one big happy family.'

'In my dreams,' Anna said softly. 'In my dreams.'

30

Saturday morning and Daisy was in the kitchen, ready to take Tom to see the whales with Cindy and Nat.

'Tom will be about five minutes,' Poppy said. 'Time for a coffee. Where are you meeting Nat and Cindy?'

'Outside the station,' Daisy replied. 'Just got time to check my emails and talk to you about... Oh, Ben's replied to my last email.'

'And?' Poppy said.

'Not happy,' Daisy said. 'Thinks I'm punishing him for leaving. Wants to talk. Promises to make things up to me.'

'Seems he didn't get the message then.'

'He'll get this one,' Daisy muttered typing furiously.

Ben, you are wasting your time. I am NOT, repeat NOT, going to marry you. I'm not punishing you for leaving me, but I've moved on – met someone else, someone special, and I'm making plans for my future – without you. I honestly wish you all the best. Have a good life, but, I'm sorry, I won't be in it.

'Well, that's told him,' Poppy said, reading over her shoulder.

Daisy pressed send and shut down her email programme. Surely that would be the end of things with Ben. She couldn't spell it out any clearer, could she?

'I just hope he gets the message this time,' Daisy said.

'So what are these plans you're making?' Poppy asked.

Daisy glanced at her sister. 'Poppy, I need to talk to you about—'

'Have I got time for a croissant?' Tom asked, running into the kitchen. 'I'm starving.'

'If you're quick. We've only got a few minutes before we have to leave,' Daisy said.

A shadow passed by the window and Anna appeared in the doorway.

'Good morning, Anna. Coffee?' Poppy offered, holding up the cafetière.

'No thanks. I'm on my way out. I just came to say Leo and I are going over to Antibes later, so please don't worry if there's no sign of life in the villa.'

'We're going to Antibes too,' Tom said through a mouthful of croissant. 'For Cindy's birthday treat. We're going on the train to see the whales.'

'I'm sure you and Cindy will have lots of fun,' Anna said. 'Come and tell me all about the whales tomorrow.'

'Can I come for a swim as well?' Tom asked.

'Of course. Now I'd better get going, otherwise my meeting in Cannes will overrun and Leo will be cross with me. Have fun,' Anna said as she left.

'She looks a bit better today,' Poppy said.

'Thought she looked dreadful when I saw her yesterday.'

'Wonder if there have been any developments with Verity and Teddy,' Daisy said. 'Maybe Nat will have some news.' She closed her laptop and stood up. 'Right, Tom, time we were going.'

'Hey, what were you going to tell me?' Poppy said.

'Talk later, sis. No time now. Come on, Tom, we'd better run if we're not going to be late.'

* * *

Nat and Cindy were waiting for them in front of the train station, Cindy clutching her pink Cannes bag and smiling happily.

An hour later, they were all finding their seats in the terracing that surrounded the whale enclosure, waiting for the display to begin. Tom and Cindy were soon excitedly involved with some of the pirates who were encouraging the audience to get into the spirit of the show to come.

'This is fun,' Daisy said. 'Just the kind of thing children love.'

Nat nodded. 'I did toy with the idea of taking them on a real whale watching boat trip out to the Cetacean Sanctuary in the bay, but Verity wasn't sure how Cindy would cope with a long boat ride.' He shrugged. 'I'm in two minds about places like this actually. Nothing will convince me that whales should be kept in captivity.' He shrugged. 'Sorry. Don't mean to be a killjoy.'

'It is an unnatural environment,' Daisy agreed. 'Changing the subject, while Cindy and Tom are engrossed in the pirates, is there any news on the long-lost son saga?'

'Heated arguments in the main. Apparently Teddy came face to face with Anna the other evening at some party or other and walked out on her. Verity has spent the last two days trying to persuade him to make contact and learn the truth.'

'Does...' Daisy indicated her head at Cindy, 'know what's going on?'

'No.' Nat said. 'She knows Teddy is upset over something but has no idea what it is. One of the arguments was over Teddy insisting that Cindy had to return her necklace, but Verity told him that was a definite no-no for Cindy's sake. She hasn't taken it off once yet, she loves it. She simply wouldn't understand why she couldn't keep it. Oh, look, the show is about to begin – here come the whales.'

Hours later when they'd seen not only the whales, but dolphins and sea lions performing, watched the baby penguins being fed and Nat had treated them all to lunch, they began to make their way to the exit.

Passing a souvenir shop, Cindy said, 'Can we go in there? I want to buy Anna a present.'

Daisy and Nat looked at each other, startled, before Nat said, 'Sure, why not? Let's go.'

Once inside the shop, Cindy, with Tom's help, decided that Anna would love a whale in a snow scene globe and happily stood in the queue with Daisy to pay for it.

'I love my necklace Anna gave me and will never, ever, ever, forget her,' Cindy said, looking up at Daisy. 'D'you think she'll remember me for always and always?'

'Oh, Cindy love, I'm sure Anna will always re-member you. Every time she shakes the globe, she'll think about you,' Daisy said, touched by the little girl's obvious sincerity and wondering whether Nat was right when he said Cindy had no idea what her parents were arguing about.

* * *

Poppy was in the kitchen when they got back to the cottage later that afternoon. 'Hi guys. How were the whales?'

'They were brilliant, Mum,' Tom said. 'I bought a poster for my room and a pot of sweets for you. Look, there's a picture of a whale on it too.'

'Thank you,' Poppy said.

'Can I go and see Anna, please?' Cindy said. 'I want to give her the present I've got her.'

'Oh Cindy, she's not in,' Poppy said. 'Perhaps she'll be back before you leave. If not, you can always leave the present here and I'll give it to her for you.'

Cindy shook her head vigorously. 'No thank you. I want to give it to her myself.'

'Tom, why don't you and Cindy help yourselves to a couple of biscuits and go watch a DVD while I get you something to eat. You will stay for tea, won't you?' Poppy said, turning to Nat.

Nat glanced at his watch. 'Can't stay too long. Verity and Teddy are expecting us back. Looking at the black clouds that have followed us home, I think it might rain soon and we haven't got rain coats with us.'

As the children disappeared to watch a movie, Daisy smiled at Nat. 'I think as birthday treats go, today was a good one for Cindy.'

Nat's mobile buzzed before he could answer. 'Hi Teddy. No, we're at Tom's about to have tea.' He was quiet as he listened to Teddy. 'She's not here anyway,' he said, before falling silent again. 'Okay. Twenty minutes then.' He closed the phone before saying, 'Poppy, I'm really sorry, but we have to go. Teddy is furious. Apparently he told Verity to make sure Cindy stayed away from here – something she forgot to mention to me. He doesn't want Cindy having any more contact with Anna before we all leave on Monday.'

'How unkind,' Daisy said. 'Cindy adores Anna. They seem to have forged a bond without even knowing about the special relationship they share.'

'I know,' Nat sighed. 'But Teddy is adamant that their friendship is to stop. I'll just go and get Cindy.'

Daisy and Poppy looked at each other. 'Poor Anna,' they said simultaneously.

'Poor Cindy not being allowed to know her own grandmother,' Daisy added.

'I'm still astonished at that turn of events,' Poppy said.

'Where are the children watching the DVD?' Nat asked, returning to the kitchen. 'They're not in the sitting room. The bedroom?'

Poppy shook her head. 'No. He doesn't have a TV up there.' She went out into the hallway. 'Tom! Cindy!' she called. 'Where are you?' A clap of thunder was the only response.

Daisy ran upstairs to look.

'No sign of them up there,' she said. 'Tom! I'm getting cross. Wherever you're hiding, please come out, NOW. Nat and Cindy have to go home,' Poppy shouted.

'Could they have gone across to the villa

without us seeing?' Nat asked. 'Hoping that Anna was in after all?'

'If they'd gone out through the boot room, yes,' Poppy answered, running towards the back of the cottage. 'This door is usually locked,' she said, staring at the open door swinging in the wind that had arrived with the thunder and the rain that was now bucketing down.

'Right,' Nat said. 'I'll go out this way and check the villa.'

'Here, take this,' and Daisy grabbed a waterproof jacket from a hook. 'You'll get soaked otherwise.'

'Even if they have gone across to the villa, they can't be inside,' Poppy said. 'Anna and Leo are meticulous about locking up the place when they go out.'

'I'll still take a look,' Nat said and dashed off into the rain.

Together Daisy and Poppy began a thorough search of the cottage. While Daisy searched cupboards, opened wardrobe doors and looked under beds, Poppy braved the small cellar rooms with their large spiders among the electric fuse boxes and discarded suitcases.

'Any sign?' Daisy asked, brushing a cobweb out of her sister's hair as they met up back in the hallway.

Poppy shook her head. 'I don't know what's got into Tom. He normally tells me where he's going to play. Oh good,' she said, glancing out of the window. 'Anna and Leo are back. Nat's talking to them and they're going into the villa. Quick, let's go over. Oh dear,' said Poppy, stopping in her tracks. 'Look who's just arrived. Teddy Wickham. I wonder how he's going to react to the news his daughter and my son are missing.'

31
_____

Anna barely registered the fact that Teddy had arrived, as Nat told her Cindy and Tom were missing. Together with Poppy, she started to search the villa, room by room, calling out the children's names. 'Cindy! Tom! Please come out, if you're here.'

In the kitchen, Leo, ever practical, took charge. 'Right. You've established they're not in the cottage. Anna and Poppy are checking upstairs here. Have you checked the garden? Tool shed, that kind of thing.'

'No tool shed or anything,' Daisy said. 'Just shrubs, the loggia and... and the tree house! I bet that's where they are,' and Daisy ran out into the garden, closely followed by Teddy, Nat and Leo.

A crack of thunder just as she reached the foot of the tall parasol pine that the tree house was built in made her jump.

'Tom! Cindy! Please come down now,' Daisy shouted. 'The storm is getting closer. It's not safe for you to be up there.' The wind whipped her words away. 'They're definitely up there,' she said as the three men joined her. 'See, they've pulled the rope ladder up behind them. She stared up at the tree house. 'I don't think they can have heard me.'

'Cindy!' Teddy shouted. 'Come down at once.' When there was no response, he turned on Nat angrily. 'What on earth were you thinking of, Nat, letting them go up a tree in the middle of a thunderstorm?'

'It's not Nat's fault,' Poppy said, as she and Anna joined everyone under the tree. 'We all thought they were in the sitting room watching a DVD. None of us have any idea as to why they decided to sneak out and come here.'

'Well, I hope you have an idea of how to get

them down now,' Teddy said. 'Do you have a ladder somewhere? Or do we have to call the pompiers?'

Anna moved close to the base of the tree. 'Cindy! Tom!' she shouted as loudly as she could. 'Please come down. We know you're up there. I promise you're not in trouble. We just want to get you indoors safe. Away from this storm.'

Everybody stared upwards, praying for a response from the children, and just as Anna said, 'I think we're going to have to call the pompiers,' Tom appeared at the front of the tree house and everyone breathed a collective sigh of relief.

'Mum, I'm sorry.'

'Just throw the ladder over, Tom, and climb down,' Poppy said. 'Cindy is up there with you, isn't she?'

Tom nodded and pushed the rope ladder over the edge. 'Mum, Cindy climbed up all right, but the thunderstorm's frightened her and she says she can't climb down.'

'OK, Tom. Well, you come down and one of us will go up for Cindy.'

Once Tom was safely down, Nat went to climb

up for Cindy, but Teddy took the rope ladder out of his hands. 'No, Nat. I'll go. You hold it steady for me,' and Teddy swiftly climbed the ladder to reach into the tree house to rescue his daughter. Several minutes passed before he reappeared with Cindy, her face blotched and red from crying, clutching his hand as they prepared to descend.

Anna, watching as Teddy tenderly held Cindy against him while he helped her to climb backwards down the ladder step by step, felt a helpless surge of love swamp her body: her son and her granddaughter. Once they were both safely on the ground, it was all she could do to stop herself from rushing forward and hugging them both. Instead she squeezed Leo's hand hard and said. 'Thank goodness everyone is safe.'

'Right, into the kitchen to dry off and hot chocolate all round, I think,' Poppy said. 'Then the two of you can tell us why you thought climbing up to the tree house was a good idea.'

'Anna, Leo. You going to join us for hot chocolate?' Daisy asked.

Anna shook her head. 'No thanks. Leo and I will leave you to it now the children are safe.'

Teddy, she knew, would resent being in her presence any longer. 'We'll see you tomorrow. Bye, Tom, Cindy. Teddy.' The last name said defiantly, out of politeness.

'Daddy, quick, can I have the bag please?' Cindy said, her teeth chattering.

Teddy took a water stained bag out of his jacket pocket and handed it to Cindy. 'Apparently this is the reason they went into hiding. Cindy wanted to be here when Anna got back. To give her a present.'

'Thank you, Cindy,' Anna said, impulsively bending down to give the little girl a hug as she handed her the bag. 'I'm so glad you're safe. Go and get warm now.'

Back in the villa once they'd both dried off, Leo poured them a glass of wine each in lieu of hot chocolate and Anna begin to open her present. A knock at the back door surprised them both and Anna listened as Leo went to answer it.

'May I come in?' Teddy asked. 'Nat is taking Cindy home and...' he hesitated, 'I'd like to talk to Anna.'

'I'll leave the two of you to talk,' Leo said. 'If

you want anything, I'll be in the kitchen.' And, ignoring Anna's pleading look, he closed the sitting room door behind him.

There was a tense silence, as Anna, determined to wait for Teddy to speak, concentrated on opening her present and Teddy stared out at the garden through the French doors, his hands clenched into fists on either side.

Finally, after what seemed like an eternity to Anna, Teddy turned to her and broke the silence.

'I'm afraid the children's escapade this afternoon was my fault. I thought Verity and I were managing to have our arguments out of earshot of Cindy but apparently not.'

'I guess children don't miss much,' Anna said, not looking at him and continuing to unwrap her present. 'Oh, how sweet of Cindy. Look,' and she held up the snow globe to look at it properly. When Teddy just muttered, 'Nice', Anna glanced sharply at him. 'So, what did Cindy overhear that made her so desperate to be here when I got back?' The question she really wanted to ask him – why are you here? – remained unspoken.

'She'd overheard me forbidding Verity to let

her come here before we leave and was afraid she would never see you again.' Teddy ran his hand through his hair agitatedly. 'While they were drying off just now, she was crying. She was determined to give you a present so you would remember her because you'd given her that necklace and she knows she'll remember you forever.' Teddy shook his head as he looked at the snow scene.

Anna shook the globe and watched the snow falling around the bright pink whale on his blue island before quietly asking, 'Does she know I'm her grandmother?'

'Well, I certainly haven't told her. And I sincerely hope you haven't.' He glared at her, before turning away and pacing around the room.

Anna watched him for a few seconds before saying, 'Are you going to tell her?'

When Teddy ignored the question, Anna shook the globe again just to give herself something to do.

Finally, as the silence between them lengthened, Anna sighed before putting the globe down on the table. Since their encounter in the cottage when Teddy had made plain his feelings towards her, she'd tried so hard to accept his attitude, to convince herself that she was happy to wait for him to come round; that it was pointless to contact him to try to persuade him to listen to her side of the story. But now he was standing in front of her, clearly unhappy, maybe she should try to break the ice – explain a few things? But where to start?

'Is this your first visit to Cannes?' she asked as he stopped to stare out of the window, his back to her.

'Yes.'

'It's ironic then, isn't it, that both you and I chose this particular year to come to the festival. Me, I came to make my peace with Philippe and to finally close an unhappy chapter that has shaped my life since I was seventeen years of age. You had hoped to meet your father. And if that had happened for you, I would have heard about the two of you being reunited because Philippe would have made sure the world knew about his son. He would have been delighted that you followed him into the film industry. I also believe that he would have wanted you and me to know each other. Instead, Philippe died and I found myself tormented by the rumours that mine and Philippe's son, whom I gave away, was in town. And now you're having to deal with meeting the mother you believe didn't care about you.' Anna sighed when Teddy made no response. 'For someone who said they wanted to talk to me you're not being very communicative.'

Teddy finally turned to face her. 'Tell me all about the man who was my father.'

Anna shook her head. 'I'm sorry, I can't. I only knew him for a brief ten days. Other people can tell you more than I can. You need to talk to Jacques, his twin, to Bernard, his best friend. They both knew him far better than I ever did.' She paused and tidied up the discarded wrapping paper. 'I can tell you about the boy I loved though. He was one of the most kind, tender and humane people I have ever met.'

'Okay, tell me about your affair then,' Teddy said.

Anna stared at him. 'It was far, far more than an affair. Philippe was my first and, until I met

Leo, my only love.' She fingered the pendant around her neck, wondering where to begin, how to try to make Teddy understand the events of forty years ago. 'For ten days we lived only for each other. The in phrase that year was 'life without limits' and it became our mantra. We knew without question that we were destined to be together for ever, living our lives to the full. I had no reason to suspect when I kissed Philippe goodbye at Cannes station after the festival closed that we would never be together again. We'd made so many plans for the future.'

Anna bit her lip and swallowed at the memory of her farewell with Philippe before continuing.

'I went back home ready to work my way through the summer to fund my college course and to wait for Philippe to return from the States. I was so looking forward to introducing him to my parents as the man I was going to marry. Six weeks later, I realised I was pregnant.'

'Did you tell Philippe?'

'Of course. I wrote and told him. But it wasn't until this week that I learned how pleased he was at the idea of becoming a father and realised how much he cared about me – and you,' Anna said.

'This week?'

Anna nodded. 'Once my parents knew I was expecting, they took control of my life. Which included intercepting my letters. Forty years ago, I was led to believe that Philippe had rejected me and you, our baby. I now know that was a lie.'

'Why didn't you keep me, bring me up on your own – especially if you loved my father as much as you say you did?'

Anna sighed. 'You have to remember,' she said, 'the world was a very different place back then. I was just seventeen – still a minor in the eyes of the law and living at home. Legally I couldn't do anything without my parents' consent until I was twenty-one. I couldn't have a bank account in my own name, I couldn't rent anywhere without them standing as guarantors and I had no money to pay rent with anyway. I was also unemployable. It was a world totally alien to the way things are today.' Anna reached for a tissue from the box on the table. 'Your grandparents refused to even entertain the possibility that Philippe would marry me. They said he had used me and that I was stupid to believe he would "make an honest woman of me", to use their old-fashioned phrase. They promised they would stand by me, let me live at home and finish my education provided I agreed to do as they said.'

Anna was silent as she remembered again the harsh terms her parents had imposed. 'I had to go away to an unmarried mothers' home, the baby would be adopted and I was never again to mention the subject to them. I fought against having the baby adopted – tried to make them feel guilty about giving away their grandchild. When I didn't hear from Philippe again, I had very little choice but to agree to their terms, which included changing my name.'

Carefully, Anna undid the chain around her neck, opened the pendant and held it out to Teddy, hoping he'd take it and really look at the pictures and the lock of hair.

'This – until three days ago – was all I had left to remind me of you and Philippe.'

But Teddy kept his still clenched hands down the side of his body and didn't reach out for the pendent, as he silently looked at the two pictures and the lock of hair.

'And in case you were wondering, the hair is yours. You had quite a mop of it when you were born.'

When Teddy didn't respond, Anna smothered another sigh.

'There hasn't been a day when I haven't thought about you; wondered where you were, what you were doing, how you'd turned out,' Anna said quietly. 'If I could have kept you, brought you up, believe me, I would have done. I hate the fact I had to give you up and that Philippe never knew you, but I don't for one minute regret loving him and having his baby.'

'No, the regrets are all on my side,' Teddy snapped, a bitter edge to his voice. 'And missing meeting my father by just a few days is probably the biggest one of all. He was the one I wanted to meet – not you – the woman who gave me away.'

Anna felt herself shrivelling under the harshness of his gaze. His eyes, a deep velvet chocolate brown so much like Philippe's, held contempt in them as he looked at her. She forced herself to carry on, to try and salvage something from this meeting.

'I suspect not knowing you was one of Philippe's greatest regrets throughout his life,' Anna said, replacing the pendant around her neck. 'But I've come to believe harbouring regrets about the past is a futile exercise. They will poison and ruin the present – and our newly discovered relationship – if you give in to them. We have to move on – get to know one another as the people our lives have made us.'

Teddy continued to stare at her as Anna struggled to express herself. 'For years I have listened to friends talk about their families, their children, unable to mention my own unknown son, to anyone. I can't tell you how happy I am now it's possible for me to get to know you. For us to be finally involved in each other's life, to be friends...'

'Whoa,' Teddy held up his hand. 'Stop right there. I'm not sure I'm ready or even want to be involved with you. It's too late for us to play happy families. As for being friends,' Teddy shrugged his shoulders, 'I don't think we can ever be just "friends".'

'We could at least try getting to know each other,' Anna said quietly.

'I have to think about what you've told me. I also need to try to forgive you for giving me away, but I'm not sure I can yet.'

'Are you at least going to tell people that you're Philippe Cambone's son? Even if you don't want to acknowledge me as your birth mother. Lay the rumours that are circulating to rest.'

'I'm not sure. If he was still alive, yes, but it seems a bit pointless as he'll never know.'

'If he was still alive, he'd have been shouting about your existence from the top of the Palais des Festivals,' Anna said. 'I know he would have been so proud to have called you his son – as I am. Why should you feel diffident about telling the world he was your father?' Anna paused. 'Besides, it's not just about you and me any longer is it? There's Cindy. Are you truly not going to tell her she's got a new grandmother?' Anna hesitated, but she had to say it. 'A grandmother who would very much like to be a part of her life.'

Anna looked at Teddy, how could she make him respond to her. What would it take for him to forgive her and let her into his life. The letters in the envelopes that Bernard had given her – would reading them help him to understand and maybe forgive?

'Wait here,' she said. 'I have to fetch something I'd like you to read.'

When she returned, Teddy was just closing his mobile.

'Bernard,' he said. 'He wants to know if I'll consider reading a piece at the memorial service on Monday.'

'Are you going to?'

Teddy shrugged. 'I told him I'd think about it.' Teddy glanced at his watch. 'I have to go. I'm due at the final screening in an hour.'

'Here, take these with you then, but please look after them,' Anna said, holding out the large envelope. 'It's a letter and part of a journal written by your father to me. I think you need to read them. It goes without saying I want them back. They may have only came into my possession a few days ago, but they are already treasured. I couldn't bear to lose them.'

'You trust me with them? Aren't you afraid to let them out of your sight?'

'Why wouldn't I trust you with them? You're my son. They were written by your father. They concern you. Hopefully, once you've read the envelope's contents, you'll feel able to publicly acknowledge Philippe Cambone as your father – and hopefully me as your mother.'

32

Sunday morning and Daisy found an empty seat at one of the cafés in front of the rue Felix Faure. Once she'd ordered her cappuccino, she opened her laptop and began to write her last festival report.

> I can barely believe it's nearly a fortnight since I first sat here soaking up the atmosphere as the Film Festival began and now it's virtually over.
>
> It's Sunday afternoon and the closing ceremony is early this evening. While the last twelve days have been filled with a spectacular

amount of glitz and glamour, there is now a general feeling of things closing down all around, an air of tiredness hanging about.

The crowds on the Croisette have definitely thinned out and bar staff and waiters are beginning to smile again. The hype is almost over for another year. Locals are playing boules in front of the restaurants and the usual Sunday afternoon craft fair has assembled around the ornate bandstand. Easels full of paintings by local amateur artists, bric-a-brac stalls and tables covered with small antiques are crowded together displaying their offerings, hoping for some celebrity customers before the festival is finally over.

Italian, Japanese, English, Russian and, of course, French voices are everywhere, but few people are still wearing their Festival identity badges and I suspect many journalists and others on the fringe of the film industry have already left. Many of the stars who have stayed on for the presentation of the Palme d'Or tonight are spending the day in Monaco, being entertained and no doubt drinking vast amounts of champagne as they watch the Grand Prix.

Another hour and Cannes will be humming again with one last official blast from the festival organisers. The posh frocks and the famous red-soled Louboutins destined for the red carpet will be being slipped into and on, for the last 'walking the walk' up the famous red carpet to hear the announcements and watch the presentation of the ultimate accolade from a film festival – the Palme d'Or.

Speculation is rife as to who will win the Palme d'Or this year, as a clear favourite has failed to emerge during the festival. Whoever wins, though, is sure of at least one evening of maximum publicity and success at the box office – although that success is not always guaranteed if the winning film is deemed to be too arty by the general public.

Daisy pressed the save button as her mobile rang.

'Hi, Nat. Was beginning to wonder where you were. Are you on your way down to meet me?'

'Afraid not. I'm over on Saint-Honorat. It's a long story, but Verity decided Cindy and I should spend the afternoon over here, out of earshot of the discussion she was planning to have with Teddy.'

'About Anna?'

'Yes. Look I'll see you sometime this evening. Shall I come to the villa or will you be in town for the closing ceremony?'

'Come to the villa. I'm planning to watch the Palme d'Or presentation on television. I've promised Poppy I'll cook lasagne for supper tonight, so I'll do enough for you.'

'See you there then. Oh, gotta go. Cindy's fallen over. Love you,' and Nat was gone.

Daisy smiled as she switched off her phone, happy at hearing the genuine love in Nat's voice. Opening her laptop again, she read through her report and started to write the last paragraphs.

As I write this, five or six helicopters are buzzing across the bay, bringing the stars back from Monte Carlo. The paparazzi still in town are forming their normal scrum at the foot of the Palais des Festival's red-carpeted steps. Fans are taking their places behind barriers, hoping for one last close-up glimpse of a favourite star.

Once the presentation of the Palme d'Or has been made, the festival is officially over. Within hours, Cannes will start the process of reclaiming the streets and returning the town to its normal everyday life.

By midday tomorrow, as the marquees begin to be lowered and the huge transporter lorries trundle in and out of town, festival organisers will already be talking about plans for next year's event. C'est la vie!

Daisy checked she'd saved the report ready for emailing later with details of the winning Palme d'Or film entered and switched off her laptop as a shadow fell across the table.

'Seen the photos of the party I emailed over? They should have arrived on your computer by now,' Marcus asked as he placed his cameras on the table and sat down. 'Join me in a glass of wine to celebrate?'

'Celebrate?'

'The end of the festival and...' he hesitated. 'I've taken a photo of a couple of stars "in flagrante" that should earn me lots of money.' He shook his head as Daisy looked at him. 'Can't tell you. Top secret, I'm afraid, for the next couple of days.'

'Oh, okay,' Daisy said. 'I'll look at the photos when I get back to the villa.'

'I've mailed the rest over to Leo and Anna. Just thought you'd like to see the ones of you and Nat.'

'Thanks. Any idea what you're going to do when you get home? I know you're freelance, but the paper put quite a bit of work your way, didn't it?'

Marcus shrugged. 'I've got a couple of short-term contracts for some glossy magazine shoots. I'll see what happens after that.' He patted his camera. 'If this photo is the winner I think it's going to be, I won't have to worry for a few months anyway. So, how did you enjoy your first festival?' Marcus asked.

'It's been great,' Daisy said. 'A real insight into

another world. Not a world I'd like to live in permanently but fun to learn about.'

'And, of course, you've met Nat.'

Daisy smiled. 'Yes – I suppose I have you to thank for that.'

Marcus shrugged. 'He's a nice guy.' He glanced at her. 'If you feel you owe me for the introduction, you could—'

'Marcus! Why should I "owe" you anything for introducing me to Nat? You almost derailed things at one point, if you remember.'

'Yeah, sorry about that. Just thought you might be willing to share some information.'

'Like?'

'How much did you find out about Philippe Cambone's long-lost son in the end?'

Daisy hesitated before answering. Should she tell Marcus what she knew?

'Not much,' she said in the end.

'Did you find out his name?'

Daisy didn't answer as Marcus looked at her speculatively.

'Rumour has it that it's Verity Raymond's husband, Teddy Wickham. Rumour also has it that his mother is in town,' Marcus said.

'I've heard those rumours too,' Daisy said, beginning to gather her things. There was no way she was going to discuss Anna's business with Marcus.

'The mother wouldn't be the woman I photographed placing a flower outside the restaurant, would it? And whose engagement party I covered at the villa – Anna Carson?'

'I'm sure the truth will leak out eventually,' Daisy said. 'But really, is it anybody's business but the people concerned? The emotional shock for both of them must be huge. I think they have the right to privacy for as long as they want.'

Marcus shook his head at her. 'You had a scoop right on your doorstep, Daisy, and you ignored it. You're really not cut out for investigative journalism, are you?'

'No,' Daisy said. 'I don't think I am. I have to go. See you around, Marcus.'

33

'Are you sure you don't want to go to the ceremony tonight?' Leo asked as he and Anna relaxed on the loungers by the pool, English-language Sunday papers discarded.

'Quite sure,' Anna said. 'Much easier to watch it here on TV. We don't have to dress up for a start! Rick was glad to have the tickets to give to a client and he'll be there to represent us if *Future Promises* should receive an unexpected accolade.'

'Nothing to do, then, with having to look at Teddy on stage for an hour?'

Anna shook her head. 'No. Talking of Teddy, I hope he hasn't forgotten I want my letter and journal back. We all disappear tomorrow to various parts of the world and I don't want to lose them – not even to my son.'

'You could always ring Verity. Ask her to make sure they're kept safe until you meet up in England.'

'I think I might do that, if Teddy hasn't returned them before we leave. I'd been praying that after he'd read them, he'd find it easier to come to terms with what happened and contact me. It's twenty-four hours now and no word.'

'I expect he's been busy,' Leo said. 'Jury duties and all that.'

'Hope that's all it is,' Anna said. 'We might have to stay down here for a few days to meet the notaire again. You don't have to rush back, do you?'

'No problem for me,' Leo said. 'My next meeting is Friday. What about Poppy though? I expect she's looking forward to getting the villa back to herself.'

'I'll ask her later. We can always go to a hotel – there'll be plenty of empty rooms in town tomorrow.' Anna shivered and stood up. 'I'm going for a shower. The sun's disappeared and I'm getting cold.'

* * *

Later that evening, as they prepared to watch the festival's closing ceremony on TV, Leo said, 'October the tenth is the official start date for the filming of *In the Shadow of Mrs Beaton*, isn't it?'

'Yes, provided everything comes together,' Anna said.

'So, could we get married in September then?' Leo asked quietly. 'September the twelfth would be a good day for me.'

Anna smiled. 'Maybe the end of September, the twelfth is a bit too close.'

'September the twelfth,' Leo repeated, 'would, I think, be perfect.'

'Too soon, Leo. It doesn't give us enough time to organise things,' Anna said.

'Book my village church – I'm hoping here that you want a church wedding and not just a civil ceremony,' Leo said. 'Reception in a nearby hotel. Honeymoon, my secret. End of story.'

Anna laughed. 'What about invitations, bridesmaids, best man, ushers, cars, photographers, cake, flowers, food, wedding dress, hair, going away outfit, shoes – and that is just off the top of my head. Even for a small wedding, there's so much behind-the-scenes stuff to do.'

'Shall we just run away then? A beach wedding in the Caribbean with a couple of witnesses.'

'No, that wouldn't be us, would it?' Anna said. 'I do see us getting married in a traditional way, but three months really isn't very long to prepare for a wedding. For a start, your village church may not be available—'

'Oh, but it is,' Leo said, picking an envelope up off the table and pulling out a piece of paper. 'Eleven o'clock, September the twelfth. The marriage of Anna Carson and Leo Hunter will take place at St Mary's, followed by the wedding breakfast at The Woodlands Country Club. The happy couple will depart at five o'clock for a secret destination known only to the bridegroom.'

Anna stared at him, stunned. 'When did you arrange all this, Leo?'

'I haven't – totally. These are tentative reservations I made before I came down here knowing I was going to ask you to marry me. Once you'd said yes, I intended picking up the phone and finalising everything. But...' he paused. 'Things – Teddy – got in the way and I knew I couldn't do it without talking to you first. The options on the church and the country club run out tonight,' he added quietly. 'Please may I ring and confirm things? I do so want us to be married. I know we'll only be able to have a short honeymoon, a long weekend at the most, I suspect, but we can have another longer one in the new year. The important thing is being married.'

'Oh Leo, I do love you,' Anna took a deep breath. 'September twelfth it is then. But, I warn you, there's a lot of arranging to be done between now and then.'

'We'll do it together,' Leo said, a happy smile on his face. 'It'll be wonderful, you'll see,' and lovingly he pulled her into his arms and held her tight as he kissed her. 'Right, you'll have to excuse me. I have some very important phone calls to make.'

As Leo picked up his mobile and wandered

into the kitchen, Anna switched on the television. 'Don't be too long, it's about to start,' she called out.

Anna watched as the opening credits of the programme showed a montage of scenes taken throughout the festival: crowds on the Croisette, stars partying, jesters entertaining the crowds, luxury yachts, famous faces smiling, and then the camera panned around to the paparazzi at the foot of the red carpet for the final time.

Last evening or not, the stars were still in full-on glamour mode. Beautiful dresses, jewellery sparkling in the flashlights, dazzling smiles were all there, as the audience for the closing ceremony made their way up the steps. The camera followed the last of the stars as they disappeared into the Palais des Festivals and seconds later the picture changed to a view of the auditorium. The compère introduced the jury as, one by one, they made their way to their seats at the side of the stage and the ceremony was underway.

'That's done,' Leo said, joining Anna in the sitting room and handing her a glass of wine. 'September the twelfth is confirmed. See, I told you organising a wedding was easy!'

Anna laughed. 'Let's hope arranging the rest is as easy. Oh, look, there's Teddy.' She fell silent as she watched her son take his place on the stage. 'You know, the more I see him, the more I recognise Philippe in him,' she said.

'I can see you in him as well,' Leo said. 'I hope he has your compassion too.'

Anna sighed. 'Verity seems to think he will eventually accept things. I just wish I could be so sure. Maybe he'll be in touch later tonight when all this hoo-ha is over.' She waved her hand in the direction of the TV. 'Or when the lawyer contacts him next week.'

'What are you going to instruct the lawyer to do?' Leo asked.

'I think the cottage should go straight to Teddy. I think under French law it has to now anyway – direct heirs take precedence over everybody else when it comes to inheriting property. I was thinking about the boat too. Unless that has to automatically go to Teddy as well, I think I would like it to go to Bernard, as Philippe suggested. Unless you have a yen for a sailing boat?' She smiled at Leo, who shook his head.

'What about the money Philippe left you?' Leo said.

'I thought we could set up a trust fund for Cindy,' Anna said quietly.

Leo nodded. 'That sounds like a good plan.'

'The only inheritance I want from Philippe is for Teddy to acknowledge me as his mother,' Anna said, turning away to concentrate on the TV, inwardly hoping that the camera would show more shots of the jury as the various prizes were announced.

More than anything, she wanted to soak up pictures of her son, store them in her memory, to be able to recall them in the days ahead, but the camera resolutely roamed around, never lingering more than five seconds on any face, except for those of the winners.

'Isn't that Helen the camera is focusing on?' Leo said. 'Sitting next to Rick?'

'Oh, Leo, I can't believe it. She's won the Prix d'Interprétation Féminine – how wonderful is that for *Future Promises*? Best actress.'

Together they watched as the young actress made her way onto the stage to collect her trophy and make a short acceptance speech in true Oscar winning style.

'I wonder if Teddy knows how deeply you're involved with *Future Promises*?' Leo asked.

'Well, he will now,' Anna said. 'Helen has just mentioned my name in her thank you speech, bless her.'

34

Daisy pushed her laptop across the loggia table and stood up, stretching her arms above her head. 'My time here is done – Palme d'Or winner's name entered and final report sent. Wonder if I'll ever report on the festival again?'

'Why not?' Poppy asked. 'Lots of freelance opportunities around, I would have thought.'

'Depends on the kind of stuff I write – not sure that lifestyle automatically includes showbiz entertainment – and also where I end up spending most time, I suppose,' Daisy added thoughtfully, looking at Poppy.

'Hey, I've just remembered you never did tell

me what you wanted to talk about yesterday,' Poppy said.

'Nat and me.'

'Ahh. Thought it might be. Finally decided he's the one, have you?'

'Given the short time we've known each other, I'm a bit frightened saying yes, but I think so. I'm still going to give freelancing a go from down here and rent the cottage as a base, but Nat wants me to go to America with him when he goes. D'you think I should?' Daisy looked anxiously at her sister.

'Definitely. Grab the opportunity – and Nat – with both hands,' Poppy replied. 'Men like him are rare. He's almost on a par with my Dan.'

'That good, eh?'

'Listen, any man who can make my little sister as happy as you've been in recent days gets my vote. You never looked as happy as you do now when you were with Ben.'

'The thing is, and I haven't mentioned this to him yet, how d'you feel about Nat moving into the cottage with me? He needs a base somewhere in Europe and the lease of his flat in London is up soon. He'll need to find somewhere to stay before going to the States.'

'Not a problem,' Poppy said. 'You're both welcome to live here.'

'Great,' Daisy said. 'Oh, I forgot to show you these earlier. Look, Marcus emailed me some pictures of Nat and me at the party. The rest have gone direct to Anna and Leo.'

'That's a good one of you and Nat,' Poppy said. 'Love this one of you guzzling champagne.'

'I am so not guzzling,' Daisy protested. 'When I saw Marcus earlier, he tried pumping me for information about Anna. Don't worry, I didn't tell him anything,' this as Poppy looked at her. 'The rumours about Teddy Wickham being Philippe Cambone's son are gaining strength. Be interesting to hear if he goes to the memorial service tomorrow. Right, as I'm on kitchen duty tonight, I'd better make a start. Tom eating with us and staying up to watch the fireworks?'

'Yes. Fête day tomorrow, so no school,' Poppy glanced at Daisy. 'You sure about staying on for a few days to help me move back into the villa before Mum and Dad get here and Dan returns?'

'So long as we make time to go shopping. Seen some shoes and a bag I covet in one of the shops on the Croisette. Feel the need to treat myself before I start counting the pennies.'

'You'll need more than pennies if you plan to buy stuff from any boutique on the Croisette,' Poppy said.

The cottage door buzzer went. 'That'll be Nat,' Daisy said. 'I'll let him in and he can give me a hand with the lasagne, while I tell him the good news about the cottage.'

Later, after Tom had disappeared indoors to watch a DVD, the three of them sat companionably outside drinking a bottle of wine.

'I can't believe how quickly the last twelve days have gone,' Poppy said. 'I'm glad I was persuaded to rent the villa for the festival. It's been fun having Anna around. You too,' she said, glancing across at Daisy. 'Thanks for your help with everything.'

'I'm really looking forward to you moving in here,' Poppy continued. 'It's going to be great having you around more – in between the two of you jetting off to the States for Nat's work, of course. Any idea when you'll go for the first time?'

Nat shook his head. 'No. Could be in a few weeks or a couple of months. My new agent just says be ready – and keep working on the next idea.'

'I hope it's not too soon,' Daisy said. 'I want to enjoy us being together – and not being tied to office hours for a bit.'

As Poppy stood up to clear the table, Anna and Leo appeared at the cottage gate. 'Hi,' Anna said. 'May we join you? We want to share our news and celebrate. Helen won best actress tonight and...' she smiled at Leo. 'We've set the date for our wedding.'

'Congratulations on both counts,' Poppy said. 'Think this calls for champagne. I'll get a bottle.'

'We've brought one over,' Leo said, holding it out. 'Just need glasses.'

'Poppy, before I forget, is it possible for us to stay a couple of extra nights?' Anna asked. 'I have to see the lawyer before I leave and it will probably be Tuesday or even Wednesday before I can get an appointment.'

'Sure. Dan isn't due home until the end of the week. My parents, who were in Monaco for the Grand Prix, have decided to stay there for a few more days before coming over here.'

'Have you spoken to Helen since she won best actress?' Daisy asked Anna, as Poppy went to get the glasses.

'No. Rick says she's in a daze. She's been whisked off to some large yacht for an interview and intends to party the night away afterwards. I'll catch up with her tomorrow.'

'So your return to Cannes after all those years has turned out to be a successful one workwise?'

Anna nodded. 'Yes. The festival has been great for business. On a personal note, it's a bit mixed,' she pulled a face and sighed. 'I expect you've all heard the rumours about Teddy Wickham being Philippe Cambone's son? Well, they're true – and I am his mother, which, as you'll realise, makes me Cindy's grandmother.'

Anna paused reflectively before continuing.

'Leo asking me to marry him is one of three personal highlights that have come out of the festival for me this year,' Anna said quietly. 'Meeting

Teddy Wickham, my son with Philippe, is another. And learning that I have a granddaughter is another.'

She took the glass of champagne Leo was holding out to her. 'Unfortunately Teddy's not as ecstatic as I am at the news of our relationship.' She sighed as she watched the fizzing bubbles in her glass. 'At least things are out in the open now, although it's going to take weeks, if not months, to finally sort things out, but I'm happy finally knowing who he is, what he's doing. Just knowing my son is alive and well after all the years of silence is, I have to tell you, an indescribable joy.'

She took a sip of her champagne before smiling and looking across at Leo.

'If nothing else, I can now follow his exploits on social media; I won't have to second guess anything. Maybe one day he'll come round to wanting to know me and then I can get to know both him and my granddaughter properly.' Anna turned to Nat. 'How is Cindy today? No ill effects from the scare she gave us all yesterday?'

'She's fine. Still refusing to take off her necklace though.'

The whoosh of a firework made them all jump and look skywards in time to see red, silver and gold starbursts explode into the heavens. The display was beginning.

'Right, folks, raise your glasses to Helen, star of *Future Promises*,' Leo said. 'And save the date September twelfth in your diaries – we expect to see you all in church.'

35

There was no reply from the notaire on Monday morning when Anna rang to try and make an appointment. She sighed with frustration as she remembered it was one of the many fête days in May.

'I know I'll probably have to come back at some stage to sign and complete things, but I really want to get things moving quickly. Hopefully most of it can be done on the computer over the internet.'

'Will they notify Teddy about his inheritance or do you have to?' Leo asked.

'The notaire will do it all officially,' Anna said.

'I must remember to phone Verity before we leave – make sure Teddy has my letter and journal safe. I keep wishing he'd...' and her voice trailed away.

'There's still time,' Leo said. 'Perhaps he'll bring them with him to the memorial service.'

'If he comes,' Anna said. 'Maybe he'll decide to boycott the event as he and Philippe sadly never met, so he has no memories of the man.'

Cannes was busy dismantling the trappings of the festival as Anna and Leo made their way later that day towards the hall where the memorial service was being held. Large trucks lined the road outside the Palais des Festivals as scene shifters went back and forth with forklift trucks loading all the paraphernalia that had been needed to host the festival.

The huge billboards erected on shop and hotel facades were being removed, while council workers were loading barriers into lorries. Men shouting, loud bangs as metal and wood hit the pavement, combined with the noise of passing traffic made it impossible to talk, as Anna and Leo dodged around the workmen on the Croissette.

When they arrived at the hall, Bernard was

standing on the steps and greeted them affectionately.

'Anna. I'm so pleased you're here. I've reserved seats for you and Leo at the front.'

'Oh – I'd rather sit at the back,' Anna protested. 'Surely the Cambones will be at the front?'

Bernard shook his head. 'Only Jacques and his wife. Agnes, Philippe's mother, is not well enough to attend. The rest of the family feel that this is very much a tribute from the film industry, which they are not a part of. Ah, here's Verity,' Bernard said.

While Verity and Anna greeted each other, Bernard asked. 'Teddy not coming?'

'He's gone back for some papers he forgot,' Verity answered, turning to him. 'Asked me to tell you if you still want him to do a reading, he's found something he'd be happy to quote from at the end of the service.'

'I am so pleased about that,' Bernard said. 'Now, you'll sit together, won't you?' and Bernard led them down through the hall.

To Anna's relief, the seats, although nearer the

front than she would have liked, were to the left and hidden somewhat behind a pillar that offered some privacy. Jacques Cambone was standing to one side and moved forward to kiss Anna's cheek as he saw her.

'Bonjour, Anna. I am glad you are here.'

With Verity on one side, and Leo on her other, holding her hand reassuringly, Anna tried to focus on the memorial sheet Bernard had handed her, but the picture of Philippe that met her gaze almost had her in tears before the ceremony had even started. As Bernard made his way to the small podium at the front to begin the proceedings, there was still no sign of Teddy. Verity telling Bernard that Teddy would do a reading had raised her spirits a little but where was he? Had he changed his mind?

Although the memorial was not a religious ceremony, the tribute did begin with a prayer offering thanks for the life of Philippe Cambone. Afterwards, Bernard introduced various friends of Philippe, who described their own differing memories of the man who'd clearly had an enthusiasm for life.

'He embraced everything with a passion,' was how one renowned film critic put it. 'He'll be greatly missed.'

Sitting there listening, and occasionally laughing at the reminiscences, Anna could only feel a strange kind of happiness creeping over her, knowing that the man she had loved so passionately all those years ago had inspired so many during his life.

She stiffened, as Bernard, once again taking his place on the podium in front of the congregation to begin to wind up the tributes nodded at some unseen person behind her.

Bernard smiled as his initial words were drowned out by a loud bang somewhere in the building, followed by a telephone ringing in an adjacent office.

'I apologise for the "off-stage sound effects",' Bernard said. 'But as a film director, I'm sure Philippe would have appreciated them and is probably even now yelling "cut".' He paused and Anna caught her breath as she watched Teddy join him on the podium, holding an envelope she recognised. 'We are nearing the end of this official celebration of Philippe Cambone's life. For many of us, he will always live on in our memories. However, the final tribute today comes from a man who sadly never met Philippe and to him I extend my heartfelt sympathy. I am so sorry he never knew the man who was my best friend, the man who will leave a huge, empty hole in my life.' An emotional Bernard moved away, leaving Teddy alone on the podium.

'As most of you know, I am Teddy Wickham,' Teddy paused for several seconds, visibly pulling himself together. 'I am also Philippe Cambone's son. Unfortunately, as Bernard said, I never met my father and until a few days ago I didn't know my birth mother either.'

Teddy placed the envelope with its papers on the table in front of him and looked around at the audience.

Anna, sitting transfixed at his words, felt a flutter of hope and smiled at Teddy as he looked directly at her before turning his gaze back to the crowd.

'When my mother did make herself known to me, I cruelly rejected her like I believed she'd rejected me all those years ago by giving me up for adoption. There was no way that I was prepared to acknowledge her. Neither did I see any point in telling the world that I was Philippe Cambone's son now that he was dead. My mother gently informed me that he would have been shouting with joy from the rooftops about me. She also told me how much she was looking forward to getting to know her son and her granddaughter. Again, cruelly, I told her that wasn't about to happen.'

Teddy paused and poured himself a glass of water from the carafe someone had thoughtfully provided, before continuing.

'But then two things happened. First, my six year old daughter, Cindy, went missing. Her disappearance for, what, no more than thirty minutes frightened me and made me realise how I would feel if I lost my daughter for real. If all contact was severed. When my daughter was finally found and I knew she was safe, I went to see my mother. She gave me these highly personal papers and a letter that had only just come into her possession to read.' Teddy held up the envelope briefly before replacing it on the table. 'I have to tell you I cried when I read them.'

He was silent for several seconds, before visibly taking a few deep breaths.

Anna, fighting back her own tears, clutched Leo's hand. 'D'you think he's going to forgive me after all?' she whispered. 'Even announce my name in public?'

Leo squeezed her hand. 'Just listen to what he has to say.'

'The second thing that happened,' Teddy continued, 'was that yesterday I chanced upon a poem called "The Gathering" by an unknown author. This poem contains two lines in different verses that stood out and made me question the decisions I was taking.

'The first line "You can open your eyes and see all that I have left" literally urged me to open my eyes and discover my unknown heritage. Another line, further on in the poem, is one I intend to try to live by in the coming weeks as I get to know and understand the circumstances that fate has thrown at me.' Teddy took a deep breath. 'And the line from the poem reads, "You can be happy for tomorrow because of yesterday".'

Teddy stopped speaking and looked around at the spellbound audience, before looking directly at Anna as he spoke.

'From what has been said here today, I know my father was a popular man, a good man, and I look forward to hearing stories about him from the people who knew him. I will have a lot to live up to as his son, but by acknowledging the woman who is my mother and who was the love of my father's life, Anna Carson, I hope I can begin to live up to the expectations I believe Philippe Cambone would have had of me, his son. Thank you.'

Picking up the envelope, Teddy stepped down from the podium and walked towards a stunned Anna.

She stood up as he reached her and wordlessly accepted the envelope containing the precious papers.

'Thank you for letting me read these.'

When he offered her his arm, she took it and,

with Leo and Verity walking behind them, they left the hall together as mother and son.

* * *

With no early morning screening or press conference to attend, Daisy had the luxury of a lie-in on Monday morning and it was nearly half past ten before she'd showered and went downstairs.

'Morning, Poppy. I could get used to this not working lark,' she said. 'Become a lady of leisure or even a lady that lunches.' She switched the coffee machine on. 'Coffee for you?'

Poppy shook her head. 'No thanks. Nat just phoned. He's on his way over. Cindy wants to play with Tom one last time, apparently, before they leave.'

'Thought he wasn't allowed to let Cindy darken our door because of Anna?' Daisy said, puzzled. 'Or has that all changed?'

Poppy shrugged. 'She's not in anyway. He'll be here soon. You can ask him what's changed. Your mobile has been bleeping for the past hour by the way. Your message box must be full.'

Many of the messages were from friends who'd heard about the redundancies at the paper and were offering sympathy. There was one from an editor she'd worked with a couple of years ago asking if she'd be interested in writing some short features and there was another one from Ben. A voice message this time, not a text.

Apprehensively Daisy pressed the listen button and held the phone out so Poppy could hear.

'Sorry I messed things up, Daisy. You sound so positive and happy in your emails. I really hope things work out for you. I've cancelled my flight back to the UK. I'll stay over here for a bit and see if I can make a proper go of things. Have a good life. Maybe we'll meet as friends one day. Love, Ben.'

'Well, that little problem seems to have gone away,' Poppy said. 'Relieved?'

Daisy nodded. 'Yes. I sort of half expected him to turn up here and try to spoil things with Nat.'

The gate buzzer went. 'Here is Nat,' Poppy said, pressing the open button. 'Tom, Cindy's here to play.'

'Hi,' Daisy said as Nat gave her a greeting kiss. 'This is a surprise.'

'Cindy was desperate to play with Tom while Teddy and Verity were out this morning. When I rang and Poppy said Anna wasn't here, I thought, why not.'

'He's still not happy about Cindy knowing Anna is her grandmother?'

'Verity says he needs to come to terms with things himself first.'

'You'll be in trouble then if Teddy finds out,' Daisy shook her head.

'I'll face that if it happens,' Nat said. 'It's Philippe Cambone's memorial service this morning, so I'm hoping, with a bit of luck, Anna has gone there and won't return until after we've left, so I'll be able to assure Teddy that Cindy hasn't had any contact with her.'

With the two children playing happily in the pool, Nat and Daisy sat down to watch them and discuss plans of their own for the future.

'When does your job with the Wickhams finish?'

'Officially tomorrow when we get back to the UK. How long are you staying on down here?'

'Mum and Dad will be here later in the week so I want to be here then. Dan gets back at the end of the week. Think I'll probably change my flight to Friday. Help Poppy get the villa ready, spend some time with Mum and Dad but leave in time to give Poppy some space to enjoy having Dan home,' Daisy said. She took a deep breath. 'Once I get back I'll start putting feelers out for work, pack up the flat and be back down here to live in the cottage in, hopefully, less than a month. Ready and waiting for you to arrive for a summer in the sun.' Daisy smiled at him. 'I'm so looking forward to it.'

'Some of the summer might be spent in the States,' Nat said.

'Exciting. When d'you—' Daisy stopped in mid-sentence as she heard the villa gates opening. 'Nat – Anna and Leo have just arrived back. Teddy and Verity are with them.'

'Cindy, Tom. Out you get,' Nat said. 'Mummy and Daddy are here. Run over to the cottage and we'll get you dry,' and he hurriedly shooed the children in the direction of the cottage, where Poppy was waiting with towels and a worried look on her face.

The children were barely dried and dressed when Teddy came over.

Everybody tensed, waiting for the explosion.

'Hi, kids. Enjoy your swim?'

As everyone looked at him, surprised, he turned to Nat.

'Would you like to take the rest of the day off? I think we're going to be busy as a family this afternoon and evening. Cindy, say goodbye to Tom. I need you to come over to the villa – Anna and I have something very important to tell you.'

'Okay' Cindy said. 'Does that mean I'm allowed to see Anna now?'

'Yes,' Teddy said. 'I don't think you can go on calling her Anna though. That is something you and she will need to talk about.'

Watching Teddy walk back towards the villa hand in hand with Cindy, Daisy said. 'Well, that sounds as if things on the Anna and Teddy front have sorted themselves out easier and earlier than Anna was expecting. I'm so pleased for Anna.'

As Anna and her new family disappeared into the villa, Nat looked at Daisy and Poppy.

'D'you two have anything planned for this afternoon? If not, fancy spending it with me wandering around the Chateau de la Napoule? Tom would enjoy it too I think.'

'Great idea. A visit to the "Once Upon a Time" fairy-tale chateau will be the perfect end to festival week. But first I'll treat the four of us to pizzas down in Cannes before we go,' Daisy said, turning to Poppy. 'Be easier if we take your car, then we can go straight along the bord de mer to the chateau.'

36

Anna's heart was thumping wildly as she and Verity organised an impromptu lunch for the five of them in the villa kitchen. As they'd walked back from the memorial service, they'd called into a favourite boulangerie, where Leo had taken charge and bought baguettes, pizzas and onion tarts, plus a large tarte tropézienne to go with coffee afterwards. Stunned by the fact that Teddy had accepted her hesitant invitation to join them for lunch, Anna had been incapable of remembering what, apart from cheese and some slices of ham, was already in the kitchen.

Leo and Teddy were now busy rearranging

chairs around the terrace table, while Cindy was back in the pool, splashing around happily.

'I can't believe this is happening,' Anna said quietly, looking out of the window at the two men. 'I mean, I know it's not all going to be plain sailing between us, but the fact that Teddy is actually here ready to talk to me.' She looked at Verity. 'I can't tell you how much his words this morning meant to me. Did you know he was going to say what he did?'

Verity shook her head. 'No. But I'm so happy for both of you. It will work out, you'll see.'

'I looked him up on Wikipedia and on a couple of film sites, a few days after I knew Teddy was definitely my son, but it was all about his professional life. I know now he's made some well-known films but nothing about him personally. Like where he grew up, when he went to America, how long he's been married,' Anna stopped. 'How long have you been married?'

'Eight years this year. I'm his second wife,' Verity said quietly. 'His first died of a brain aneurism just after they were married.'

Anna looked at her, stunned into silence for

several seconds. 'I wasn't expecting that. Poor Teddy.'

'You both have a lot to learn about each other, but Teddy won't hold back now he's determined to do the right thing by everyone.'

'I was wondering why you were inspired to write to the Cambones this particular year and not before?' Anna asked quietly.

'Ah, now I think I'll leave that for Teddy to tell you,' Verity said.

'Okay,' Anna said, not wishing to probe. She already knew more about her long-lost son than she'd ever expected to learn. There was plenty of time to learn more. 'Are your parents still alive?'

Verity shook her head. 'Sadly no. They both died in a car crash three years ago. They adored Cindy, but she was so young when it happened that I doubt she'll remember them.'

'You must miss them,' Anna said softly.

Verity nodded. 'One of the reasons I'm so family orientated these days. You never know how long you've got them for.'

'Shall we start to carry things out to the terrace?' Anna picked up plates and cutlery and handed them to Verity. 'If you take these, I'll ferry some of the food out and come back for the rest and the glasses.'

Once everything was out on the table and Leo had opened a couple of bottles of white and rosé wine, Verity called Cindy out of the pool, dried her and helped her to put on shorts and a T-shirt. Cindy insisted on sitting next to Anna because, 'Anna's my friend and we're leaving soon and I don't know when I'll ever see her again,' and heaved a dramatic sigh, which made everyone laugh.

'Sorry folks.' Verity shook her head. 'Can't think where she gets her diva-like attitude from.'

'We have something important to tell you about Anna,' Teddy said. 'Something that means from now on Anna will be part of your life.'

Cindy gazed at him round eyed.

'You know Granny and Granddad adopted me when I was a tiny baby because my real mother couldn't take care of me and she wanted me to have a better life, well...' Teddy took a deep breath. 'Turns out that Anna is my real mother and your granny.'

'Anna's my granny like Granny Eliane already is? I'll have two grannies? I don't have to give Granny Eliane back, do I? 'Cause I love her too.'

Teddy burst out laughing. 'No. You get to keep both. You do have to decide what you are going to call Anna though – and Leo – because when they get married soon he'll be your granddad.'

Cindy put a hand to her head and groaned. 'Two grannies and two granddads, we're going to get in a muddle.'

'That's why you have to decide on different names,' Teddy said patiently.

'My daughter Alison is making me a granddad at the end of the year,' Leo spoke quietly. 'She's suggesting they call me Pops and that Anna might like to have the nickname Lolly. Have to admit I'm getting used to Pops, but I'm not sure whether Anna is keen on Lolly, especially when you say the two together – Lollypops.' He glanced across at Anna, who was trying to keep a straight face.

Cindy jumped up and down on her chair with excitement. 'Lolly and Pops, Pops and Lolly, Lollypops.'

'Okay, well that's a definite hit,' Teddy said.

'You all right with the name Lolly, Anna? Or would you prefer something a bit more traditional?'

Anna smiled. 'Yes, I'm fine with Lolly. Pour some wine, Pops, and we can toast our new names.' No way was she going to admit to anyone that she would have preferred Cindy to call her something that really indicated their relationship. Something like Nana or even Grandma. But it was only a name in the end, it was nurturing their new friendship into a proper relationship that counted.

Lunchtime passed in a buzz of conversation and lots of laughter. Anna had to keep mentally pinching herself that she was sitting at the same table as her son. Lots of information would slowly seep out in the future, filling in the gaps in their knowledge of each other, but right now she was content to just ask the odd question or two and learn about him.

'Why the name Teddy? Is it a nickname that's stuck? Or were you christened Teddy – if you are christened.' Something else she needed to learn about her son.

'I was christened Edmund Matthew Philip,' Teddy answered. 'Edmund for me, Matthew for my dad and the English version of Philippe because...' he shrugged. 'Dad and Mum thought it was the right thing to do.'

'Philippe would have been thrilled to hear that,' Anna said quietly.

'Teddy is a diminutive of Edmund and also because...' Teddy continued, grinning at her. 'Because apparently I was plump and cuddly like a teddy bear!' Teddy glanced down at himself ruefully. 'Which is something I don't seem to have grown out of.'

'So your dad is Matthew and your mum is Eliane' Anna said.

'I hope the three of you get on when you meet.' Teddy looked anxious for a moment.

'I'm sure we will. I intend to ask Eliane about all the embarrassing things you got up to as a child that I can't ask you,' Anna said, laughing at the look on Teddy's face.

It wasn't all one sided though. As they sat there enjoying coffee and slices of the tarte tropézienne, Teddy surprised Anna by asking a question about her own parents.

'Did they ever regret not seeing their grandson grow up?'

Anna closed her eyes and bit her lips. Should she sugar coat her parents' attitude towards her all those years ago? Or tell him the truth about not just their sheer obstinacy over her pregnancy and his birth, but how vindictive, mean and downright cruel they'd been in the way they'd treated her? In the end she opted for a sanitised version; it was too long ago to drag it all back up in depth. Besides, it was a generation away, involving people he'd never known. Would never know.

'They never acknowledged you in any way,' Anna said quietly. 'After you were born, I returned home, finished my education, got a job as an office assistant with a small film company and started to secretly save money so that I could leave home and be independent. A week after my nineteenth birthday, I left home.' She took a deep breath.

'After that, contact was limited to the occasional phone call and a Christmas card. They died ten years ago within a month of each other.' Anna didn't add they'd treated her as a distant relative after she left home; that she could count on the fingers of one hand her visits to see them in the intervening years; that they had never congratulated her on the success of her career,

'I'm sorry that my existence caused you such pain,' Teddy said quietly, reaching out to hold and squeeze her hand. 'It's unbelievable that anybody could treat their only child the way they treated you.'

'But your parents were kind to you?'

Teddy smiled. 'I couldn't have asked for better parents. Sorry,' he rubbed his face in anguish. 'I didn't mean that you and Philippe wouldn't have – if circumstances had been different I'm sure—'

'I'm glad you feel like that,' Anna interrupted. 'I'm not offended, just happy that what I prayed for happened. I wanted you to go to a loving, caring couple who would give you a better life than I could give you at the time.' Anna hesitated. 'There is one thing I'd like to know though – why try to get in touch with Philippe now after all these years?'

'I've always known I was adopted and when I was about eighteen, I did mention to Mum and Dad about trying to find my biological parents.' Teddy swirled the wine around in his glass. 'Dad was fine about it, said they'd expected me to be curious, but Mum,' he shrugged. 'She was clearly worried about me rejecting them, even though she never tried to persuade me not to look. In the end, I decided it would hurt her too much if I started looking, so I didn't.'

Anna was silent for a second or two. 'So what changed this year?

'Dad was diagnosed with diabetes by a new doctor at our local practice who didn't know I was adopted. This doctor said the disease could run in families so Dad should tell his son to be aware and have regular checks. It made the three of us realise that maybe for medical reasons I should try and get in touch with my biological parents. Just in case there was anything nasty lurking in the genes.'

'When you talk to Jacques, you'll be able to ask him. You are going to talk to your uncle, aren't you?' Anna asked.

'Strange having an uncle who is my father's twin,' Teddy said. 'But, yes, I am going to talk to him and to Bernard. It will have to wait though until we come back for a visit. We leave tomorrow for the UK and I have quite a schedule lined up for the next few weeks.'

Teddy finished his wine and placed the glass on the table before looking at Anna seriously.

'I need to say something. I hope you will meet Mum and Dad sooner rather than later and that's the thing. Mum is my mum and I'll never stop thinking or calling her that. Which means—'

'Teddy, stop right there,' Anna said. 'You are her son, she brought you up, she loves you. The fact she didn't give birth to you is immaterial. There is no way I would want to come between you and her. I'm happy for you to call me Anna – or even join Cindy, in calling me Lolly.' Anna smiled at her son. 'I really, truly don't mind. All I care about is having you, Verity and my grand-daughter in my life from now on.'

EPILOGUE

FOUR MONTHS LATER

Wandering through the Duty Free zone of Nice airport before boarding the flight to the UK, Daisy smiled happily to herself. So much had happened since the last time she'd been in there, sniffing the perfume before treating herself to a small bottle as a final treat from the Film Festival.

Nat had left with Cindy and the Wickhams the day after the festival finished, while she'd stayed on for another week to see her parents and talk to them about her future. A future that seemed to them to be uncertain to say the least. Her mother had been the one to voice her worries.

'Finding work as a freelance will take time.

Are you sure you've got enough money to survive on in the meantime. Dad and I will, of course, help you if you need anything. And are you sure about Nat? You've only just met him and I know Poppy likes him but you barely know him. To even be thinking of going to America with him so soon,' and her mother had shaken her head.

'Mum, I know it's not going to be easy but I've got lots of contacts and I've got enough money put aside to live off for several months. I'm sorry you've not had the chance to meet Nat but when you do I know you're going to love him as much as I do. As soon as I get back next week I'll bring him down to meet you, okay?'

Her mum and dad had taken to Nat on that visit as Daisy had known they would although her mum admitted to still being worried about her.

'But I can see the two of you are great together and will work things out between you,' she'd said.

Two days after Nat had met her parents, Daisy had waved him off at the airport to catch his flight to America. She had so much to organise in the next few weeks that they'd decided however much she wanted to accompany Nat on that first trip it wasn't possible. For the next few weeks she had to concentrate on clearing her flat out and giving notice, sorting the stuff she needed to take to Poppy's, updating her contact list and letting editors know she was now freelance and available, pitching ideas to various magazines and newspapers in an effort to get some work lined up and finally, but by no means least, she had to get herself back down to Cannes and Poppy. Her dad came to the rescue there, offering to drive her down, meaning she could take the things she wanted rather than leave them in her parents' garage.

She and Nat Skyped each other every day — mid evening for Daisy and breakfast time for Nat. When the studio Nat was working with on his script wanted him to stay on longer they were both disappointed that the separation would be longer than they'd anticipated.

'Next time you're definitely coming with me,' Nat had said.

It was the middle of July before Nat returned, by which time Daisy had settled into the cottage, got into a working routine – although Poppy had a way of disrupting that some days — and was enjoying her life in the south of France. Nat coming home was the last ingredient to complete her happiness. While Nat worked on his second script, Daisy wrote the commissions she was successful in pitching for, and gradually her freelance career was gaining ground. Life was good.

'Can I help you, Mademoiselle?' The assistant's voice jolted her out of her day-dreaming.

'No thanks. I'll leave it for now,' and Daisy took a final sniff of the tester bottle before replacing it on the counter and turning to face Nat who had joined her. She looked at her watch.

'Think it's nearly time to board,' she said, smiling at him. Nat nodded.

'We've got a few moments. That's your favourite perfume, isn't it?'

Daisy nodded. 'I've still got some left. When I land a really big feature commission I'll treat myself to another bottle.'

Nat smiled at the assistant watching them. 'Please.' He took out his credit card after pointing to a bottle of perfume and held it out. 'My treat.'

Daisy leant in and kissed him on the cheek. 'Thank you.'

A couple of minutes later they were making their way to the aircraft with Daisy holding Nat's hand and clutching her duty free bag in the other. She glanced at him before saying quietly. 'Just think, a day after Anna and Leo's wedding we'll be at Heathrow catching a plane for the US – together,' she said. 'Who'd have thought it all those weeks ago at the Cannes Film Festival?'

* * *

12th September

Standing in the front bedroom of Leo's cottage, Anna saw Daisy and Nat, hand in hand, making their way under the lychgate and along the path leading to St Nicholas in the Field Church, where, in half an hour's time, she would become Mrs Leo Hunter.

Five minutes earlier, she'd seen Leo's pregnant daughter, Alison, and her husband tread the same path, and now Poppy, Dan and Tom were being welcomed by one of the ushers. Bernard and his son were the next to disappear into the church.

Anna smiled to herself. It was almost unbelievable how things had fallen into place over the past few months, just as Leo had insisted they would.

'It's because it's meant to be,' Leo had teased her twenty-four hours before, when he'd moved out to a room in the village pub so they could follow the tradition of not seeing each other the night before their wedding. His son, Luke, who was his best man, had flown in yesterday evening from Dubai and the two of them had spent the time together.

It wasn't just the wedding arrangements that had slotted almost seamlessly into place over the last four months. Everything, even if it hadn't exactly gone like clockwork, had been relatively easy to organise. Things like selling her house, moving in with Leo, sorting out her work schedule for the new film, even shopping for a wedding dress had been relatively stress free thanks to Alison, who had insisted it was her duty as a soon-to-be stepdaughter to be allowed to help choose the dress.

She and Leo had even managed a couple of weekends away, but for Anna the best weekend had been the one when Cindy came to stay. Then there were the family visits to Teddy and Verity, visiting Alison and her growing bump, with Leo. The last few months had been some of the busiest and happiest in Anna's life.

And then there was the phone call to Teddy's parents. Anna had been apprehensive when Teddy had dialled the number, spoken to his mum and said, 'Mum, I've got someone here I'd like you to say hello to,' before handing the phone to Anna.

But she needn't have worried. Eliane was kindness itself and her gentle lilting Welsh accent had smoothed away Anna's fears. There hadn't been time to get to Carmarthenshire to meet them in person before the wedding. That would happen next month, once she and Leo got back from their short honeymoon.

Downstairs, a door banged, jolting Anna out of her reverie. Thirty seconds later, Cindy burst into the bedroom.

'Lolly, Lolly, we're here. Can I put my dress on?'

'Not until you've given me a cuddle, young lady,' Anna said, holding out her arms for Cindy to run into.

'I'm sorry we're late,' Verity said, following Cindy into the room. 'Traffic. Honestly, you'd think we lived fifty miles away not fifteen.'

'No problem. We've got plenty of time. You're looking very glamorous. I love your hat,' Anna said. 'Where's Teddy?'

'He dropped us and walked down to the pub to check on Leo and Luke. Make sure they've got everything – like the rings! He'll be back here soon.'

'Come on then, Cindy, let's get you dressed,' Anna said. 'Then you and Mummy can walk to the church and wait for me.'

A few minutes later, Anna said, 'Cindy, you are the most beautiful flower girl I've ever seen. I'm so proud you're mine.' Placing the halo of silk daisy flowers on to Cindy's head, she gently clipped it into place, before dropping a gentle kiss on the little girl's head. 'Go and have a look in the mirror – see how beautiful you look.'

'Is your dress pink too?' Cindy asked as she twirled in front of the dressing table mirror.

'No. I did think about a pale pink one but decided it was really your colour,' Anna said, crossing to the large wardrobe and taking her own wedding ensemble out.

'Can I give you a hand dressing?' Verity asked.

'Please. Lots of hidden buttons down the back that I can't reach,' Anna said, slipping the Grecian-style gown made in the palest of pale yellow chiffon off its hanger and over her head. 'What d'you think?' she asked anxiously. 'I wanted something special but felt I was a bit too old for a traditional wedding gown. Alison said it was a perfect dress for me.'

'Anna, it's beautiful and so are you. I know Leo will be stunned when he sees you walking towards him. You look amazing,' Verity said. 'Anything in your hair?'

Anna shook her head. 'No. I'm just going to carry a simple posy, which is in the kitchen with

Cindy's flower basket. Oh, I think I can hear Teddy.'

Downstairs, Verity collected the flower basket and she and Cindy kissed Anna before leaving for the church.

'We'll see you there,' Verity said.

Left alone with Teddy, Anna suddenly felt shy and was glad when he took charge.

'We'll give them a head start and then we'll set off,' he said, glancing at his watch. 'If we walk slowly, you should be a fashionable five minutes late.'

Looking at Teddy, handsome and immaculate in his morning suit, as he checked the cottage doors and windows were locked before they left, Anna felt a sudden rush of happiness. Followed by a need to put a certain thought into words.

'If is the biggest word in the dictionary, but if Philippe and I had managed to beat the odds, marry and raise you, I doubt we could have done a better job than Eliane and Matthew. I'm so proud to be able to call you my son and I wish Philippe could see you today. He'd feel the same.' Anna bit her lip in an effort to stop her emotions getting the better of her. 'I just want you to know that I'm proud to call you my son.'

Carefully Teddy put his arms around her and gave her a gentle hug before placing a soft kiss on her forehead.

'I know,' he said quietly. 'But I'm glad you, at least, are now in my life.' Several seconds passed before he gave her a final hug before pulling back slightly to look at her. 'You okay?' When Anna smiled tremulously at him he released her.

Come on then, Lolly,' Teddy said, happily using the name Cindy had bestowed on her. 'Let's get you married to Pops,' and he handed her the posy of flowers before ushering her out of the cottage and slamming the front door securely behind them. Together they slowly made their way along the path, through the lychgate and on into the church.

Standing in the church porch as Verity made a couple of last minute adjustments to Anna's dress and Cindy jiggled from one foot to the other, desperate to start throwing rose petals, Anna saw Leo waiting for her by the altar.

She turned to Teddy. 'I can't believe how much

my life has changed in the past year. When I met Leo, I didn't believe things could get any better, and then you happened.' She was silent for a moment. 'We've come a long way in the last few months, haven't we?' she said. 'Who would have thought my own son would be walking me down the aisle to marry the man I love.'

'It's a whole new stage of life for us all,' Teddy said. 'After years of wondering, I know my real roots. Now, I'm sure you are going to be very happy married to Leo, but, remember, Lolly, I'm here if you ever need me.'

Anna smiled tremulously. 'I still can't get used to hearing you call me that, but I do love it so.'

As the organist began a joyful rendition of the Wedding March, Teddy took her by the arm and, at the side of her son and behind her granddaughter joyfully scattering rose petals at her feet, Anna began her walk down the aisle to marry Leo.

ACKNOWLEDGMENTS

As always, my thanks go to the team at Boldwood Books: Nia, Amanda, Caroline my editor, Jade the copy editor and Rose the eagle-eyed proof reader – you are all ace and thank you for making my books the best they can be.

Thanks to my online writing friends and fellow Boldwood authors, who boost me up and keep me sane when I'm in need!

My heartfelt thanks too must go to you, the reader – without you, I wouldn't be doing the best job in the world. Receiving a lovely email from someone who has read and enjoyed one of my books is a wonderful feeling.

MORE FROM JENNIFER BOHNET

We hope you enjoyed reading *Rendez-Vous in Cannes*. If you did, please leave a review.

If you'd like to gift a copy, this book is also available as an ebook, digital audio download and audiobook CD.

Sign up to Jennifer Bohnet's mailing list for news, competitions and updates on future books.

http://bit.ly/JenniferBohnetNewsletter

Discover more escapist reads from Jennifer Bohnet:

ABOUT THE AUTHOR

Jennifer Bohnet is the bestselling author of over 10 women's fiction novels, including *Villa of Sun and Secrets* and *A Riviera Retreat*. She is originally from the West Country but now lives in the wilds of rural Brittany, France.

Visit Jennifer's website:
http://www. jenniferbohnet.com/

Follow Jennifer on social media:

facebook.com/Jennifer-Bohnet-170217789709356
twitter.com/jenniewriter
instagram.com/jenniebohnet
bookbub.com/authors/jennifer-bohnet

ABOUT BOLDWOOD BOOKS

Boldwood Books is a fiction publishing company seeking out the best stories from around the world.

Find out more at www.boldwoodbooks.com

Sign up to the Book and Tonic newsletter for news, offers and competitions from Boldwood Books!

http://www.bit.ly/bookandtonic

We'd love to hear from you, follow us on social media:

facebook.com/BookandTonic

twitter.com/BoldwoodBooks

instagram.com/BookandTonic